Praise for
The Horned Women

"Matheson skillfully intertwines traditional Irish folklore with contemporary themes, creating a narrative that's both enchanting and relatable."

—Erik McManus, Breakeven Books

"What a fun, witchy little read! The Horned Women takes a creepy old Irish fairy tale and spins it into something fresh, smart, and totally charming. I loved Maura — she's got that "holding it together with duct tape and coffee" energy I can seriously relate to — and seeing her face off against twelve different horned witches with nothing but folklore, stitching skills, and pure mom grit was just so satisfying.

Christy Matheson writes with a cozy, heartfelt vibe that makes even the spookiest moments feel grounded and real. It's a quick read, but it really sticks with you. If you like your fairy tales with a bit of chaos, a little magic, and a lot of heart, you'll love this one."

—Gina Rae Mitchell Reviews

"Christy Matheson takes ancient folklore and breathes wild, bloody life into it, conjuring up a story of grief, anger, magic, and survival.

The atmosphere is thick with shadow and myth: dark woods, whispered warnings, the gleam of horns; I was spellbound. The characters are raw, fierce, and painfully real. Maura is a woman who refuses to be quiet and refuses to be broken. She may not be unscathed but she has more than enough tenderness for her children to balance the rage she feels when anyone threatens them."

—Claire's Reviews

"Matheson deftly illustrates the love of a mother for her children and the relationship between a mother and her stepchildren..."—Karla, Bookish Life

"Matheson did a wonderful job incorporating unique elements into this story while still staying true to the source material! ... You're going to find this story extremely riveting until the very last page!"

—Shawn, Mr Geek Book Reviews

the
horned
Women
and
Other Stories

Contemporary Retellings of
Irish Fairy Tales

THE CASTLE OF KILKENNY: FAIRY TALES BOOKS 1, 2, & 3

CHRISTY MATHESON

THE HORNED WOMEN AND OTHER STORIES

ISBN 13 Paperback: 979-8-9920274-5-7

Cover design: Christy Matheson and Elaine Aucoin Schroller
White tree illustration: iStock/usankova312;
Other cover illustrations: BookBrush
Interior formatting: Elaine Aucoin Schroller
www.elaineschroller.com

THE HORNED WOMEN By Christy Matheson
Copyright © 2024 Christy Matheson.
ISBN 13 eBook: 979-8-9920274-0-2

THE WHITE DEER OF KILDARE By Christy Matheson
Copyright © 2024, 2025 Christy Matheson.
ISBN 13 eBook: 979-8-9920274-1-9

THE KNIGHT OF THE TERRIBLE VALLEY AND AIDEN OF FLORIDA By Christy Matheson
Copyright © 2025 Christy Matheson.
ISBN 13 eBook: 979-8-9920274-2-6

THE TWO RINGS By Christy Matheson
Copyright © 2025 Christy Matheson.

v08212025

Also by Christy Matheson

The Castle in Kilkenny Fairy Tales

Book 1: *The Horned Women, A contemporary retelling of an Irish fairy tale*

Book 2: *The White Deer of Kildare*

Book 3: *The Knight of the Terrible Valley and Aiden of Florida*

Book 4: *The Squire and His Magical Library*

Book 5: *The Knight and His Magical Armlet*

Book 6: *The Boat on the Lake of Regret*

Book 7: *Oona and the Swan*

Book 0.5: *The Leprechaun and the Castle* (only available through author's newsletter)

Magical Libraries (only available through author's newsletter)

In *Feisty Deeds: Historical Fictions of Daring Women,* "The Inner Good"

Contents

About this Book

The three Castle of Kilkenny Fairy Tales in this book have a historical setting with a contemporary frame. Through one fairy tale after another, American folklorist Maura and her children rely on creativity and love to solve their highly unusual problems. And through one adventure after another, they try relying on something new...each other. But whether it is because Maura has the Second Sight or some property of the castle itself, the boundary is thin between our modern world and the ancient folklore...

In *The Horned Women*, the only things that American folklorist, Maura, wanted from her contentious divorce was custody of her two young children—and an Irish castle. She ended up with more than she bargained for, including her ex's teenage kids, plumbing problems, and now...twelve horned women carding and spinning in her living room. Maura is determined to use her knowledge of folklore to keep her otherworldly visitors away from her children...but is a stepmother's love enough to save the grumpy teens?

In *The White Deer of Kildare*, all Maura wants is a peaceful Christmas in her Irish castle, but her ex is threatening her with family court, and her second grader has invited a strange—completely unclothed—friend,

CHRISTY MATHESON

to spend the holidays with them. Oh. And the friend's dog, which is not actually a dog but probably one of the white deer of Celtic myth.

Maura distracts herself from her husband's threats by trying to discover why a Fae deer is in her kitchen, when the two accidentally end up in the Ireland of ancient myth. The White Deer was the human queen of this castle, but she has husband trouble too. Can Maura help her new friend, and will she ever make it home to her children?

In *The Knight of the Terrible Valley and Aiden of Florida*, Aiden's little sister has been kidnapped into a magical world. Armed with nothing but a wet mitten and a hurley stick, he's determined to bring her home...

Sixteen-year-old Aiden Robinson is just trying to learn to play hurley and fit in with his new Irish classmates, when a mysterious stranger snatches his little sister, leading Aiden and his not-quite-friends into a world that definitely didn't exist yesterday. Aiden doesn't care if he's slipped into a fairy tale, he just needs to get his baby sister home—before his stepmother notices she's gone and never trusts him again.

But that night, the wise woman has a weird message from Aiden's real life, and his other sister follows to "help him." Now he's got twice as many sisters in danger, and his magical weapon is the...Hurley Stick of Daylight—?!

Aiden's got to learn to be a hero (and apparently how to play hurley) if he's going to survive the Terrible Valley and get both sisters home alive.

BOOK 1
THE HORNED WOMEN

Dedication

To everyone who has ever been a thirteen-year-old girl
or loved a thirteen-year-old girl,□
and most of all, to my own girls who are no longer thirteen.
I have full confidence in you.

The Dorned Women

I finish stoking the fire and push myself to my feet, slowly, as though I were already a crone. I haven't gotten nearly enough done for today, but that's the way it always is now. The workmen have gone home—leaving the back stairs half-finished and the plumbing main off—the little kids are blessedly asleep, the kitchen is tidy, and I can finally sit down. Maybe I can mend the kids' uniforms quickly and steal a few minutes to work on my beaded embroidery.

I let my gaze travel around the room, still not quite believing this is real, that I belong in a building so full of history and myth. Walls of local sandstone tower beyond the glow of the lamps, faded tapestries, coats of arms. This is the oldest part of the castle, and some nights I can almost hear the whisper of the generations that have come before me, all the way to when this was a wooden fort.

Despite my exhaustion, I can't help but smile. After all this—quitting grad school, Roy's "situations" leading to an entire year of divorce proceedings—and just look at me now. A little nobody from South Boston, and the sole proprietor of a castle. A castle! Dating from the medieval period, and still livable. Almost.

I reach for my mending—wait. I haven't locked the front door, and there's four children in the house. Pulling my sweater close, I hurry beyond the warm radius of the fire. The hallway angles slightly, and then I can see the entryway light and feel the draft whisking under my skirt. Is that noise nearby? Like laughter, or the trilling of a lark or a violin—I pause with my hand on the latch of the peep-out door. I'm already chilly, and that will just let in a blast of cold air and rain, when it's almost certainly just an owl or a truck driving past. I'll put the crossbar in its jambs, and then no matter what's out there, it can't come in. I pull my hand from where it is tucked in my sweater to reach for the heavy oak bar, and am startled by the clatter of tumbling glass.

"Hey Mum, are you down here?" Aidan calls.

Drat.

"Coming!" I hurry towards the kitchen before the teens break something else. The castle floor plan has kitchens and sculleries and still-rooms in the wing to my left, but I need a National Trust grant to restore them. Or something; yet another thing I haven't had time to research. Meanwhile, there's a useable kitchen shoehorned into one corner of the Great Hall.

I open the door. Aiden is picking up pieces of broken mason jars we use for drinking and dropping them in the bin, his younger sister Kaylee is standing in the middle of the floor glowering at her phone, and the kettle is whistling. I switch off the burner so the chaos dims a little. So much for my tidy kitchen! I've gotten my own kids to bed, but apparently I've got two more to deal with.

"Hey, Mum." Aiden stumbles over the word, his smile awkward. He pulls the cuffs of his Seattle Seahawks sweatshirt over his hands.

"Hi," I say, trying to sound cheerful. I appreciate the thought, but I am not his mum. When we lived in the US he called me Maura—if he had to call me anything—but I assume he wants to fit in with his Irish classmates. "Needed a midnight snack, I guess?"

"It isn't midnight," Kaylee argues.

"Okay." I take a breath. Here we go again. "You're right, it's not."

"Ugh, where did it go?" Kaylee is talking to her phone.

Her long blonde hair glimmers under the dull kitchen lighting, reminding me forcibly of Roy's first wife. Unlike her mother, Kaylee's roots are starting to show under her highlights. Since we've moved to Ireland, I've had no time to find a hair salon to maintain her look...although come to think of it, Kaylee hasn't asked me to go.

"It's 9:43," Aiden says, as though the precise time could avoid further conflict. He clunks the bin back in the corner and picks up his plate, containing ice cream and the last piece of apple cake.

That's fine. I made the cake for eating. I can always make another one.

I sweep up the last shards of glass from the floor. Don't want the little ones cutting their feet in the morning. Then I fetch the rag and wipe up the circles of ice cream that the carton left on the counter, then scrape the cake dish into the trash and stack it in the sink. Too bad the workmen turned off the downstairs water main so they can fix the bathroom, so I can't wash anything tonight. It makes me grumpy, watching tomorrow's chores add up, and I reach for Aiden's cup.

"Hey, Mum?" Aiden flushes with the too-easy blush that I know he abhors. "We can get that. You're not our servant."

That niggles, because in some ways, I do still feel like a servant around Roy's family—and even though they came with me, his older kids still feel part of his world. But I'm trying not to let my ex loom over me anymore, so I brush off the feeling and try to make a joke. "You'd think a place this big would come with staff, wouldn't you?" I laugh, but Aiden's smile barely twitches. "Maybe some magical ones, right?"

Aiden glances around the room. "Like...the teapots in *Beauty and the Beast?*"

There are serpentine gargoyles carved into the rafters, but the only teapots are the ones I bought from the homeware department at Dunnes.

"Something like that." I dump the last of his cocoa in the sink and stack the cup.

"I want a lamp to clean my room," Kaylee says, without looking at us.

I have a degree in comp lit and half a doctorate in folklore; I don't know how I ended up with children whose mythology comes from Disney.

I don't know how any of this happened. Me in Ireland with Roy's first four children, while he skips off to have his fifth. I wish his new wife the luck of him.

"Kaylee wants to make that." Aiden points his fork at his sister.

Still glowering, Kaylee holds her phone towards me, an Instagram video flickering. "It's pudding. See? In a mug."

Now they're both watching me, but I'm not sure what they're waiting for.

"Can she...make it?" Aiden's voice wavers.

"Of course." I've never given them any indication to think they can't use the kitchen, for Pete's sakes! "What do you need? Flour? Baking soda or powder?"

Kaylee reads the ingredients out loud, and I gather the dry ingredients and find a microwave-safe mug. I wait to see if she wants any other help, but she props up her phone and starts scooping and pouring. The tinny voice walks us all through the recipe over and over as Kaylee stops and starts the video.

"How is chemistry?" I ask Aiden. It seems like the sort of thing a good mother would ask.

"It's way harder than back in Florida," he answers, and stumbles through more details.

I nod and mm-hm. I don't know why they aren't both still in Florida. I can't help but glance at Kaylee, who hates the rain and has a constant sniffle and is embarrassed by wearing a school uniform. She hates the dark and all the corners around the castle are dark; we have dozens of lights on those chunky timers, and she also hates the cold so she keeps the space heater in her bedroom going full blast, and I don't complain even though electricity is wicked expensive here. By the end of a long day—and they're all long—I can barely remember why I wanted to move out here, and I have never had any idea why Aiden and Kaylee chose to come with me.

"Dammit!" Kaylee slams the microwave door.

Aiden and I both jump.

Kaylee bangs the mug on the counter, smoke pouring out.

She crosses her arms, glowering.

She sniffs.

It might be that her nose is running because of the cold, or because of the constant dust or the black sugary smoke. But that might be a wee quiver of her chin, and she might be feeling sad. Thirteen is still a child, I remind myself every day.

"You can try it again," I suggest, trying to sound positive.

"I can't. The cup's ruined."

"I'll wash it. Look, here's another mug."

Kaylee restarts the video. My mother would have said, 'if you keep looking like that your face will get stuck that way,' but it was never very helpful so I resist saying it to Kaylee.

As usual, I can't find anything to say to Kaylee. After all, she never says anything to me.

I start folding a basket of rags and towels, making stacks on the chrome-and-formica table. My knees hurt from standing all day, but I might as well do something useful while I'm waiting for the second round of pudding.

Aiden jostles the camping jug on the counter, making an echoing empty slosh. "Oh, sorry, I forgot to refill this. Do you want me to fetch water now?"

He opens the back door, the one that goes directly into the courtyard with the well, and a strange feeling slides down my spine. It is just an owl; no one is laughing out there.

"It's raining," Kaylee says.

"We can wait till morning," I answer.

Aiden nods and closes the door. I fold another towel, feeling silly for letting the night get to me.

"Thank you, though." It sounds like an afterthought, but I mean it. Not being able to use the kitchen sink is a huge frustration, but at least Aiden can carry in a bigger tub than I can manage, and he has been willing to help... if I remind him.

Aiden checks the kettle on the stove, and the soup pot next to it. "There's water in both? I think that's enough? Are you going to want tea?"

"It's fine." I laugh weakly. "I'm just one person; I don't need more tea than fits in the kettle." At this rate, I'm won't have time to stitch and sip anything, anyway.

"Oh, shi—oot!" Kaylee stabs her second pudding and stomps her foot. "It's all *globby!* And weird! And it smells bad!"

"You can make another one." Aiden sounds much more encouraging than I did.

Will I have to stand here through another whole pudding? For pity's sake, Oona is only six and she can microwave her own oatmeal, and Oliver often mixes up pancake batter while I cook. I don't know how Kaylee is managing to ruin five-ingredient pudding.

I touch my pocket, thinking I will find an easier recipe, but I left my phone upstairs, playing a sleepy-time meditation for Oliver. Never mind. I just get a new mug, and Kaylee turns her video back on. Aiden stands by the window, drumming his fingers.

"You don't have to get the water," I repeat. To be honest, I kind of don't want him out there at night. My grandmother always used to talk about the second sight, but Roy scoffed at such things; I'd almost forgotten the shivers I used to have–visceral reminders of a different world layered on top of our own, as soft as shadows.

But last week, Oliver wanted to fill his own water bottle directly from the well. He took his flashlight but came back saying that he couldn't find the spigot or any of the stainless steel pump housing that sits on top of the old stone circle. There was just a bucket, he told us, white with the rim painted black. Kaylee told him he was stupid and I said to watch her language, and soon Oona was wailing and Kaylee stomping, and that was before the workmen turned off the pipes so I just filled Oliver's water bottle from the sink and forgot about it.

But maybe we should fetch water in the daytime, just to be safe.

Out in the Great Hall, the grandfather clock strikes ten.

"Didn't I shut that thing down?" Aiden says. "It wakes up Oona." The deep chimes resonate up the grand staircase to the wing where the little children are sleeping.

"It rings every night at midnight," Kaylee answers. "Just midnight."

"How can a clock ring once a day?" Aiden asks. "I mean, just wondering."

I do not care about their squabbling. I'm folding a towel and watching the green numbers on the microwave, counting down as my pleasant solo sewing time disappears. Single parenting my own kids is hard enough, I didn't ask for two more. I put away the hand towels, unable to stop from slamming the cupboard door.

Kaylee snaps open the microwave.

"Did your pudding come out any better this time?" I manage to smile.

Kaylee shrugs. "Maybe. We're out of milk so I can't try again." She clatters through the drawer and pulls out a spoon. "That was fun."

She meanders out of the kitchen without meeting my eyes. I am not sure if that comment is mocking me or she means it. She didn't act like she was having fun.

Almost done. I wipe up the flour and sugar all over the counter. Not because I'm a servant, just because I want the kitchen done and the kids in bed.

"Are you fixing the kids' uniforms tonight?" Aidan asks.

"Yes." I shake the rag in the sink.

"Could you...could you fix something for me? It's just little. Nothing much."

I shouldn't take my mood out on Aiden. "Of course."

"Really? 'Cause, if you don't mind, you could do like you did on that gray skirt of yours. The kids all like it."

I'm surprised. "The one with all the colors? Visible mending?"

He nods, flustered but hopeful. He pulls his denim jacket from a chair under the table, where he clearly stashed it waiting for me.

"That's fine." I take the jacket and finger the rip, deciding what I can do. I put my hand on the light switch, waiting for Aiden to come towards the door. "Ready?"

"Um...yeah. But..." He pulls out another jacket, this one cream and soft gold. "Kaylee also wanted a bee? Like those ones you did on the pillowcases? She put a safety pin in the spot she wanted."

If Kaylee wanted a bee on her jacket, Kaylee could possibly manage to compile a complete sentence, look me in the eyes, and say it.

"Um...if it's okay? It would be really cool." He gives me that tentative smile. "Please?"

I take it and manage not to sigh. "Of course. I'm happy to do a bee." It means I won't get to my own project tonight, but maybe stitching will work its magic, filling me with positive thoughts while I work, binding her heart to mine.

We walk out of the kitchen together, saying goodnight, and Aiden heads towards the grand staircase while I turn towards the living room. I stoke the wood stove again, and settle in my comfortable, cozy, wonderful chair. Bliss!

I'll save the fun sewing for last. I pull out Oona's uniform and start pinning. My mind can wander as my fingers adjust the seams for her narrow torso, and I fall into daydreams. Oona adores being in Senior Infants, in the same school with her brother, and her anxious habits are fading. Oliver is anxious about fitting in, but Oona is making friends easily for the first time in her life. I worried that leaving her father would make her cling to me even more, but I think she has intuited that we are safe here. The waist and side seams close under my needle, and I have only the hem to finish.

"Open, open!" someone calls, and I am half out of my chair when I realize the sound is from the front hall, not bedroom wing. It must be—

My stomach plummets. I don't know who it could be. One of our neighbors, with some kind of country trouble? Footsteps clatter towards the living room, so I suppose I forgot to lock the door. What if—

A woman clumps into the shadows on the far side of the Great Hall and I am flooded with relief. She has a bag under one arm, a bulky sweater, and looks so normal and unthreatening compared to the visions that leapt into my mind. I'm not sure why she would just walk in, but I have to remember that this isn't an American city filled with high crime. Neighbors probably walk into each other's houses all the time here.

"Welcome," I say with a blank smile, falling back on habit since I'm discombobulated. Roy brought home a lot of odd friends. "Did you need help with something?"

The woman glances at me and flops into the chair by the fire. I think her name is Mrs Doherty, who lives down the road and we met at the church craft fair. She is tall and frowning, with scraggly gray hair and—

Is that a horn sticking out of her disheveled bangs? But of course it's October, so it might be a Halloween costume, although usually it's just the children who dress up here...

Whatever is happening here, no good comes from starting an argument, so I smile again. I've gotten good at acting nice while I was married to Roy, no matter how I felt inside.

The probably-Mrs. Doherty glowers at me as she snatches items from her bulky sack. Maybe it's a hat, like the visors with room for a ponytail, or a headband under her hair. She's got so much hair, it certainly could hide one. I catch myself staring and drop my eyes to the brushes in her hands.

This is familiar ground. I can talk about this, and maybe everything will make sense in a moment. "Oh, you've brought over some carding? It's always more pleasant to craft with company, isn't it?" I try to smile. If I act like everything is calm and normal, hopefully she will act calm and normal as well. If I stay calm, she won't bother the children. "I do love working with natural fibers." I hope she will respond, but she just pulls at her batt so I keep chattering. "I tried carding, too, a few years ago. I found local wool, and learned all the steps to card and spin it. I didn't have enough for weaving, but I knitted a baby sweater. Have you watched the Sheep to Shawl competition? Amazing, isn't it..."

Okay. I don't actually think this is my new neighbor Mrs. Doherty. And I'm really not sure about that horn. All the more reason to stay composed.

"Where are the women?" not-Mrs.-Doherty snaps, staring towards my front door. "They delay too long!"

What women? Oh—I suppose it might be a craft circle. That would explain why she didn't greet me, because I'm sewing and she thought I was part of the circle too. It's the second Wednesday in October, and it's perfectly possible that some local women have used this castle for their crafting club on the second Wednesday of every month for years. Why not? I've already noticed that the whole neighborhood has a proprietary feeling about the castle, which I understand completely. Roy's money bought the property, but it's their history. Hosting a craft circle is a great way to give back to the community, really; I just wish I had known about it ahead of time. And maybe had some input about the meeting time.

Or maybe I'm dreaming it all? Maybe my imagination finally did run away with me. Or I fell asleep mending.

Before I can introduce myself, there is more clattering, heavy shoes on flagstones, something dragging. I really thought I had locked the door, but that must have been last night. Or wait, I remember reaching out, but then the mason jars fell.

"Welcome," I say as the second woman enters. My voice comes out tentative.

They must be meeting in costume. That's a perfectly rational explanation for... more horns? Maybe it's a theme?

The second woman ignores my greeting and snaps, "Give me place!"

Did I lock the door or did I not? Did I go to the kitchen before or after the bar fell into place? My armpits prickle and I can smell my own sour, anxious sweat. Why didn't I lock the door?

I gesture towards the sofa, but the second woman thumps her spinning wheel down next to the first. I drop my eyes to Oona's uniform, trying not to stare. This woman is short and neatly dressed, her hair pulled into a smooth bun, so there is nothing hiding her forehead.

Nothing to hold those two horns in place.

Two!

This is more than Halloween or a strange call in the dark or a whispery feeling on my spine. Although come to think of it, if I stop filling my head with justifications, I have a lot of whispery feelings on my spine, and everywhere else. I try to use that way of relaxing my vision that used to work as a child, but I come up with nothing. I've been in Roy's world for too long...

Cringing under the memory of his chuckles, once again feeling helpless and useless, I say nothing as the third woman enters. Three horns and a lap loom, and she draws up a stool next to the spinning woman, even though I don't keep stools in the living room. Roy would come up with a logical explanation, and he would laugh at me for being afraid of old women.

"Open, open!" calls a new voice, thin and reedy. I recognize the sound of the wooden bar lifting, although it's on the inside of the house and none of us are near the door.

I must be dreaming. Making up problems that don't exist, like Roy often accused me.

But the draft when the door opens is real. The swoosh of a car on the highway is like every other night. This is definitely Oona's uniform, with the same chalk marks I used this afternoon. And if everything else is real, maybe these are not ordinary women, maybe—

A low voice calls to my door as the fourth woman takes out wooden knitting needles.

Maybe these women have been having their craft circle here for a very long time. Centuries.

If they are real, what do I do next? My heart is pounding with fear, but they haven't actually done anything bad. They haven't attempted to pass beyond the Great Hall and do anything to the children. If my instincts are right and Roy's mocking is wrong, then these are fae—and the Irish fae are often demanding but not always evil.

The fifth woman comes in. She has five horns and a drop spindle.

And if Roy were right and the fae are only in my imagination, there are still more of them than me. I couldn't physically force them to leave my house, and I'm told if we call 999 to expect it to take an hour or more out here. Besides, I left my phone next to Oliver. I'm not going to go fetch it; it's definitely a better idea to keep an eye on these women.

Not daring to make a fuss, I return to Oona's hem. The door thumps and clatters, and seven more women file into my living room, one—by—one. Each has a tool for working wool, and each has one more horn than the last. Pretending to keep my eyes on my thread as I knot it off, I count twelve horns bristling from the forehead of the woman nearest me.

I don't know what to do, so I rethread my needle and mend Oliver's school pants. My son snagged it while sliding down the hill getting covered in dirt. Like children do. Normal second graders, in normal schools. I stitch and listen, listen and stitch.

I have to decide what to do next.

The women mumble short comments to each other, perhaps in Irish or perhaps I am just too unsettled to decipher their accents. I don't understand, but this is definitely real. The women make the room smell of wool and fennel, bump into a picture frame and send it clattering to the floor, make a breeze when they flap out their skirts to sit. Speaking of sitting, I arranged this big drafty room with only two recliners, a little rocker for Oona, and one couch, which is enough seating for one woman and four children. Now there are twelve people—plus me—seated in a circle, and all of them have chairs and stools.

The clock whirrs and the chimes strike eleven. Startled, I stare at Oliver's pants, which are somehow already finished, my familiar stitches making neat rows up and down them. I know sewing is meditative, but the last hour seemed to just vanish.

Since there is nothing else to sew, I knot the final stitch and snip my thread. I am tempted to sit and stitch all night, staring into the fire and waiting for someone to tell me what to do. I need to take some sort of action and wake myself up from this odd daze.

"Would you care for some tea, perhaps?" I speak over-loudly, since none of my guests have acknowledged me yet.

Twelve heads turn and twelve pairs of eyes stab into me.

"Yes, mistress," says the first woman. "Go fetch it."

"Gladly." I smile as I rise. If tea will keep them content, I will make as much tea as they can drink. Fortunately my chair is closest to the kitchen, so I do not have to move any closer to them.

I flick the kitchen switch, relieved when the lightbulbs turn on in the usual way, even though one is bright white and one is more yellow and ordinarily that irritates me. I take a slow breath, annoyed that it trembles as I exhale. I yearned to move to Ireland because I loved the folklore so much: another layer of truth exists next to our world, sometimes separate and sometimes touching. There's no reason to be upset just because what I have always believed has turned out to be true.

I have always imagined that the stories were real, so it isn't the fae themselves that worry me. It's having them in the house with my children.

I turn on the gas under the kettle and the pot, blowing on the burner that's always stubborn to light. As I fetch trays and mugs and teapots, my mind seems to clear. The Irish canon rewards bravery, cleverness, and obedience to the elder's wisdom. There are twelve horned women in my living room, and I just need to keep them away from my children. That's all. So I'll ply them with tea, keep the fire warm—and keep my eye on them.

I put sugar bowls on the trays, but we're out of cream. Maybe they won't notice. The kettle whistles, and I turn off the burner, but the pot isn't boiling yet.

The Irish canon also rewards a mother's love and loyalty, and that much I can do. In this dragged-out divorce, I have been through every shame and accusation, and weathered them for the sake of my children. I have been through fire for Oona and Oliver, and I am hot with certainty that we will get through this night safely, too.

Think, Maura. I have a dozen horned women in my living room. There are two possibilities here: one, these are wise crones, and showing them gratitude and hospitality will pave the way for their wise advice. Or two—

In the living room, the women start singing, their voices darting under and over, shrill and canting. I find myself scooping herbs from a ceramic pot with no recollection of the last few minutes or where this pot came from. I shake my head, hard, and start singing "Hallelujah" by Leonard Cohen. Oona has been obsessed with it lately, although Kaylee rolls her eyes and makes fun of her, and I let her alternate the playlist with Taylor Swift. I sing some of that, too, with a little shimmy. Nice and twenty-first century.

I tip the kettle over the herbs, and they bloom into a bright red color. I stare, and stare...

I shake my head hard, turning away from the acrid smell and forcing myself to start singing again. My thoughts move more freely again.

Option two is looking more and more likely. These are evil fae. The crones, the mother, and the innocent—my job in this story is to keep these horned women away from my children.

The children, the children, the children.

As I carry the trays back to the Great Hall, I barricade my mind with memories of my children.

The night when Oliver was born and my whole world was filled with color that I had never known. And Oona's birth; the pain, the ecstasy, Roy holding us both.

I remember us kicking leaves as we walked through the park, one sticky little hand in each of mine. Oona's laugh as I pushed her on the swing, up to the moon, visit the stars. Oliver's face when he brought me home a holiday-themed glob of construction paper and popsicle sticks, and then later with spelling tests and double-digit addition.

My memories fortify me all the way around the circle of horned women, pouring tea and passing mugs.

Twelve, sitting in order from one horn to twelve. I must keep them here, far from Oona and Oliver. I let my love throb, and I feel so strong and clear-headed that I have faith I will be able to protect them.

They do not speak to me, so I settle back in my chair to keep an eye on them. I pick up my mending, and the fuzzy texture surprises me. I blink, startled. This isn't a primary school uniform.

It's Burberry wool, one denim sleeve flopping out from underneath. Kaylee and Aiden! I forgot them entirely!

My heart sinks. Four children to care for, and I don't have years of love for my stepchildren, who aren't even really my official stepchildren. Resentment boils through the thoughts tumbling into my mind.

They are old enough to take care of themselves. I should focus on the little ones.

We all know what stepmothers are like. If I'm stuck in a folk tale, there's no point in me trying to be good.

If I forgot them already, then it must mean my love—tepid and hesitant at best—isn't going to be enough to protect them anyways.

Suddenly, I'm hot and angry with guilt. How could I forget them, even momentarily? I didn't ask for Aidan and Kaylee to live with us, but I thought I was trying my best. Apparently my best isn't much good.

Worst of all, I can't help thinking that if things get worse, maybe I could give Kaylee to the witches. Maybe that sacrifice would be enough to save the other children. And even more worst of all, the idea of that gives me a rush of pleasure, as though any part of this is a competition and any part of me would relish victory over a thirteen-year-old.

This is awful! I don't have to give in to thoughts like these.

I flatten one hand across the cream-and-gold wool and pick through my embroidery threads. I did a whole set of bees for the pillowcases last year and my fingers know how to do this practically without thought, which is just as well. I need my wits if we're all to survive this night.

I am determined that we all survive this night, including Kaylee. If a stepmother must betray her children, then I must rewrite that story.

I thread my needle and backstitch an oval for the bee's body. Some of the women are humming now, someone laughs, the spinning wheels whirr, and my mind is blurry.

It helped to hold onto memories of the little ones, so I need happy memories of Kaylee now. It isn't easy to keep her close to my heart, but I'm an intelligent woman. More to the point, Roy has spent years teaching me how to keep myself guarded. If I know that, I can also choose to open the gates to my heart. It might not be easy to love Kaylee, but I can make the choice to do it.

Until this month, I've mostly only seen the older kids at Thanksgiving, one week in the Bahamas every February and two weeks at the lake house every July. My mind flickers through Kaylee picking a fight with toddler Oliver, Kaylee scrolling her phone during a dinner I spent hours making, Kaylee demanding that her dad buy her some expensive gadget.

No. Is it the witches making me think like this? Surely I can do better. My fingers fly back and forth, filling the bee with bright golden satin stitch. That's when I notice that there are no piles of batts next to the carders; the spools on the spinning wheels are not growing fat; the traditional crios belts are not extending from the loom and snaking towards the floor.

I wrap the thread on my needle and plunge it above for a pistil stitch, then a second, and raise it to my eyes. I rub it. Yes, there are two cute little antennae. Yes, the whole bee is now yellow.

We are all crafting, but I am the only one in this room who is creating something.

I have a whole repertoire of fancy stitches for my bees, but right now I just choose simple and quick. The horned women can influence my thoughts, but they can't change the fabric so I must sew my love for Kaylee into her jacket. Do I love Kaylee? No time to think of that now. I load two needles with black thread and work quickly, filling in stripes and outlining wings. The witches are murmuring among each other, and I can feel resentment pummeling me. Kaylee told her mother about all my working-class gaffes. Roy only took a few days of vacation a year, but Kaylee demanding all his attention. Kaylee sniggering about how much weight I gained after Oona was born, and Roy giving her all my designer dresses, which were one thing he bought for me, one thing he liked about me, and then Kaylee spilled sauce poivrade all over the yellow one.

I stitch faster and let the thoughts fly past like gnats, annoying but insignificant. They do not define Kaylee, and I will not let them define me.

I take a few careful stitches in silver-white, suggesting the wings and defining the rump. One last tiny stay stitch.

Simultaneously, I snip my thread—

"Mistress," says the Woman of One Horn—

And I realize that although I have never witnessed Kaylee being kind, neither have I witnessed an adult being kind to her. There's something—

"Make us a cake," orders One-Horn, and I find myself rising to my feet. I cannot stop from walking into the kitchen and reaching for my biggest bowl. I resent the horned women's interference, for I wouldn't be foolish enough to disobey twelve witches. Those fairy tales never end well.

Which story are we in? Perhaps if I keep them busy until dawn, they must leave and my children will be safe.

Or perhaps I must sanctify. I stack the cake pans and bless them in the name of the Father and the Son and the Holy Ghost. The Christian gods have been in Ireland for a long time, but it doesn't feel quite right. I scoop flour and think of Demeter, the harvest. Yes; this is a women's story. The mother and the crone. Isis, be with us, I whisper to the eggs. Izanami, raise my family with this baking soda. Freyja, love as sweet as this sugar and my husband's tongue on the night we conceived. My spoon circles: Asase Yaa, Umay, Frigg; protect my children. Mór Muman, this is your butter, your land, and I am a mother as you are a mother. I turn on the oven; Pelehonuamea, burn the evil from my hearth.

I stare at the batter, gloopy and dense, and cannot think of any more names. I suppose I was making a simple cottage pudding, something I have often thrown together during one episode of Octonauts. But it needs liquid.

I open the avocado-colored fridge, but the milk jug is empty. Oh yes; Kaylee and her microwave puddings. Just water will do.

I hold the measuring cup under the tap and spin the handle for a whole minute before I remember the main is turned off.

The kettle—is empty. The pot. I jiggle the camping jug. I have forgotten something. The jug, what about the jug?

Aiden! Aiden is the one who fills the jug. And I had forgotten about him entirely. Entirely!

I am filled with a sick sense of foreboding. My throat is parched, and I tip the jug forward so the last bit pours into my glass. I drink it down, this water that Aiden has fetched for me, and try to make some sense out of this jumble.

The horned women are busy but make nothing. The opposite of their bitterness is acceptance; the opposite of their barrenness is creation.

There it is—I have mended the clothing for three of my children. I have stitched down my feelings for them, and even Kaylee is perfectly clear to me now. I see the little tremble of her chin when her pudding came out wrong, and I see now that she didn't dare ask me for help because her own mother never even let her try.

The witches compelled me into the kitchen this time. Their hold on me is growing, and I am flushed and shaking with the knowledge that I must complete Aiden's mending before they make their next move. Eating is a spell of its own; I have a bad feeling about this cake.

Hands stumbling, I bang the pans and scrape the top of the bowl, leaving the floury blob. I open the oven door (it creaks) and slam it closed.

Head down, I shuffle back to the living room. "Mothers, your cake is baking," I tell them.

They squeal and chitter with anticipation, and I slink back into my chair. Aidan's coat. I must finish his repair before they notice my deception.

I do not look up while I sew this time. I choose my threads quickly: pale blue like Aiden's eyes, turquoise like the sea outside the Florida mansion where he grew up, deep blue for the pure water he fetches for me. My heart is pounding, but my hands know this work and do not tremble or dawdle. When I finish a running stitch around the tear, I bring the denim to my face to check the sewing. I breathe in the smell of Aiden: fresh air, Sublime Gold shampoo, his own musky sweat. I am ashamed that he has been calling me 'Mum' for almost a month and I have never held him close enough to know his smell.

I feel the witches' influence tug at my mind as I slide the patch and darning egg under the denim. Aiden ruined sneakers on the second time out, sneakers so expensive they could have paid for my college wardrobe.

Aiden warning Oliver about all the ways he wouldn't be popular in kindergarten and making him cry. Aiden throwing up for one entire trip to Hawaii, until I couldn't wash the smell off my hands and—

Hey. This is ridiculous. Who could resent a child for vomiting?

With my ground stitches in place, it's time to add running stitches over the top in all the different blues I have chosen. Blend it together. Repair the damage. Mend what you can, Maura.

My brain is bleary with magic and stress and also plain exhaustion. Has the clock struck midnight yet? Oona always wakes me by six.

I don't have enough memories of Aiden to weave into his coat. He's always been quiet, gone into his room or played on his Switch when Roy started raising his voice. I know I must weave in my memories to hold tight to my love, so I pull out the heavy artillery, the memory that always makes my heart pound and my throat tight, even when there are not twelve horned women in my living room:

My divorce from Roy took an entire year, and we had to appear in court again and again. It is not that I am litigious. It was because Roy had not properly finalized his first divorce, and she was claiming his assets and Roy had a new pregnant girlfriend to care for as well. And his money is all family wealth so his brother was involved as well. The way I was raised, the whole thing was shameful, so I retreated into myself and held onto two requests only: I wanted full custody of Oliver and Oona, and I wanted a castle in Ireland.

That last demand sounded foolish, even to me who had dreamed of it all my life. But Roy really owns a great deal of property, and I was entitled to a great many parts of it. Since no one could decide who owned how much of all these houses and companies, they were delighted that I would cede my share in exchange for a single solitary property. My lawyer insisted that Roy throw in necessary furniture and upkeep for thirty-five years. But even once that was sorted, I still had to sit there while Roy argued with his first wife and his brother, and his girlfriend cried dramatically and the judge rubbed his temples. And then on what we all hoped would be the final day, the judge went down all the custody agreements one last time.

Roy's lawyer and my lawyer had worked them out amicably in mediation. I thought there were no surprises.

I was knitting on a side bench, my braid frazzled and my jacket creased from Oona's clinging tantrum when I left her at kindergarten, trying to appear politely uninterested in the endless bickering. Roy's older kids entered the court room, accompanied by no fewer than four women in designer suits and perfect hair.

"So, um, yeah," Aiden addressed the judge. "You said we were old enough to make our own choice. This time. Um, your Honor."

Kaylee trailed behind, examining the sparkles on her nails. I never know what she is thinking.

"That's right, young man," the judge answered, his pen ready. "Do you want to maintain the current arrangement?"

Aiden scratched his ear. "We'll both go with Maura," he said. "Full time. Um, yeah."

The entire courtroom went so silent that you could have heard a butterfly's wings unfurl.

One of the women with them clicked forward, perfectly poised in wholly impractical four-inch heels. "I'm their psychiatrist. I have discussed this at length with both siblings. Here is my report supporting the decision that Aiden just announced to Your Honor."

And then everything erupted. Back then, I was too numb to feel anything at all. Now, I go over the memory every night before I fall asleep, and the part I hold close is when Aiden glanced around the courtroom, panic growing in his too-young face, until his eyes met mine.

I kept my expressions shuttered back then. But Aiden had seen something, and he smiled, just a little, and he hugged his arms close to himself, just a smidge. And he made it through that awful afternoon, repeating his words every time he was asked.

I'm going with Maura. I'm going with Maura. I'm going with Maura.

"Where's our cake?" screeches One-Horn.

"I don't smell a thing," complains Two-Horn.

"Is the mistress lazy?" demands Three-Horn.

I stab my stay-stitch, slide the needle under, and snip my thread before I speak. It isn't my best work, but Aiden's jacket is mended. I can feel him now, his tentative smile, the way we are finding things to laugh about together, the way he brings me his literature homework and asks me questions with trust in his eyes.

It is not just Aiden I am feeling, it is us. A relationship that I didn't even realize belonged to me.

"Good mothers, let me fetch it," I answer, rising to my feet, eyes cast downwards. I rush to the kitchen, their hackling chasing me down the passage. I have a scant few seconds to come up with an excuse or a lie.

I slam the door behind me, my eyes scanning the kitchen desperately. Every mythology has its own central themes, its own types of warnings and its own particular unhappy endings. The thing is, the Irish canon is particularly bad about children.

It is bad about the fae stealing children, and there are twelve fae in my living room while my four children sleep upstairs. I must make the right choices, but there are as many stories as there are story-tellers, and there is no way to know which one I am in.

Kaylee's pudding. The microwave. Maybe I can cook up the cake really fast.

I dart across the kitchen, but as my hand tugs the microwave's handle, sparks begin to fly. Its lights all flash, randomly, frenetically. I slam the door and back away. It isn't unexpected that electricity doesn't work right—

Then the entire microwave starts blinking and flickering. First with green light, then the whole thing disappears for a second, is back, gone and back and...gone. All that's left is a little puddle of grease on the counter.

"Dammit!" I swing my fist and thump the counter. Now I'm mad. This isn't abstract any more.

It's one thing to try and raise four children—all wealthy and American—in a drafty, half-ruined castle in Kilkenny. It's another to try to do it without a damn microwave! I'm going to be drinking lukewarm tea and eating lukewarm food for the rest of my life! How will Oona make her oatmeal packets for breakfast—

Never mind. We need to survive till breakfast time, which is looking uncertain. Enough with the microwave. Maybe I can just throw the batter in the oven, maybe in little pieces like cookies and it will cook faster.

But it's so cold in the kitchen that the butter didn't mix in properly, so the batter is mostly flour with globs where it's stuck to the egg. I set the whole bowl on the warm stove and beat that spoon as hard as I can.

The clock in the hallway whirrs, plays its song on out-of-tune chimes, and strikes the hour. Midnight. It is their time now.

"Mistress, is there a problem?"

The voice comes to me as clear as day, and when I look up I can see straight to the horned women. It is as though the wall between us is nothing but mist, or ice, or old-fashioned glass with its bubbles and waves.

"Where is our cake?" screeches Five-Horn, and my feet carry me back towards them as though I am a yo-yo, the bowl cradled in my arms.

Their magic does not compel my words, and I have an idea. "We are out of milk, and I have used the water for your tea. Is there any left? I can mix the batter with your tea."

Their eyes fixed on me, the three closest to the teapots each reach out an arm, lift the pot, and tip it over a cup. The pots are all empty, and the gestures all are in eerie synchronicity.

"Go fetch some water from the well," Six-Horn orders.

"Yes, mothers." I drop a fumbling curtsey, and am allowed to return to the kitchen. Okay, the well. I didn't want to leave the house with the witches and children inside, but the well is only a dozen steps from the kitchen doorway. The courtyard has castle walls on all four sides, built up over the centuries. This well has been here since before the time of Christ, and I have always liked it.

Okay. I can do this. I don't need to fill the whole heavy jug, I just need a couple of cups. Some for the cake, and some for my parched throat. I plonk the mixing bowl back on top of the stove and grab the teakettle.

The handle comes off in my hand and the kettle falls back onto the stove, breaking in half.

It's a metal kettle. This is not normal.

I use both hands to lift the pot, cautiously, but it shatters into a dozen pieces. Usually, my cheap clearance pots hang from wrought-iron hooks, but the hooks are empty. I open the cabinet with our dishes, only to find a heap of broken crockery. Same with my baking drawer. How about the low cupboard, with Oona's plastic cups—they're...gone.

Horned Women, with every passing minute I am liking you less and less.

We've barely moved in, so there's not much more to look for. I glance at the mixing bowl with the gloppy batter; I could take it outside and put it under the tap...

That gives me a bad feeling. A very bad feeling. I don't take the time to analyze it; I assume there is some folktale that my subconscious remembers. But it would be quick, I could run, I could make the cake. I must finish the cake!

I am holding the bowl and halfway to the door by the time I realize I am doing exactly what I decided against.

"No! Stop." I pause, twitching towards the door. Song works better; I figure out lyrics with the word "stop" and when I sing a couplet I am able to obey myself and set the bowl back down. I must trust myself.

Roy would laugh at me, but I am making the choices here. Not him. Not the witches.

That invisible string draws me back to the living room. Fine. They have some power. But I will hold onto my own.

"I have no vessel to fetch the water," I tell them.

"Take a sieve, and bring water in it," orders Seven-Horn.

I curtsey again, with a bubble of hope. There are dozens of stories about a sieve becoming solid once a supernatural creature tells a human to fetch water with it.

"And don't come back until you do!" she cries to my receding back, and the others all cackle and chortle.

The sieves in the stories were probably not like mine, faded green plastic with a too-long handle so the basket wobbles and sags when it is full. I slip on my fleece and shoes and carry my sieve to the well. Please, my children be safe. I'll be quick.

I find the flashlight in my fleece pocket and shine it up into the well, and find the bar and the crank and even the bucket with a painted rim just like Oliver described. But when I shine my light down, the water is sparkling only a little way below the top of the well. I don't need to figure out the pulleys and bucket, I can reach down and touch it.

As I draw in slow breaths, I realize how much the witches have clouded my mind. The air smells of wood smoke and elderberries, rotting leaves and wet stones. I close my eyes and look back to girlhood-Maura, the joyful confident Maura at Indiana University, the Maura who knew she could feel the shivers of the world that barely touches our own. I let my fingertips of my left hand trail in the water, and lift the other towards my children's bedrooms. Their lights are out, but I know they are there. Sleep little ones. Do not come downstairs tonight.

If I trust myself, I know that I love them. All four of them. I draw that love around me like a cloak, like the wisp of smoke when I blow out Kaylee's Lilly Pilly candle, fastened closed with one of Oona's sticky kisses.

I can feel that love, a spider-light thread from my fingertips to their hearts. The gray sandstone wavers, just a moment, and I recognize this shiver. I can feel their heartbeats.

Two heartbeats. I close my eyes and reach deeper, searching for Kaylee and Aiden.

I can still hear the witches in the Great Hall, which is the front side of this courtyard. Our bedrooms are upstairs in the second wing. The third side is falling apart; I asked the workers to nail boards across the entrance to our tower, because all four children want so badly to explore it. Behind me, the fourth wing is storerooms and garages.

I cup both hands in the water and drink. It is clean and sharp, like fine wine with the memories of herbs and minerals in the edges of the mouth. I drink again and again, four handfuls.

Come on, Maura! Four heartbeats! Find them all! Try harder!

I glance back towards the lighted living room. Although the sitting area is past the kitchen, I can almost see them, the silhouettes of women in dark gowns, their hands carding and spinning, the shadows of their horns dancing in the firelight. I need to act before they come outside and start making choices for me.

I dip the sieve in the well. All the water pours out, just like you would expect.

I dip it again and again. Try putting my hands over the bottom. Try wrapping my skirt underneath and running towards the kitchen door, but it only soaks my skirt and leaves the sieve empty. I try carrying water in my hands, which become frigid and stiff. I dig through my fleece pockets; maybe there's a plastic bag, a candy wrapper, something to block the holes, anything anything anything. I must be more clever than this trap they have set for me.

If I can dip water into the broken shards of a pot, I could fill the mixing bowl tablespoon by tablespoon. I turn back toward the kitchen, but my feet stick. I yank myself, but the momentum only knocks me to my knees, my palms hitting the flagstones and I cry out in pain, or maybe fear and despair and self-loathing. I cannot solve their puzzle, I cannot escape their trap.

The clock strikes one.

This is the deepest depth of the night; I have hours to keep them busy until dawn closes the gates between our worlds.

"It seems the mistress has forgotten us," says One-Horn.

When I raise my head, once again, it is as though I am looking through medieval glass, slightly distorted, but the light shines clearly. Except this time, I am also looking through my own tears.

"We must make the cake ourselves," says Two-Horn.

"If the mistress has no milk, then we will mix the cake with blood," says Three-Horn.

Damn Kaylee, damn her three stupid puddings and burning the edges and she didn't even share and now we are out of milk!

"I know where the children are," says Four-Horn.

"Maura, you're being foolish," I say aloud, pushing myself onto my knees. It's 2024; no one would ever think of saving enough milk to make a cake for witches in the middle of the night! And if anyone could think such a thing, it would be me, the folklorist, who knows something about saving milk. The teens only know Disney.

Besides, I'm the adult. I'm responsible.

"Let us go find them," says Five-Horn.

"They will be delicious," says Six-Horn, and they all rise.

"Stop!" I scream. I stagger onto my feet, but the only direction I can move is back to the well. "Stop! You may not pass! Stop!"

Unperturbed, they all file out of the Great Hall, into the corridor to the grand staircase that curves around both sides of the Elizabethan hall. Up the first seven steps. Like a ballet dance, they part, one taking the right and the next the left, in perfect unison.

"Stop!" I cry again, but my voice is weak and trembling. It is obvious that they do not hear or perhaps they just do not care.

The first witch draws a silver blade, the second a lamp, and the two lines reunite as one. This is the hallway that leads to the bedrooms. To my children.

I am responsible. Responsible for their lives, their innocence.

Roy's mother told me I couldn't do it, four children and a foreign country and me full of these useless ideas. My own mother said I would have another think coming, trying to parent without Roy's money solving all my problems. Aiden and Kaylee's mother said a dozen things, each worse than the last. No one wanted me here. No one trusted me.

I sag down on top of the stone wall. My hair is falling out of its braid, my legs shaking under my wet clothes, my numb fingertips trail in the water. The plastic sieve tumbles at my feet, as useless as I am.

Two-Horn opens the door to the big bedroom and One-Horn glides in, holding the blade above her head. I can see Oona now, sleeping on the right, and Oliver tucked into his bed on the left.

Wait. I can see. Through the walls.

This is some kind of magic. The Horned Women are not listening to me, but the house itself is. And that thread—that thread that I stitched between my children and myself—

I lift my hand, and I feel it. I breathe the air, I touch the stones and the water, and I can find my baby. There is Oona, not through a glass darkly, but her heartbeat as close as when she used to nurse at my breast.

Seven-Horn holds up a lantern, Eight-Horn pulls Oona's arm from beneath the blankets, and Nine-Horn kneels beside Oona's bed with a crystal bowl in her hands.

I have nothing to sew, but I must find my own strength. A song has power, a verse, a rhyme, but what can I say? I cannot command the witches. The house is too large, too old, for me to change. But perhaps I can command my children. Fly away? Fight? Those seem foolish.

One-Horn slashes her knife through the air, glinting in the lantern-light. The silver tip dives into my baby's wrist and red spurts onto One-Horn's white hand and drips into the bowl.

My baby, her blood—

> *"Child who was born to me,*
> *Do not let your blood run free…"*

My words are tumbling and fumbling, a half-question at the end of the sentence. It's the way I have been talking to Roy for years now, trying to be kind, hoping to influence him. It's the way I talk to Aiden and Kaylee and the handyman. I hate it, I hate who I have become.

The Horned Women look up, as though they have noticed some presence besides themselves.

Oona's blood is still dripping, but it is no longer gushing.

I try again, stirring the well-water, gripping the stones, pulling anger and love into my lungs and transforming them into a clarion call.

> *"Child who was born to me,*
> *Do not let your blood run free!"*

Oona does not stir, but the drips slow, then stop. She lays as though a marble statue, but I can feel the torpid beat of her heart.

Nine-Horn holds up the bowl and the others inspect it.

"That is not enough for our cake," says Ten-Horn.

"We must collect more," says Eleven-Horn.

"Our cake must be a delicious feast," says Twelve-Horn.

"And we must have enough to share," says One-Horn, and she turns to Oliver's bed.

They move quickly, but this time I am prepared. It is terrible to watch one's child in pain, and I wince away as the blade pierces my sweet boy's tender skin. But I keep my gaze steady and I make my voice strong:

> *"Child who is born to me,*
> *Do not let your blood run free!"*

The dripping stops quickly, and they collect less blood than they got from Oona. Visibly irritated, they repeat their statements and head down the hallway.

I am too busy thinking to pay them much attention. I can say my rhyme before they get to Aiden, but obviously I cannot say the same thing. What power I have is rooted in love and in truth.

"Child who has chosen me, do not let your blood run free," I try, but I can feel that they are just words. My rhyme for Oona was yanked from my heart, from my womb.

"Child of my heart..." But he's not, we don't love each other yet. *"Child who I honor and respect..."* I'm never going to rhyme that. *"Child I swear to protect and defend..."* That has no meaning because I have given him nothing; nothing of my true self. I have dealt with school paperwork and folded his laundry, but I have guarded my heart. I have not even asked Aiden what he likes to have best for dinner.

Two-Horns opens Aiden's door. She does not know the way it always sticks and drags, and it takes her three tries to get inside.

One-Horn raises the knife above her head, but the blade is no longer shiny. It is dark with the blood of my children, and I am burning with anger. Aiden's face is sweet and young on the pillows, and he is such a good kid, and he chose to be here. No one else thought I was anything, but Aiden trusted me and this heat, this rage, this power emanates from the magma of the earth and radiates through my entire body—and this is love.

"Child who chose me, all above,
Let me enwrap you in motherly love…"

That is all true, it is all Aiden. My thread spools out and catches him, but now I need to say my truth for him. Except I do not know my own truth, not for these two children.

One-Horn plunges her knife into his arm, and Nine-Horn pushes her bowl closer. His blood splashes down. No no no, it is too fast, and I want—

"I want you beside me for days and for years,
Do not shed blood and"

—rhyme with years, rhyme with years—

"do not cry tears!"

I'm not getting nominated for the next poet laureate, but the house or the air or their souls hear my passion, and his bleeding ceases.

"Is that enough?" asks Twelve-Horn.

"I want a good cake," says Eleven-Horn.

"There is one more child," says Ten-Horn, and they turn to file out of the room.

But my mind is racing faster than their dance-like pace, and Kaylee's room is down and around the corner. I'm getting the hang of this, but what is the truth for Kaylee? She did not choose me, I did not work for her. She is just—aha!

"Dear child who is broken,
I am thankful you stayed,
Each day I am grateful for the choice you have made."

It catches her, like a bee flying from my fingertips and spooling the thread of my love around her. Poor Kaylee, who didn't want to leave her school and is chronically cold and scared of the dark, but every single adult in her life is even worse than this, and she just wants to make her pudding and I am enraged, irate, incensed that yet another person is trying to hurt her.

The Horned Women turn into her corridor, and Seven-Horn holds the lantern while Two-Horn reaches towards the door.

"Door!" I scream. *"Please hold fast!*
Lock! Fall in place!"
There is a thump and a clatter as Two-Horn shoves.
"Protect my sweet child from pain and disgrace!" I yell.
Two-Horn pulls and yanks, but the door does not budge. Nine-Horn blows on the lock. Eight-Horn kicks it. Seven-Horn searches up and down the hallways for a different entrance.

I am exultant, my heart pounding so hard I can hear the rush in my ears. I say the whole rhyme again, my voice quiet and steely, like the way I wish I presented myself to the world.

"Dear child who is broken,
I'm thankful you stayed,
Each day I am grateful for the choice you have made.
Door! Please hold fast!
Lock! Fall in place!
Protect my sweet child from pain and disgrace."

"We cannot get through," says Six-Horn.

"We have enough, though barely," says Five-Horn, examining the bowl.

"Let us go and bake our cake, our cake!" shrieks Four-Horn. They file away, and the walls grow dim then solid.

My children are safe, for now. But what happens once that cake is cooked?

I stand and test my feet. I can walk around the well, but I cannot leave it. I fill my hands and take a step away, but as soon as the water drains I am pulled back. Now I can see the Horned Women in the kitchen, but the normal way—through the window. I think they have forgotten me, but the compulsion she spoke earlier remains in place. Don't come back until you fetch the water. I am still trapped, but everything has changed. I have changed.

I am connected to something, and I speak to it. "How can I fetch this water?"

A woman's voice answers me, low and resonant. "Take my yellow clay and moss and bind them together, and plaster the sieve so it will hold."

This would seem like it is obvious, but I have only ever seen this courtyard with paving stones and pebbles and shiny steel. Hm, perhaps the moss was cleaned when they installed the pump? I walk around the well, shining my flashlight, dragging my fingertips into the corners and between the stones. It is well-worn stone, but I find bits of clay here and bits of moss there. Just enough to plaster the sieve. Slowly, but hopefully fast enough.

I dip the sieve in the well. Water drips but holds. I walk towards the house, one step, two, three, four. Twelve steps and I am at the door. The cake is baking and I pass through the empty kitchen, exulting in my freedom. Cold water drips down my wrist, and I smile. I passed their trial, and I recognize that the well and the spell have given this water other-worldly powers, and now it is mine.

I find myself in front of the grand staircase, but this time I am not propelled by the compulsion of the witches but the compulsion of my heart. I debate what to do next, the dribbling water braced on one hip, flickering my flashlight up and down the stairs. The rest of my water might leak out before I reach the children, and besides, in the fairy tales blood must atone for blood. Water will not be enough to revive them.

But the house will listen to me. I dash water from one banister all the way to the other.

> *"Stairs, obey my will and drink your fill!*
> *Test the heart of anyone who passes.*
> *Let none set foot who wishes ill.*
> *Protect my little lads and lasses."*

I feel the settling in the house as it absorbs its new purpose. That should do it.

The clock strikes two. I can smell the first whiffs of cake, and it is more sweet than any pastry I have ever made. Nothing at all like frying up blood pudding. There is cackling in the living room, and I run into the courtyard.

I lean on the well, the stone rough on my palms. "How do I send the Horned Women away?"

The answer comes again. "Go to the north angle of the house, to the very top of the tower. Cry into the wind three times, and say 'the mountain of the Fenian women and all the sky over it is all on fire.'"

The Fianna are the ancient warrior bands who follow Fionn mac Cumhaill, and the Fenians can refer to them or—more often nowadays—the Irish Republican Brotherhood who fought for independence in the early twentieth century. The Fenian women could be either, I suppose. I trust the well and I trust myself.

Now that I know what to do, I am filled with urgent panic. I race to the other side of the courtyard, hoping that the tower stairs have reverted to the same period as the well, when they were solid and functional. But no, they are just like the workmen left them; blockaded by plywood and 2x4's, and my flashlight shows pebbles and stones littering the stairs. There's probably bats, or badgers.

I never wanted to go up there. But that makes me think of the children, the light in their eyes when they begged me to let them explore. For once, all united.

I pull at the first board, but it holds fast. I yank harder before remembering this is ridiculous. I must use my head.

I drag over a planter to climb on, but when I try to upend it the lemon tree fights back, stabbing my face with leathery branches and the block of soil stuck to the terracotta. Finally I get it out, my skirt now muddy and my hands smarting. Standing on the planter, I can just grip the top of the board and use the 2x4's to step on. I stick the flashlight in my mouth, although it tastes acrid and is probably all over germs. I scrabble and pull, my palms growing raw from grabbing at the unfinished plywood. I pause at the top, a board cutting into my stomach and ribcage, to check the other side with my flashlight. There are tumbled stones which I can use to scramble down, which is easier as long as I don't think about more of those stones falling on me. I aim, swing my legs over, and let go. It scrapes my thigh so painfully that I have to stop for a moment, gasping.

The smell of the cake is everywhere now. The walls are tight on either side of the tight spiral staircase, hemming me in, spider webs glob onto my face and something larger might jump out any minute. I find a stick and wave it in front of me. My pulse is pounding to hurry, run, quickly, but I force myself to climb carefully, shining my light back and forth to check for debris. If I slip and fall or get attacked by a badger, then I will not be able to fulfill my instructions, protect the household, and revive my children.

The door at the top of the tower is half-broken, but with all my strength I can shove it just enough to squeeze through. The wind catches my damp skirt and tangled hair, carrying such a scent of freedom that it makes me laugh out loud. The forest spreads out below me, the quarter-moon flits through gossamer clouds. Here I am! Even the smell of the cake cannot reach me here.

I cry out three times, half in fear for my children and half in anticipation. Clutching the stone balustrade, my hair flapping around my face, I shout the words that I learned from the well.

"The mountain of the Fenian women and all the sky over it is all on fire!"

The Fianna come from the north beyond the moon, calling and laughing to each other on the wind. They fly on broomsticks and ravens and by their own sheer will; in the distance, in the distance, and then swooshing past my tower. I think they are both kinds of Fenians, although it is hard to see. They are screeching war cries in Irish and English, waving shillelaghs and hoes but also pistols and sewing shears.

They descend on the Great Hall, flying at the windows and door and vanishing instantly. I circle the tower to watch, but the walls stay solid and I can only guess what occurs within. I assume they are battling the horned women, and I am delighted. They make a great deal of noise.

After some time (three minutes? thirty?), the front door opens and twelve figures rush out, their line as neat and precise as ever. Then, a dozen blurry figures fly out of where the clerestory windows ought to be. Anxiety breaks through my exultation, as I imagine presenting Roy with the bill for every window in the Great Hall. He might call his lawyers in, for that, and I don't ever want to see a lawyer again, but how can we get through the winter with all the windows broken?

Come to think of it, I didn't hear the sound of shattering glass. Maybe they passed through like shadows.

Come to think of it, if I can wake the children and keep the Horned Women away, then I should be grateful for anything else. I should be, but lawyers are scary.

All is silent.

I can't stop now.

I make my way slowly down the staircase, each step shuddering into my knees and hips. I am so tired, and the stone is so unforgiving. Finally, moonlight in front of me—the delicious smell of the cake assaults me. The kitchen window is straight across from me, and I can see it on the counter.

But first, the plywood barrier. I groan. This time, with the witches gone, there is no adrenaline to help me reach higher or pull harder, just the dull awareness that I cannot stay back here all night. The children need me, their heartbeats slow and faint. My feet keep slipping when I try to climb the boulders. I grab for the top of the plywood and it hurts so badly, rubbing all the raw places. I haul myself up and can't help but cry. The plywood juts into my stomach, rips my legs. It all hurts, it is not fair; my anger has drained away and I am nothing but pain and exhaustion. Plan, Maura. I've got to land on the planter, not hit the paving stones and smash like an egg.

I catch it, landing hard with my balance wrong. I jump off the planter before I can fall, twist one ankle and tumble into the lemon tree.

Okay. That's done. Okay.

I limp back to the well, rubbing my fleece sleeves across my face. I sink onto the rim of the well, one arm around the post, the other fingers dangling. The cool water feels good on my hands, and I take a drink and splash my face. There. I am better. I must be better. Mothers do not have the option to give up.

"You have only one question remaining." The well startles me by speaking first. "Ask wisely, Maura."

The clock strikes three.

An owl hoots in the woods; a truck passes on the distant highway; I feel the heartbeats of the children sleeping in their beds. Other than the insidious smell of too-sweet cake, it is a normal night. I have time to sort through all the stories that I know and choose the right question.

"How do I protect this house so the Horned Women cannot return?" I finally ask.

"Ah, Maura, that is what you need to know. Listen carefully. Sprinkle your child's foot-water on the threshold outside the front door. Drop the crossbeam of the door into its jambs, and tie it in place with four threads from your four children's mending. And break apart the cake that the witches have baked, and place a bit in the mouth of each child who cannot wake—but do not eat even one crumb yourself, Maura."

"Thank you, oh, thank you! I shall do as you bid. Thank you." I bend and kiss the stone, then hurry towards the house, half-forgetting my scratches and aches. None of that will be difficult! I have made the magic and now I just need to tie it together, and we will all be safe. Safe!

I limp up the grand staircase, already planning what I will make for breakfast. I will call the children in sick from school; after all, they have lost a lot of blood. Waffles, I think. With thick Irish bacon and whipped cream and imported Vermont maple syrup.

Foot-water is from a time when children went barefoot and washing feet was a ritual. But Oliver, who tore his school uniform sliding down hills, does not disappoint. Under the covers, his feet are nice and grimy. I keep a bowl under the bathroom sink in case of vomit, and fill it with warm water. The plumbing in this wing is still working fine. I wash Oliver's feet—he does not stir, but the water goes a satisfying gray. I march downstairs and splatter it on the threshold, saying a rhyme for good measure. First step done!

The living room is an absolute disaster. Lamps are broken, spinning wheels cracked apart, picture frames splintered and shards of glass sparkling across the hearth. My sewing basket is knocked into a corner, tangled up in the mending. I find a working lamp. It takes a little while, but I sort out my needles and the threads I have used tonight. Four threads: girls primary uniform blue, boys primary uniform brown, gold for the bee and blue for the water.

It is satisfying to drop the crossbeam into the jambs, even though it stings my hands. My cold, scraped fingers stumble, but I am good with thread and I manage to get them tied. I put my hands on my hips, admiring my handiwork. I love that those delicate threads can hold the oak crossbeam in place, so it cannot leap to the witches' call. Two steps done!

The clock strikes four.

Now, just for the cake. And my children will wake! I long to kiss each one, even the big kids. I push open the kitchen door. The smell hits me and my stomach growls.

It's going to be delicious, but not for me. The nightlight in the corner is enough; I just want to get through this quickly. I place the cooling rack on the counter, put one hand on top, and flip the pan over.

And I find my hand almost at my mouth, clutching a fistful of cake.

"Maura! Stop!" I laugh, almost in surprise. I might be hungry—okay, starving—but the cake isn't for me.

I break the cake to put pieces in the pan, but I want to eat a chunk. I drop it, but raise my palm to lick it.

No.

I wipe my hands down my skirt, more desperately now. What is wrong with me? I lean forward, inhaling that blissful smell—and almost dip onto the counter and grab cake right in my mouth.

No!

I back away, clutching a kitchen chair to ground myself. This is ridiculous! Just break the cake into pieces. One into the mouth of each child. It will wake them from this strange, marble sleep, which is what I want most in the world. All of that love pounding through my veins, and the answer is right here. It's easy!

Except what I want most in the world is to eat that cake.

I am a strong woman. A smart woman. I can do this. Just bring it upstairs to my children.

Three times, I cross the kitchen and start to break the cake. Three times, my hands and mouth and arms disobey, trying to eat eat eat just one bite just one.

Cake in my hand—I cast it to the floor. Slap my own cheek. I pick up the cake with my left hand, a kitchen spoon poised in my right so I can whack my hand if it tries to feed me.

Want—I whack it.

Bring the cake towards my mouth.

Whack. This time I cry out.

My left hand is throbbing, but still pulled towards my mouth.

Whack, whack, whack. I am sobbing now, pain cutting through my fear and frustration.

I drop the cake and retreat behind the table, as though the flimsy thing can hold back the raging beast inside of me. I want that cake I want that cake. I drag the table and chair towards me, blocking myself into the corner, clutch the windowsill behind me, my left hand barely able to grip. My hair is flinging in my face like One-Horn's, I am sobbing and do not dare let go of the windowsill to wipe my snot away. My sweaty fingers slip free and I launch myself onto the table, which shudders under my weight. I need to get to that cake! I start crawling forward, the table swinging like a rowboat. Either to feed it to my children or to myself, I must have it!

The overhead light floods the room, white and yellow.

"What's going on in here?" Kaylee says. "It's been really loud tonight."

Oh yeah. Kaylee is not turned to marble sleep, because the Horned Women never touched her. I slide off the table onto a chair, trying to pull myself under control.

Kaylee's eyes are wide with fear, and she clutches her bathrobe tight. Her gaze swings to the counter, and she recoils. "What is that mess? And it smells disgusting! And don't say I'm yucking someone else's yum, because no one could like that smell! It's like dead skunk!"

"It smells...disgusting?" I can barely breathe through the ambrosia that assaults my nostrils. I am hungry and my hands are stinging and my ankle is throbbing and my thighs are frozen and chafed and splintered under my torn wet skirt. I just want that cake, but I have to think.

Kaylee doesn't even want the cake, which means that this yearning is for me, specifically. I cannot complete this story by myself.

The crone, the mother and...the maiden.

"Kaylee," I say, "I need your help."

I expect her to cringe, but instead she stands a little taller. "You need me? Can I do something? It's like...really there's a problem in here."

"It's really a problem," I agree. I feel a little more like myself now that I'm talking to Kaylee.

"Did you see the living room?"

"I did. We can sweep in the morning. But right now...Kaylee, I need you to take this cake upstairs. Your brothers and sisters are all..."

"Enchanted?" Kaylee offers.

"How did you know?"

"I looked for you in your bedroom, first. Oona and Oliver are just, like, laying there. They look weird. And there's dark stuff on the covers." Now Kaylee cringes a little, but just a little.

"Yes. One bite of this cake will restore them, and Aiden too. But listen, Kaylee—take the whole thing. Every single crumb. Don't leave any of it here."

"You trust me to do that?"

Motherhood is coming back to me, and I manage a reassuring smile. "You are the only one who can do it. I know you can, Kaylee."

"I'd better get some water." Kaylee pulls the wash-up tub down from the shelf—where did that come from?—and hurries to the well and back. She leaves the door open, and the fresh air clears my mind a little.

I clutch the table while Kaylee does a meticulous job of cleaning up the mess I have made, the counter and the floor and even wiping off the cooling rack so not a smudge is left.

"What do I do with the rest?" she asks, rinsing her rag. "What doesn't fit in their mouths."

"Flush it down the toilet," I say. It will meld with the castle's water and drain into our septic field, one with the land. The well can manage the evil cake.

"All right." She puts a paper towel over the cake pan to hold all the pieces in. "I'll be right back. Okay? Okay! Here I go!"

"There you go." I manage another smile. "You can do it."

Kaylee doesn't like the dark even in her own bedroom, she doesn't like the sound of the rain dripping from the eaves, and she refuses to light the fire because she's afraid she'll get burned.

But she must be brave, just the way she has been brave enough to stay this whole long month in a world that feels hostile at every turn.

Kaylee leaves the kitchen.

I draw a breath.

And another.

And something occurs to me. Kaylee can feed the three children, wake them all, finish the enchantment so the witches cannot return, and there still will be cake left over! There's no need to flush it down the toilet. I can have a bite. That's reasonable. I will make sure they are all awoken and safe. After the children have had their share, I can have a little. That is what mothers do; have the last sweet nibbles when their children are done. That is not selfish.

I rise from the table, wobbling a little on my bad ankle, and head for the grand staircase. Kaylee has turned on the lamp at the top of the hallway. "Wait, Kaylee!" I put my hand on the newel post and search for her upright figure. "Just a minute! Don't flush it away! Wait!"

It hasn't been long, so she can't be done yet. I step up the stairs, leaning on the balustrade to support my bad ankle—

And fall down again. Well, that was stupid.

I push myself painfully to my feet and start up the stairs again.

And fall.

How ridiculous! And I'm starting to get mad. I just need to get up and find Kaylee! I just want a bite of that cake!

I fall.

I hear Oliver, the sort of mumbled exclamation he often has in his sleep. His natural sleep, because he's had the cake, and all the children will get their share, I just want the bit that is leftover. That is not selfish!

"Let me have the leftovers!" I call, to Kaylee and the entire house. "Just save one bite for me!"

I try to step over the first stair, but fall again. I try on my hands and knees, but it is like climbing ice. I cannot make any headway; I just slide to the floor again. Everything hurts, but I am determined! I have done everything tonight, I must do this last thing! I try to pull myself up with the banister, but I collapse back down; I clutch and jump and flail. My knees are bruised and I am sobbing and I am leaving smears of blood with every grab. I don't understand, I am forgetting something, I don't know, but I must get up to my children, I must have that cake!

I wail her name, "Kayyyy-leeee!"

No one answers.

My head drops to the stairs, aching and throbbing. They are just normal stairs. I go up them every day. I will try one more time.

Smack, bang—I avalanche to the floor. The cake and my children, I must—

Above me, I hear the whoosh of a pull chain toilet, and everything is over.

I don't care about getting up the stairs.

I don't want to eat.

Everything hurts.

I curl into myself, cuddling my aching hand against my chest. I am cold, it is dark, and I cry. Silently. I have failed.

"Maura? They're sleeping now, the normal way. Maura!"

Footsteps on the stairs, poom-poom-poom-poom.

"Watch out for the—" I do not know what to say. I do not know why the stairs keep throwing me down, but Kaylee does not trip.

"Oh my god."

I hear the sob in her voice, and I am aching with guilt. It is too much, she is too young. I have failed.

There's a drag and a clunk and a click, and a lamp turns on over us. That's what Kaylee thinks of first, turning on the lights, and right now it's a darn good idea. I open my eyes and try to push myself up.

"Maura, oh my god! You're gonna be okay. I'm sorry. I'm sorry, Maura." Her hands on my shoulder, arm around my waist. She scoots us both, her lithe body pressed against mine. "Come here. I got you a blanket. It's one you made, it's really soft, I'm sorry, but I stole it for my room. Here you go...Mom."

She wraps us both in the blanket and we scoot against the wall. She drops her head onto my shoulder and I lean my cheek against her hair, both of us sagging and holding up the other. She clutches the quilt around us with one hand, and holds my hand with the other. I adjust the blanket so it covers our feet. We are all tucked away.

"It's okay, sweetie," I say.

"It's okay," she tells me.

We hold hands, tight. Nothing is okay.

The clock strikes five, and I hear a sound in the distance. It is a call of rage and vengeance.

We both tense.

"Open, open!" screams the voice, and eleven others echo the cry. "Open, feet-water!"

"I cannot," comes a reply, child-like and ghostly. "I am scattered on the ground, and my path is down to the Lough."

Kaylee shivers. I hold her tight.

"Open! Open, wood and trees and beam!" they scream.

"I cannot." This voice is deep and mournful. "The beam is fixed in the jambs, and my power is tangled in the threads."

"Aha, but we will have you yet! Open, open, cake that we have made and mingled with blood! You cannot refuse us entry, for the blood belongs in this house!"

"I cannot." This wailing, aching sob comes from all around us, shaking the stones beneath our bottoms. "For I am broken and bruised, and on the lips of the sleeping children."

"Ah! Ah! Ah!" The Horned Women scream and pound the walls, but I can feel that the stone does not give way. "We must retrieve our spindles and looms tonight, or we have lost our circle forever! Forevvvv-errrrr!!"

Kaylee and I bury our heads and hold each other fast as they pound and scream, scream and pound. Dawn comes late this time of year, but when it chases them away they will be gone. We will burn every scrap of spindle and loom, carding brush and knitting needle.

Kaylee shakes with quiet little—not even sobs, like that little sniff, that little chin quiver when her pudding didn't come out. I've learned to guard my heart, and Kaylee has learned to guard her feelings, and tonight all our guards are broken.

"Is it enough?" she whispers.

"The walls are strong. The door is closed." I squeeze her. "You did a good job."

"Really?"

"Forever! Forever!" the Horned Women cry. "Open, open!"

"I cannot." The deep voice.

"Really good," I tell Kaylee. "You were perfect."

And I realize what was good—her heart. I put the sanctified water on the stairs and asked them to test the hearts of those who pass, and they let Kaylee by but kept me on the floor.

What was in my heart? If I had gotten that cake, what would I have done to my little lads and lasses?

I shiver and Kaylee pulls the blanket tighter. The Horned Women scream and sob.

A few hours ago, I couldn't wait to sit down. Here I am, and I am definitely sitting, but this is not what I had in mind at all. I snug Kaylee close and hum to block out the noise. She murmurs words along with my tune, and I realize it's "Hallelujah."

The clock strikes six and all goes quiet.

We lift our heads, turn to look out a window. The sky is not bright, but the darkness has grown pale.

"What happened?" Kaylee asks.

I tell her the whole story. I leave nothing out.

"I don't think that cake was good for you," Kaylee says solemnly.

I can't help it, I start to laugh. And giggle and chortle and laugh some more. "I don't think it was," I agree, and Kaylee laughs with me, our breath warming us both.

"Look what I found when I was breaking it apart." She twists to reach into the pocket of her robe. "I washed them in the sink so there's no crumbs, but I didn't put them away so I wouldn't give one to the kids by accident. I forgot about them."

She opens her palm, and I shine my flashlight right at it. It is filled with little shiny pale curves, like toothpicks or puppy teeth, with a tiny ridged spiral.

"They're horns," she says. "Baby horns."

We count. There are thirteen.

"That would be for me," I say. I am horrified, but it finally makes sense. "It was a trap for me." I was not crazy or evil. "If I had eaten the cake, I would have become Thirteen-Horn."

"Don't touch." She closes her hand.

"They aren't calling to me now. It was just the cake."

"Okay, but still. I'm not taking any chances." She shoves them back in her pocket. "I'll bury them in the garden as soon as it's light. No wait. I'm not telling you where they're buried."

"Don't tell me, but I think I'm safe." I lean my head back against hers, feeling her relax into me.

"But we almost lost you." She sounds little and young, like she is. "If we didn't have you, that would—that would suck. It would suck elephant balls!"

I don't want to think about what Thirteen-Horn would have done to the children; it didn't happen. I'm still me, thank heavens. "I'll still be around, to make you scalloped potatoes and decorate for Christmas and—and love you every day." I swallow hard. I said the big word. I meant it.

It feels good, loving Kaylee.

"You remembered that I like scalloped potatoes," she says, in awe.

I'm worried that she's frightened of being left alone, and I'm not really essential. "But of course, if anything happened to me, you could always go back to your mother. Roy would take the little ones. Even without me, you guys are—"

"Now that," Kaylee interrupts, "that would suck dinosaur balls. Brontosaurus balls!"

I laugh again, and put both arms around her and she buries her face in my neck and laughs and cries and we hold each other tight. Maiden and mother and crone, and we have defeated the crones and kept our family safe. The edge of dawn glimmers at the top of the window.

"Hey," Aiden calls from the landing, mid-stairs. "For some reason, I couldn't sleep. Anyone want some tea?"

We do. Oh, how we want some tea.

"Will you make it, please?" Kaylee says, perfectly polite.

"Sure." Aiden ruffles his hair and yawns. "I just need to fetch the water."

Just like it is an ordinary morning. A new day, in my beloved ruined castle with my beloved children.

All four of them.

"Thank you," I answer. I have a suspicion that the well is going to behave for Aiden.

As for me, we're going to burn the looms and spinning wheels, and then just use a push broom to shove all the other debris out of the way. I'm going to ignore it. We can spend the day upstairs; my bedroom is big enough for all five of us, and Aiden can bring in his computer so we can watch a movie. Disney's fine.

We can deal with the Great Hall tomorrow. I'll send a bill to Roy for any damage, and if he makes a squeak I will stare him in the eye and remind him that I'm raising an awful lot of his children.

And then, I'm going to buy a new microwave. I don't mind dealing with jam on faces and algebra homework, but I draw the line at drinking lukewarm tea.

Besides, Kaylee can make a damn fine microwave pudding. I have full confidence in her.

BOOK 2
THE WHITE DEER OF KILDARE

Dedication

This one is for our sons.
Our world needs loving and confident warriors.

Chapter 1

Raindrops slide down the windscreen of the Peugeot, and condensation creeps up the windows as we let the minutes tick by. We got to Cork airport early, but Aiden and Kaylee haven't changed their minds. No way, no how are they getting on that plane back to America.

Aiden lifts his phone and snaps a picture of the distinctive swoop of the departures building, then turns and gets me in the frame. Ca-tip. Ca-tip. He hunches and his thumbs fly over the screen.

"Okay," Aiden says. "Done. It's official now."

He's trying to prove that I did my best to drop them off, but I know it won't be enough. The teens' biological parents are both going to blame me for violating the custody agreement.

Within seconds, my phone buzzes against my leg. In the back seat, Kaylee's pings, then dings, then chirps. Aiden, who at 16 always plans ahead, switched his to silent mode before unleashing the storm of recriminations. I should have done the same. I close my eyes and lean my head against the cold window. Buzz, buzz, chirp, ding.

"Are you sure you won't get out..." My voice can't turn this into a question.

"Have we missed the plane yet?" Kaylee demands.

"No," Aiden and I say together.

We sit without talking. More pings.

Amber: Please.

Please please please please please.

One mother to another. Please.

In my heart of hearts, I sympathize with Amber. I'd want to see my children for Christmas, too. I'd already be devastated if they chose a custody agreement with their former stepmother rather than with me. Then add losing Christmas together? I'd be dying. I feel so badly for Amber, but it's not like I can force two teens to board an international flight.

"Kaylee, are you sure?" I twist to look at the 13-year-old in the back seat. "It's just a few days. Your mother really wants to see you."

Kaylee leans forward, curtains of blonde hair meeting to hide her face.

"You can come right back to Kilkenny," I say. "We can wait to celebrate Christmas until you get back. Don't you want to see your mother?"

"You're stupid!" Kaylee rears forward, flailing a hand against my seat.

I wince.

"Stupid stupid stupid!" she shouts.

"Enough!" My voice is sharp and jagged.

She is breathing heavily, but I don't look back. I'm barely holding my composure. Another text buzzes, and I'm not surprised to see my ex-husband's name.

I never tried to get custody of Roy's older kids. I just wanted mine. The two we made together; the children I've held every day of their lives. I barely knew Aiden and Kaylee before I was awarded custody of my step-kids last summer. Aiden surprised the court by requesting that they go with me, and I have figured out he said that because Kaylee wanted him to, but I still don't know why. I just try to do my best for them.

Kaylee makes a little sniffling gasp.

"It's okay," Aiden says. He twists back towards his sister, pats her knee. "It's okay. Maura just has to say it, remember? She has to show the grownups she's doing her part. That's why I sent the picture. She won't make you go."

"She will!"

I stare at the raindrops rolling down the window. This conversation isn't for me.

Kaylee sucks in a sob. "She just wants her own kids for Christmas, you know she does. She doesn't want either of us. She probably won't even let us in the house again."

Aiden sighs. "Kay-bear, Maura would let anyone come for Christmas. She'd invite her worst enemy if they were at the door."

"But don't you want to see your own mother?" I can't help it.

"I like the *decorations* better at the castle!" Kaylee shouts. "I spent all *month* clearing the dining room! I want to *stay*!"

"Okay." This is as much as I've gotten out of her. I know it's not the whole story, but I can't do any more.

Kaylee's phone pings a series of different tones. She says a word that I do not officially allow her to say, and I hear the little song that means she's shutting off her phone. I glance at the rearview mirror as she tosses it into the boot, bumping off their suitcases and clattering down the metal frame of the car. When she meets my eyes in the mirror, her face is flushed and her lower lip stuck out.

I bet it felt good to do that, but I have to deal with the adult stuff here. I swipe open my messages. I don't owe anything to Amber, her lawyer, her brother, or the kids' psychologist—all of whom are texting me—but I do need to answer Roy if I want to keep custody of my children.

Roy: At the airport! Good job, Maura. I know Kaylee was being difficult.

None of your location trackers have moved.
Did Aiden leave his phone in the car? Why is he showing in
the parking lot?   You're all showing in the parking lot.

The next few are mostly that word that I don't officially let Kaylee say, interspersed with my name. His aggression makes me frightened and shaky, and I close my eyes, visualizing the physical distance between us... an entire ocean and continent. He can't get me here. If he gets too mean, I'll be like Kaylee and turn the phone off.

Please be respectful, I type.

There, I'm standing up for myself. Roy can't see my wet eyes or the way I'm biting my lower lip.

Roy: Sorry.

I take a breath.
Aiden passes a Kleenex without looking at me. Kaylee shuffles her feet and sighs.

Roy: I know Kaylee can be a handful. Sorry babe.

Oh for—! I am not his babe. He has a newborn with another woman. And I don't know how to reply without making it sound like I'm agreeing to blame Kaylee for everything. Don't get me wrong, I'm totally frustrated with Kaylee. She's been sulking and stomping all week, and I've tried and tried to have a rational discussion about this but she just says that I don't understand, and I argue I can't understand if she doesn't explain anything to me, and I swear I have kept my voice calm and level. Every. Single. Time.

Roy: Listen, this is putting me in a pretty bad place.

Oh, you don't say? Poor Roy. Maybe you should have thought about this before going through three wives in a decade.

Roy: So, could you just... Like pick up Kaylee and put her on the plane? Aiden will follow. You're bigger than Kaylee. You could get her out of the car.

My mixed feelings incinerate in a flash of rage.

Me: I will not! I do not use physical force on children, even when they're toddlers!

Roy: Aw, that's not true, babe.

Me: It is!

Roy: Oh yeah? I remember back when Oona was screaming herself sick, and you'd hold her poor little hips and force her into her carseat. More than once!

Is he seriously correlating putting a one-year-old in a carseat with dragging a thirteen-year-old through an entire international airport, and then what? Physically holding her on a plane until it takes off? I stare at my phone, seething.

Roy: Maura?

The word wiggles and sparkles. He's tagging me in the conversation right in front of my face.

Me: I'm sorry. But no, I can't force them out of the car.

Roy is going to keep showering me with texts until I don't know which way is up. I never figured out the right way to argue with Roy. He's going to start back in on the custody agreement, but my understanding of having custody is that I put the kids' needs first. And they need me.

I put the key in the ignition and glance in the rearview mirror. "I've got to get home before the little ones get home from school."

"Are you leaving me? Just leaving me at the airport here?" Kaylee's voice is panicked, breath fast, eyes wide. She clutches her seatbelt, as though someone is actually coming to drag her out of the car like a recalcitrant toddler.

Oh god, what have the adults in her life done to this poor child?

I switch off the engine and twist around.

Aiden puts his hand on his sister's knee. "Um, Kay-bear? We're both in the car. We're together."

We're all leaning into the middle of the Peugeot, and I can smell Kaylee's coconut hair gel and Aiden's nervous sweat.

"Have we missed the plane yet?" Kaylee turns to the window.

There's a hum and we all turn to watch a jet take off, our eyes tracking it into the air. That's not the one, but they're supposed to be at the gate by now. Even if they ran, even if they got special treatment, they couldn't make it through all the checkpoints before boarding.

"I've got to be there when the little kids get home," I repeat.

"Then we'd better go," Kaylee says.

I toss my phone to Aiden, press the clutch, and turn the key in the ignition.

Aiden turns it around in his hands, looking for the button to power down, and I'm sure there are more texts from Roy and Amber visible on my lock screen.

I wonder if he misses his mother.

***

Flustered by everything, I make a couple wrong turns driving out of Cork. With our phones all shut down and all the maps with them, I can't make sense of the streets. Roy's voice echoes in my head, *You never did have any sense of direction. You're not practical, Maura.* I yank the Peugeot towards an exit but change my mind—too late—the driver behind me slams on the brakes and then peels out around me, narrowly avoiding an accident. Heart pounding, I lurch down what is almost certainly the wrong road, almost stalling before I remember to downshift. Third, then fourth. Accelerate. Take a breath, Maura.

Roy is right. I can sew and cook and tell stories, but I'm no good at anything practical. Look, I can't even get them on an airplane.

"Uh, Mum?" Aiden rustles next to me. "I think you can take that turn. Up ahead, by the church? Yeah, that'll get us around."

I'm not his mum, but the word is starting to sound right to me. I focus on traffic, shifting at the right times, and Aiden tells me which lane and which roundabout exit, until we make it back onto the little county roads we both recognize. I breathe a sigh of relief and dare to check the dashboard clock.

Dang. School's already out, so I've got to beat the carpool home. I press the pedal and take the corners at Irish speed. Luckily the rain is tapering off.

Our castle is nearly an hour inland from Cork, along the twisty roads and rambling farmland between County Kilkenny and County Tipperary.

When I was a little girl in Boston, dreaming of living in a castle, I imagined being perched on a misty mountain or the surf crashing below rugged cliffs. When I was 31 and my husband left to live with his pregnant girlfriend, I couldn't sleep and kept browsing eclectic real estate listings and imagining living somewhere, anywhere, that I didn't have to look at him anymore. My lawyer kept *saying what do you want, you're in a position to ask for things*, and one night at three am I found a castle on Savills. It had a working roof and kitchen and was in a country that spoke English. I want that, I said.

It turns out that you cut across the corner of a cow pasture to get to my castle. Hardly the romantic setting I imagined, but it belongs to me and I love it fiercely. And on the upside, I don't have to worry about little kids falling off a cliff.

I take the turn from the south at the same time as the carpool hurtles around the curve from the north. We bounce down the gravel road, the Ford van behind me, and through the gap in the looming whitethorn hedge. In the early Saxon period, this castle ruled an entire kingdom, but nowadays you can stand in the tower and see lorries driving by.

I pull to the side of the parking circle to give Claire O'Connelly room to turn the van around. I see the shadow of children's heads bouncing around inside while Aiden and I get out and stretch. Kaylee slams her door and pops the trunk.

Mrs. O'Connelly comes towards us, smiling in her bland way. "Nice to have the holidays, innit? Kiddies all home for Christmas."

"Lovely." I smile on the outside, although Kaylee and Aiden are at the wrong home for Christmas and I can't stop worrying about it. Roy's probably called the lawyers by now, but I can't have him trying to take Oona and Oliver. I'll have to figure something out.

Kaylee throws a backpack on the wet gravel. "I decorated the Long Gallery." Scowling, she points a finger to the wall above our heads.

Mrs. O'Connelly and I turn obediently to look; Kaylee has that effect on people.

"Well then, that's lovely." Mrs. O'Connelly gives the van door an expert yank. "I brought Oliver's friend Oisín no problem, but text me first the next time you're going to need an extra seat, won't you?"

What friend? Did I schedule a playdate and forget about it? I apologize automatically.

"No worries." Mrs. O'Connelly smiles. "It'll be great fun anyhow, Oliver having a friend to stay for the whole holidays."

Now wait. I am positive that I did not invite a child to come stay with us for two weeks.

Eight-year-old Oliver jumps down with his gap-tooth smile and a Jurassic diorama in one hand. "Hi, Mum!"

Another little boy follows, with an equally round face and equally wide smile. "Hi, Oliver's mum!"

They both roar like dinosaurs, throw their arms around me, and pretend to eat my jacket.

I'm a little stunned. I stare after them as they take off in a wild loop around the Peugeot and into the shrubbery, diorama waving. Aiden helps Oona with her overflowing bag of kindergarten art projects and heads inside with her, but Kaylee is as shocked as I am, her mouth gaping as she watches the boys run.

"Now then, Maura"—Mrs. O'Connelly sidles closer to me, her brows lowering—"I know you Americans have all these problems with race, but this isn't the time or place. His name is Oisín, which is a nice Irish name, and he sounds just like we do. So he's a nice Irish boy and never you mind the color of his skin, you hear?"

"Of course not. Of course."

Kaylee meets my gaze, eyes round as cookies. We aren't shocked by the rich brown of Oisín's skin, we are shocked because he is buck naked and no one else seems to notice. We saw some strange women a few weeks ago,

Kaylee and I, but that was in the middle of the night and inside the castle. Right now it's four in the afternoon and we're talking with a pragmatic mother with a van full of primary school kids. This is normal life, right here, right now.

"Oh, and I've got his dog too." Mrs. O'Connelly trundles around to the back of the van.

What the ever-loving—? This child I have never heard of has brought his dog?

"Wouldn't want to leave her in town now, would we." She opens the gate and pets something inside. "She a lovely girl now, innit? Traditional breed, the deerhound." She steps aside and snaps her fingers, and the animal leaps gracefully to the ground.

"Bye, puppy!" the children chorus from inside the van.

Kaylee and I exchange another look.

That is not a dog.

Right then. A custody argument with my ex was only the beginning, and this is not going to be a normal afternoon at all.

Chapter 2

While I spread peanut butter on graham crackers, I convince Oona to choose one drawing to tape to our avocado-green fridge, and Oliver to loan his friend some clothes. They claim that Oisín is already wearing the school uniform, but I think the boy will be warmer when he's wearing something visible. The deer stands by the sink, watching me thoughtfully. Sometimes out of the corner of my eye, I can see a shaggy frame around her face and an arc of fuzzy tail.

"You don't need to do the dog thing with me," I tell her after the kids have clattered away. "I can see through it." My grandmother used to tell me I had the Second Sight. Although Roy convinced me that was nonsense, since I've moved to this castle I keep seeing things in a different way. And this time, I'm not afraid like when the Horned Women came.

"Me neither." Kaylee stomps in and dumps a tangle red and green bunting on the table. "I can see you're actually this weird-colored deer, and that you're following the boy around because you're taking care of him, not because he belongs to you."

That's an insightful conclusion, and one I hadn't articulated to myself. I shouldn't be surprised that Kaylee is particularly attuned to anyone who cares for children.

The deer nudges the pile on the table with her muzzle, then sneezes.

"I can't figure out if I should untangle it, or wash it first," Kaylee says. She's been finding bundles of decades-old decorations in the attic all month.

Before I can tell her that the washing machine will just tighten the knots, the deer yanks a corner with her teeth. The whole thing spills onto the floor, where she uses her front hooves to loosen the loops. She cocks her head, extracts a mistletoe-themed handkerchief with her teeth, and returns to the tangle.

"That's helpful," Kaylee says. "Thanks."

I find a few carrots in the fridge, and after a moment of contemplation add a gingerbread cookie and put the plate on the floor. Sorting napkins and bunting is a particularly housewife-ly task, and if I were stuck in a deer's body I would miss cookies. The deer takes a nibble and returns to sorting.

Kaylee crosses her arms and raises her eyebrows at me. "What is it with you and weird textile-related guests? See, it's good I'm not going to Florida. She seems nice enough, but you wouldn't want to be the only one here who knows what's going on."

I give Kaylee's shoulders a squeeze, although she doesn't lean towards me or soften. I know my next words are important. Kaylee deserves to make her own choices, and it's up to me to worry about the custody arguments.

"I love having you here, Kaylee, and it will be nice to share the holidays together. I'm just worried about how much your mom misses you. That's all, sweetie." The pet name still feels awkward, perhaps because she never acknowledges my affectionate gestures. But sometimes a mom just has to act the part until the feelings follow, so that's what I'm doing.

***

The Great Hall of my castle is original. Our living room is set up around its ancient hearth, and previous owners have installed modern windows and hidden the electrical wiring under mason-work of its blond local stones. After the Second World War, the owners jerry-rigged a kitchen into the back corner of the Hall, but the rest of the front wing has fallen under a layer of dust and disrepair, waiting around like Sleeping Beauty.

It has been a hundred years, and our castle was apparently waiting for Kaylee. Ever since she and I had a misadventure with some Horned Women a few weeks ago, she has taken a proprietary air for these abandoned rooms. I don't think she cleaned anything in her life before she came here—when I first reminded her to tidy her bedroom and en-suite she gaped at me like I'd lost my mind—so I get an endless stream of questions for every task she tackles, but she's willing to put in the elbow grease. We worked on the Long Gallery together, but then when December got busy for me she did the dining room all by herself, and now has decided that the winter hols mean we're going to eat there. It's just as well; the kitchen is cramped enough, and with Oisín and the deer we are never going to all fit around the Formica table.

While I serve the little children, Aiden pours the water, and Kaylee jabs her finger around the room and describes what each piece is and what she did to it. She's looked up historical furniture and tells us the period for the vast oak table, mismatched chairs, and slightly broken glass chandelier. The vast carved china cabinets are stocked with Ikea dinnerware.

Kaylee is describing how a Norman Rockwell-esque poster covers some damp stains on the wall when Oisín interrupts.

"What's Christmas?" he asks, fork poised halfway to his mouth.

Oliver bursts out giggling.

"But you knew about the other decorations, why not Christmas?" Kaylee asks.

Oisín pops mashed potatoes in his mouth. "I thought it was for Solstice," he mumbles. "I was glad you guys celebrate it too."

"We don't—" Oliver begins, but stops. His class has been studying the traditional celebrations.

All of my children are at the edges of their seats, heads cocked, eyes full of possibility.

"That's it!" Aiden thumps down his water glass and grins. "We did Christmas in America, just because everyone did Christmas. Right?"

All of the children agree.

"We're moving on. We're a Solstice family now." Aiden flashes me a grin, blushing. "Okay, Mum?"

I don't think I've ever heard Aiden speak this definitively, and I like it. And despite my guilt about Amber, I like that we are a "we."

***

Over the next couple days, I dive into trying to discover the true identity of the white deer and the little Black boy with no clothes. I have half a PhD in folklore, and it might as well do someone some good.

I have to admit, it's a way to distract myself from worrying about custody issues. Roy's style of argument really unsettles me, a barrage of compliments and endearments and then a sneaky hook buried in there. I can't tell what's real and what's not.

I've seen advice in the divorce groups to make your first holidays alone something special, but that's easy for me. I've always had ideas for things to bake and stories to tell, sitting around the fire listening to music and crafting together, but those were never Roy's priorities. I glow with satisfaction at our noisy, bustling home, but every time I hear the teens' laughter and meet their smiling faces I am struck with guilt. I like having them here, and they're helpful and fun besides, but that's a privilege I shouldn't have. I feel like I've cheated.

Roy and Amber think I've cheated too, as their barrage of texts and emails makes clear. Ordinarily, I couldn't help but spin in mental circles worrying. But now I've got the deer and Oisín to think about, and I decide that I will only deal with custody problems three times a day: 10 am, 1 pm, and 4 pm. Then it's family time.

After pouring through Irish folklore and online lists, I make some discoveries. The name Oisín means "little deer," and I thought there was an Oisín who had something to do with Fionn mac Cumhaill, but oddly enough I cannot find a single reference to it any more. The only Fionn stories I can find are from his later life.

In the kitchen, I make raspberry tea for myself and the deer (mug for me, basin for her), and read her the list I've compiled of mythological Irish female names. She watches me, cocking her head as I go through the B's and M's.

"Saba," I suggest, and she hops in a circle, nudges my arm, hops in another circle, and prances out of the room. When she returns, she is carrying one piece from the Three Kings set we have in the front window, and drops it on the table in front of me.

I pick up the little crown, turning it around in my hands. "You're Queen Saba, then? There's a story there, for sure."

She bobs her head stiffly, then rests it on my arm in a gesture of affection. I rub my hand down her muscular neck, thinking how hard it must be for her to have a conversation with a deer's lack of physical expression. I must harness the castle's power to help her. I know her name now; surely I can figure out the rest.

Saba might have been a queen, but she is still first and foremost a mother. She extends her vigilance to my children, nudging the boys and baring her teeth if they leave Oona out of their games. She can't do anything that requires hands or speech, but she follows the children outside when they play, lays on Oona's bed when she is afraid to be by herself in the dark, and helps Kaylee sort even more decorations.

One night before dinner, Oona pops out of the downstairs bathroom.

"Did you flush and wash your hands?" I'm carrying the casserole to the dining room.

"Yes!"

But Saba blocks Oona's path, sniffing suspiciously. She nudges Oona back towards the bathroom.

"Maybe just try one more time," I suggest.

Oona heaves a gust of a sigh, but I hear the tap turn on behind me.

I set down the casserole, and can't help but smile. I hadn't realized how lonely I was; how hard it is to worry about everything in a household where no one sees you. Being lonely is better than the tension of living with Roy—a million times better, I'm not complaining. But it's been a hard few months, and someone else reminding my daughter to wash her hands is a real gift.

***

I have extra time during the day, because Oisín takes the children to play in the "nice peaceful valley" nearby. I didn't know where he meant, but Aiden goes with them the first day. After hearing about the Horned Women, he is doubly cautious.

"It's fine." He shrugs. "It's just in the woods between us and that big house with all the windows. I mean, there's never been a valley there before, but it's sunny and pretty and there's lots of berry bushes."

He's eyeing my krumkake cookies (I like all kinds of traditional food!) as I pull them off the mini waffle iron. One breaks as I roll it and I pass it to him. The way his face softens into a smile makes my heart soften, too. I'm so lucky to spend the holidays with this sweet soul.

"But can they get back?" I ask. "Are they safe?"

Aiden nibbles. "I think so? You can see this castle and the McMansion the whole time. I went in and out on all the sides of the valley, and everything stays where it should be. If you stand on top of our garden bench, you can see them playing."

I am relieved. I pass him another broken cookie. "That sounds safe enough. You're a good boy, to check all that out so carefully."

He shrugs. "It's nothing. Anyone would do it."

But we both know that his father wouldn't bother.

With the extra time I have, because Saba and Oisín are with my kids in the afternoons and Saba is helping with bedtime, I have time for both writing my lawyer and researching animal/person/fae enchantments in folklore. Neither endeavor is particularly successful.

Saba's disenchantment isn't going well, but at least I like folklore better than Roy. A whole lot better. I research different theories, and we test them out after the kids are in bed. We go to the well, which obediently becomes medieval but does not transform Saba. Herbs, both smoked and in a pot of tea. Poems and songs; ones that I find in mythologies, and ones that I write myself. That worked to free me from the Horned Women, but does nothing for Saba. I try to have us sleep at the oldest part of the castle, waiting with my songs and a thermos of possibly-magical tea, hoping that the dark of the night or the apex of the moon will help. But once it starts to rain, Saba tugs on my jacket and headbutts my rear end until I am all the way upstairs in my bedroom.

"All right," I tell her, laughing. "That message is clear enough."

Saba swings her head back and forth and prances out of my room, kicking the door shut behind her. I can imagine her saying "go to bed" but wonder what would come next. "Go to bed, you silly fool!" or "go to bed so we can have a good day tomorrow," or "go to bed, there is no value in fighting my curse."

As for Roy's threats, my lawyer thinks I don't have a problem, especially with Aiden's time-stamped photos proving that I had them at the airport in plenty of time to make their flight. My lawyer thinks this is a sulky teenager argument, not a bring-it-to-the-judge argument. Roy's four million daily texts tell a different tale.

I know the rules of Roy's game. No matter if the court upholds my custody in the end, if a judge orders Kaylee and Aiden and I to appear in court back in the US, then they win. Amber will see her kids. Roy will be telling me what to do. And Kaylee won't get the peaceful Irish holidays she has worked so very hard to create.

Chapter 3

It is the day before Grianstad an Gheimhridh, the day the sun stops. My household is as busy as a hive full of bees, as full of opinions as the woods full of crows. I don't really care what we do to celebrate Solstice; their enthusiasm lights me up more brightly than any sun.

Oliver wants to open the presents that have been piling up in the old scullery, but Kaylee says that presents from Daddy are just stupid. Aiden wants to go to Knockroe Passage Tombs and see the solstice sunbeam, like at Newgrange but local to us, while Kaylee argues there will be lots of people there and she wants only our family together. Oona just wants to eat pancakes, and Oisín wants to eat everything. Kaylee joins me in the kitchen, rolling pie crust, her tongue out in concentration.

"Knockroe dates from three thousand BC and is only fifteen minutes from our house," Aiden says, stirring the minestrone.

"Me, me!" Oona cries, and he lifts her up, propping her on his hip so she can peer into the pot.

"But we'd spend the whole morning getting on coats and driving," Kaylee says.

Aiden says, glancing at Oisín with a little smile. "They have mulled wine and mince pies."

"I want pie!" Oisín responds immediately.

"I'm *making* you pie," Kaylee tells him.

"Pie, pie, pie!" Oisín starts marching around the kitchen, Oliver giggling right behind him. Saba blocks their way before they can knock into anyone at the stove, and I find carrots and vegetable peelers to keep those little hands busy.

I've never seen the older kids argue, and I'm proud of Aiden for standing up to his sister. No matter how much you love someone, it doesn't make for a happy relationship when only person ever gives in.

After lunch, Aiden leads an expedition to gather oak and holly and evergreen boughs.

"Don't worry, I won't let Oliver hold the saw," he tells me, while Oliver jumps up and down trying to grab the saw.

Kaylee has cleaned several wreath forms from the attic, and I use alcohol wipes to put up those 3-M hooks on the mantlepiece and door and window frames. The main fireplace is big enough to roast an ox, but there's a wood stove installed in the middle and that's what we usually use. Aiden puts Oisín on his shoulders with a flashlight, and they call up the chimney and eventually decide it's not blocked.

"Yule log, yule log, yule log!" Oliver chants, and it takes all five of them to wrestle it into the house, oak leaves fluttering under the furniture. Saba paces anxiously while I laugh and take pictures.

***

By late afternoon, we've put greenery in every nook and cranny of the Great Hall, wreaths on the doors, candles in the windows, and the whole castle smells of mulling spices. Kaylee spent an hour decorating the dining room table for tomorrow. I'm not allowed to look, so we decide to eat dinner in the Great Hall. It's soup and rolls for tonight, all the fancy food for tomorrow, but the kids think this is hysterical to get to sit on cushions and set their bowls on the coffee table.

I walk through, brushing breadcrumbs into a napkin, resting my hand on each head. The smooth brown hair of my bio kids, Kaylee and Aiden's fluffier and blond, Oisín's tight bouncy curls. Saba meets my eyes, and I can feel her happiness, the friendship shimmering between us.

This is what I always wanted. Right here.

I carry the rolls back into the kitchen, and my eye is caught by my phone lighting up on the counter. When I see Amber's name, for once I am not feeling defensive. I let my own rules slide, and swipe up to read her texts.

When I get back to the living room, Oliver is wiping the table while Kaylee gets out the craft baskets.

"Good news." I nod towards the teens. "Your mother is coming to Ireland. She wants to see our castle, and she'll join us for Christmas."

"No!" Kaylee drops a box of markers with a crash.

Saba leaps to her feet, hooves scrabbling on the stone.

"Honey, it's all right." My smile goes tight. "Solstice is what matters to us, right? We'll have that, and then she'll visit for a day or two. I'm sure she'll stay in a fancy hotel in Kilkenny, you'll only have to see her a few times, but she'll be satisfied and—"

"No!" Kaylee throws a paintbrush at the wall. "I don't want to see her!"

"It's a compromise—"

"You don't *understand!*"

"Kaylee, honey..." I take a slow breath, hoping she will do the same.

"It's not tonight or tomorrow," Aiden says quietly.

Kaylee crosses her arms and turns away from me, but at least she's not yelling. Saba taps across the room, ears flicking. Slowly, she slips her head under Kaylee's elbow, and Kaylee allows her close.

I know Kaylee has big feelings, but I want her to think about other people, too. "Honey, every day as a family is so precious. These holidays feel so good, and next year will be too. If we had this for years, and then one year you refused to see me again, it would...really hurt. Just think about how your mother feels..."

Kaylee rubs Saba's neck, her posture stiff.

Aiden starts picking up the markers. "I don't think that's how...like... it really works."

"But it does," I protest. "That's how mothers feel!"

"What about fathers?" Oliver says. "Because Daddy doesn't want to see us for Christmas."

"I'm sure he does..." Now I'm backed into a corner. "He just...can't." Since he has a new baby, and a whole new family. Roy always does like newborns the best.

"My father's not here either!" Oisín chirps. "Sometimes I'm kinda mad at him."

Saba's head swerves around, but her deer-face has no expression.

"Me too," Oliver says.

"Me too," Aiden agrees, keeping his face away from me. "But come on. Let's just do our crafts and have our family evening."

"I'll put on the music," Kaylee says.

"Can we finish our ornaments tonight?" Oliver asks, bouncing up and down.

"You don't have much left to do," I say, giving up on the conversation. "Just stitching the outside." I start to sort through the craft basket.

Aiden puts the markers back on the coffee table, his shoulder brushing mine. "Are you going to let Amber come?" he asks softly.

"I don't think I can prevent her," I answer, and the words he said in Cork flash into my mind. *Maura would invite her worst enemy to Christmas.* Even though Amber isn't my enemy, I won't turn her away.

"Okay." Aiden sighs. "It's not tomorrow, anyways. We'll manage."

"Exactly. We'll manage." I appreciate this attitude.

He picks up a sheet of translucent kite paper and begins folding it, and I turn the music back on. It's time to be happy.

A few days ago, I cut out two green felt wreaths for each of the children. They've spent the last couple evenings learning decorative stitches, then adding sequins, buttons, and beads. This afternoon, I layered in some wool roving and pinned the two decorated pieces together, and now all they have left is do is to go around it in a blanket stitch. We sit on the rug, Oona and Oisín pressed up against my shoulders, as I demonstrate the stitch over and over, and then they each pick out a color of perle thread.

Oona and Aiden wanted to do a wool felt ornament too, but they both finished the first night. Now Kaylee is working on a pom-pom project with an old box of Red Lion yarn, and Aiden is working on intricate folded paper stars. Saba settles herself by the fire, on the comfortable mat of old blankets that Kaylee arranged. She sways her head to the Enya, but seems to prefer the jigs and reels from Cherish the Ladies.

I thread the needles for Oliver and Oisín, chattering as they surround their wreaths with wild, loose stitching. They can't wait for me to thread the hanging loop, then choose places to mount their masterpieces.

"Come help me with pompoms," Kaylee says, casting an appraising glance on Oliver's hopping. "I need fourteen more before bedtime."

The boys dive over to meet her challenge. I tidy up their work boxes and turn to help Oona. She's been working slowly with a very specific creative vision, involving lots of things that sparkle.

For a moment, I can't see her, and Oona always stays close to me. There she is, on Aiden's lap, his long legs stretched out on the carpet. His arms are around her, both their heads bent to the crooked wreath in her hands.

"Oh, thanks, Aiden," I say, reaching out my hands to my daughter. "I can take over now. Are you stuck on the blanket stitch, honey?"

They both look up. Oona does not move.

"Um, I think we've got it," Aiden says.

"I don't want to take you away from your star-making," I say. He's got a metal-edged ruler and everything. It's a good project for a high school boy who likes geometry.

"We're okay," Aiden mumbles, and turns back to Oona's wreath.

Oona lifts her chunky needle and accidentally pokes his arm. They both giggle.

I guess they look happy enough, so I finish tidying the crafts and glance around the room. The boys are chattering with Kaylee. No one needs me.

I pick out a sheet of undyed wool and the shears. I'm not starting anything important. Just keeping my hands busy until someone calls me. I keep worrying about Amber, picking out flights to Ireland, wonder how it would feel to see my kids for the first time in months, the heartbreak if they didn't welcome me. Before I know it, I have cut out the silhouette of a deer.

I check out the kids again. "Oh, Aiden, that's not how I teach the stitch. She can do it on her own." He has his hand over Oona's, but she won't figure out the way to do it if he is guiding her. "It's slower at the beginning, but let her—"

Aiden doesn't look up, but he moves his hand a few inches away from Oona's.

"Do you want me to help?" I ask.

"We've got it," Oona says, imitating the inflection that Aiden used a minute ago.

All right then. I look down at the wool in my hands. I guess I might as well cut out a matching deer, and make a stuffed ornament like the kids' projects. I pick out a variegated cream thread and a milliner's needle.

"Tell us a story?" Kaylee turns down the music.

I was at the graduate folklore program at UCLA, before I fell madly in love with Roy and then fell pregnant. I gather my thoughts and tell one about midwinter, the Mean Ceimhreadh, and Saba creeps closer. Then Kaylee asks about Saint Wenceslas and Oisín wants to hear one about the Fianna, and we all stitch and wind yarn and sink into the stories I know by heart. Worries about Amber and missing fathers fade into the distance, and it's a good evening.

"All right." I glance at the clock, my smile soft. "It's about bedtime, and looks like perfect timing." Oona just finished her ornament, and Kaylee is tying off a loop of colorful pompoms.

I start to stand, but Oliver giggles and pushes me back into my chair.

"We've got this," Kaylee says. "You can take it easy tonight, Maura."

Aiden is pushing himself to his feet. "I'll bring you a cup of tea."

"There's no need, I can—"

"We've got a surprise!" Oona giggles. When the little boys shush her, and she puts her hands over her mouth, eyes sparkling.

"All right...well, that's very generous." I sit back down, but I feel awkward. What am I supposed to do with myself?

"You too," Kaylee tells Saba, petting her as she heads towards the stairs, all three little ones bouncing along behind her. "Stay here."

I meet Saba's gaze, feeling a little better now that I'm not the only one stuck in the living room.

Kaylee has left yarn scraps and scissors all over the coffee table. Obviously, I can't leave it like that. I'm almost done tidying when Aiden arrives with a steaming Santa mug.

"Thank you, honey." I take the cup, inhaling the smell of oranges and spice. "But are you sure you can manage bedtime by yourselves? I don't mind."

He looks away, rubbing his toe on the carpet. "It's okay. Kaylee and I have it all planned." He points to my chair, still not meeting my eyes. "You go ahead and sit back down. That deer ornament? It's looking good. You can finish it up really pretty now."

I do enjoy letting my needle roam, just finding what fits the project in the moment. But I feel guilty, putting the bedtime work on the teenagers.

Aiden leaves the room before I can argue. I sigh and obey him, settling back with my tea and my stitching. Saba lays her nose on her forelegs, flicking her ears. She looks content.

The music has turned to carols on the Celtic harp by the time I finish my sewing. I examine it, pleased. Yes. Any more, and it would become too fussy. The children's ornaments are already hung around the mantle, five wool felt wreaths expressing their preferred colors and level of attention to detail. I hang the deer to the side, where she can keep an eye on the wreaths, and put another log in the stove. The children are surely asleep by now, and the evening feels too pleasant to go up to my room. I settle back in my chair, curling my fingers around my now-cold mug of tea.

"You're being too hard on Aiden." A woman's voice speaks calmly.

I jump. "What?"

Saba's head is raised and she is looking directly at me. "You tried to take Oona away from him three times. It is important for a young warrior to learn to nurture, as well. Let him care for his sister."

The deer's muzzle does not move, but I am quite certain that Saba is speaking to me. "A young...warrior," I repeat.

"Of course." Saba flicks her ears. "He is fostered at this castle so he learns the skills of leadership, no? And the warriors who spend time with little children are the ones who do not burn entire villages in order to punish their enemies."

"I don't approve of burning entire villages." My mind is in a blur, but I'm quite sure of this.

Saba does not give me a moment to catch my breath.

"Exactly. And while we are discussing matters"—Saba's ears flicker rapidly—"why don't you just attend sunset at an Cnoc Rúa? The sunbeam goes through the ancient stones then, too. And perhaps they still serve mince pies. Pick up your little information-teller box and find out."

"My...my phone's in the kitchen. But I think you're right...I saw something about that—"

"Very well then. Oona will have her pancakes. Kaylee will have her family together. And Aiden will see the miracle of the returning sun." Saba recrosses her forelegs. "As for our two boys, I don't believe they care what happens as long as they are in the middle of a loving family. Preferably with something sweet to eat."

Our two boys—the words give me a wave of happiness that washes away any lingering concern about having a conversation with a deer.

Because even after years of baby play groups and small-talk at preschool concerts, I've never had a mom friend. I've never had anyone refer so calmly to "our" boys, never had anyone care about how Aiden was developing.

"My father once took me to an Cnoc Rúa for Solstice," Saba continues. "It was ancient even in our time. And your big girl, the one with the golden hair?"

"Oh—Kaylee—"

"Yes. She needs experience with the children, but you should make her tidy up her own work." Saba jerks her head at the coffee table. "She must learn how to become a good wife. Just because she is rich, do not let her become lazy. But that Amber who speaks to you through your little box"—Saba snorts like a horse—"I am not impressed with her. If she sends you her daughter for fostering, then she must trust your judgement. That is part of the agreement, everyone knows that! You are doing the work to raise Kaylee, therefore you have the right to make the decisions on her behalf."

I have not thought of it this way; I have only thought about Amber's rights. "You don't think that Amber deserves to see her children for Christmas?"

Saba tosses her head. "I think that any good mother puts her own wants below the needs of her children."

"I agree." I am confident about this. "But—"

"But nonsense. It is clear that Kaylee is learning her duties while she is with you. I see your face when you talk about this Amber person, and you do not believe that she will benefit Kaylee."

I laugh. Despite the strangeness of this conversation, it feels good to talk about my parenting decisions. I feel stronger already. "Amber certainly didn't teach Kaylee to clean up after herself! Do you know what happened,

the first week we lived here and I said it was time for the children to tidy
their own rooms?"

"Do tell!" Saba twitches her tail eagerly. "I wager that little Oona went
right to work and that big girl gave you sass."

"Her maid always cleaned her room at home."

"All the better that her mother sent her to foster with you!"

"Oh, her mother didn't send her." Too late, I realize I shouldn't be airing
our family's dirty laundry.

Saba makes an encouraging, sympathetic noise.

I stare down into my mug. Well, drat them all, anyways! I don't have
anyone to talk with, and I know Amber and Roy have both gossiped about
me.

"Aiden decided they would live with me," I explain slowly. "Or maybe
the two decided together and Aiden said it out loud." I explain about my
divorce, the moment when everyone expected the judge to rubber-stamp
the current custody agreement. "Amber had her kids full time, Roy got
visitation rights, and as the ex-stepmother I would have had nothing—but
Aiden said they would live with me. Even though it meant moving to
Ireland. Even though everything, he would not back down. Amber fought
for one week at Christmas and one week in the summer, and Roy got a
week at spring break and all four children for a week in the summer."

Saba continues to question me gently, leading me through the story,
and I realize that Aiden and Kaylee never actually agreed to the visitations.
Aiden kept asking the judge if they got to make the decision and the judge
kept saying yes. I can see Kaylee in the courtroom, full makeup on her sulky
face, one hand always touching the back of Aiden's suit jacket.

For the first time, I realize that perhaps Aiden was asking if they could
decide not to do the visits. For the first time, I wonder if I am betraying
what they thought was the judge's promise—what they thought I was
promising them.

Saba seems to think that the judge is the same thing as a druid, but she is not surprised by a woman's right to leave her husband. "I did not realize all the children had the same father. I am not impressed with him either." She lowers her head. "If you are fostering all these children, he ought to provide more ladies-in-waiting. These machines for washing and pumping water do much of servants' work, but there is no substitute for having other women about to support you while you are raising children."

"Well...no, there isn't." Tears well in my eyes, startling me. Was I really this lonely? "It's normal, nowadays, to raise children without ladies-in-waiting. Without even having friends nearby." I glance at the deer. "I guess the castle seems kind of empty."

"It's absurd! They have added rooms since I was queen, but you have no one to keep you company. Your father and your husband do not do you enough honor." Saba scrabbles, hindquarters up and then leaping to her feet. "But you are fostering my son as well, and my husband is also derelict in his duty to Oisín. I have neither gold nor power among the druids, but let us see what I can do." She begins nosing around the room, touching the evergreen boughs and nibbling a leftover cookie. "Not here, no, not here. I have ladies-in-waiting, I must send you a few, where is the crossing..."

"Saba—!" I stand, anxious. "It's fine. We don't want a crossing to your time, because then there will be no one to care for the children."

"No, no, we will stay here, you and I." Saba keeps pacing, tapping the unburnt Yule log with one hoof, nuzzling the grandfather clock. "Besides, I had my own enemies. Your time is much better, and I do like those washing machines. And the little information boxes, very clever."

"Do you know how the castle works?"

"I can feel there is something in this room."

"If the children wake up and neither of us are here—"

"Hush, Maura. I am just fetching some ladies to wait upon you. I never know when I might be called elsewhere, so I must complete my duty tonight." Saba comes up to the coffee table, bumping against me.

I put my hand on her shoulder as she knocks over the craft basket, but I am not worried. Unlike the children, Saba always puts back the things she touches.

"Aha!" Saba nudges the pompom chain. "This is full of Kaylee's passion, and she is a very passionate girl. Besides, Oisín was working on it too, and his energy is—"

Saba breaks off to lift it in her teeth. She gives her head a little toss, and the pompoms fly through the air, looping over her head and brushing my arm—

Thin winter sunlight suddenly streams through the clerestory windows. This is my Great Hall, and it is no longer empty, the walls no longer stained by time. There are rushes below my feet, I am holding hands with a young woman with bright gold hair, and my other hand holds a Santa mug half-full of cold Celestial Seasonings tea.

The castle has surprised us both.

Chapter 4

M en in wool cloaks and furs are toting long boards, which they prop on barrels while women lay out wooden bowls and pewter goblets. Weaving among them are the ladies-in-waiting that Saba mentioned, visible by the multiple colors in their léine and their air of confidence. Lanky hounds meander among the bustle, similar to the shape that Saba used to disguise her deer form.

Human Saba is slightly taller than I am, very upright, her eyes very round and brown. Her skin is white—not a euphemistic "white" like mine, but white like a piece of paper or bleached linen. It is startling; slightly inhuman. Glancing around the room, a couple of the others have a complexion like hers, a few are fair and blond in the Saxon style, and most are either Black like Oisín, or olive-skinned and black-haired. As a historian, I am fascinated; I suppose this is a period when the different waves of migration are all present.

As a mother...this is not good. Not good at all. Still holding Saba's hand, I twist and look all around both of us. We are both dressed in appropriate ancient-Ireland garb—although I suspect mine is an illusion—but Kaylee's pompom garland is nowhere to be found. I sip my tea. It tastes like the Mandarin Orange Spice I was drinking before, but it does not transport me back to the 21st-century.

"Saba?" My voice comes out half-choked.

She turns to me, her face lighting up with a smile. "Maura, dear! Aren't you excited? My husband and his men will be back in time for the Solstice!"

I understand her, and I am vastly relieved. Whatever language they are speaking here, it is just as clear to me as Saba's grasp of everything we said in modern English.

"Do you remember me?" I ask. "Do you remember why we are here?"

Saba cocks her head. "It is fuzzy to me. We must have come through the Veil. But don't worry!" She squeezes my hand and grins. "I remember that we must stay close together, and I must do something to help you. Oh, don't fret, my dear!" She touches my cheek, and her hand is strangely pale but a perfectly normal human warmth. "Whatever you are worried about wherever you are from, it is not happening now. And once my husband is home, he can consult with the druids and advise you."

I nod, thinking. Irish folklore says that multiple versions of the world exist in the same plane, like veils laid across the land we see, sometimes crumpling and shifting, fae and human interwoven. In all the stories where a human ends up in the world of the Fae, when the human returns home they are in the same moment that they left, so hopefully that will be true for me.

I simply must manage to return. If I am killed or enchanted or persuaded to stay forever, then I won't exist back home, either. The children will wake, alone with no adult in the castle. Aiden could keep them alive for a few days, I'm sure, but he can't drive a stick shift to get groceries or anything. The children have Amber and Roy, two adults who should be able to provide for them, but I am beginning to understand that those are dreadful options to the children themselves.

"Don't worry." Saba smiles again, more tenderly. "Even if my husband cannot help you, he has been invited to Dún Ailline to celebrate the solstice. The High King will know what to do."

I struggle to remember my history, which is suddenly essential to my survival. "The...high king of Leinster?"

Saba nods cheerfully. "Yes, the king of Rí Laighín is my uncle, and has many powerful druids in his kingdom. Although I cannot recall the details from your time, I know that we owe you a great deal. I will not forget."

I feel a little better. Saba is powerful in this world, and she is still loyal to me. Either I will find my way back through this castle itself, or we will travel to Kildare and Saba's uncle will help me.

"Very well, then." I take a deep breath and look around the bustling hall. "Let us help prepare for your husband's homecoming! It looks like we are having a feast."

Saba flashes me another breathtaking grin, and leads me into the melee of preparation.

***

It turns out that Saba's husband is Fionn mac Cumhaill himself, returning from war up north. I am going to meet the greatest hero in Irish history! I have had lunch with scholars who spent decades compiling stories and history about this man, not to mention all the hours I spent snuggled in bed with Oliver reading the Tomie de Paola book about Finn McCool. Besides, surely someone so powerful will be able to help me return to my children.

I follow the other ladies-in-waiting to Saba's chambers. They seem perfectly sanguine about me appearing out of nowhere, as though inexplicable things happen all the time. This part of the castle is built of logs and earthen ramparts, in the area where my front wing will be. But when we get to Saba's chambers—she has the best position at the end of the wing, with the most light—I am drawn to the window like a moth. Light glows through the horn panels, but one pane is already ajar so I push it open. There, that hill! That is my silhouette, the shape of my world. The red sun is dipping in the same spot against the horizon as it was yesterday afternoon, looking out my own windows. I shiver with delight.

Since the time I am here will pass in the blink of an eye for my children, why not enjoy myself? I'm glad I live in a time of modern hygiene and medicine, but as a historian I am beyond thrilled. I am looking at the textiles in their original colors! I will hear the bards perform tonight! I will speak with a real druid!

"Lady Maura, will you help me with this cloth?"

I turn from the window quickly, apologizing for not doing my part, but the other women laugh off my worries.

"It's a fine castle, is it not?" asks Maeve, blonde and confident. "We all were overawed by its grandeur when we arrived."

The ceiling is low and dark with smoke, the walls are rough timber and woven reeds. There is only one bed in the room, and palettes which will be rolled out when it is night time; apparently a dozen women sleep here. The space before this—there are no hallways, each room goes into the next—is set up with looms and spindles, and the fires have gone out when the women were called down to hear that Fionn was returning, and the breeze sneaks through the windowpanes and under the edge of the roof, so it is possibly 40 degrees in here. And this is overawed by grandeur!

I am so excited. Of course it's a little terrifying, but this is exactly the kind of thing I used to dream of...a little girl reading books to escape her bland life.

Meanwhile, I am helping Maeve fold the coverlets. The other women are busy around the chamber, preparing the clothing, filling wash basins, putting out a goblet of mead and cheese at Saba's place.

"Is there anything different where you are from?" Maeve asks. "We can help you with what you need to know."

I take a deep breath. Oh, is there ever! But if I ask too much, I will put them on their guard. There are half a dozen ladies-in-waiting, and they seem kind. The youngest is perhaps Kaylee's age, barely out of girlhood, and the oldest is...much younger than I am.

"Where I am from, we do not have the...white people," I say, hoping this does not sound too strange to them.

Several chorus that they do not have White People in their villages, either.

"They are the ones who shift between forms," Ailbe explains. She is quiet-spoken yet sure of herself, with smooth black hair, dark olive skin, and dramatically slanted eyes. "Most are born that way, but some are caught in a spell or a curse, and the color drains out of them."

That makes sense, since I already know Saba has a deer form. "Do they just have one shape each? Or can they change to anything they wish?"

Ailbe shrugs. "We only see one form, but I do not know if they have more choices. Probably the more powerful ones can control their shape, but they do not share their secrets."

"It's just as well." Maeve laughs. "I am just an ordinary girl. I want to spin fine thread and drink fine ale, and not concern my head with danger!"

The others laugh, and just then Saba arrives. We turn towards the business of adorning ourselves for the feast tonight, and the chamber is soon a-flutter with long sweeping fabric in a dizzying array of bright colors.

Just like Oisín dressed himself perfectly well in Oliver's clothes, my hands automatically know what to do with the garments that Saba hands to me. I slip on the undergarment which I remember is called a tunica, soft next to my skin, and raise my arms as smiling Maeve lifts a close-fitting léine over my head. The tunic pools in colorful folds onto the floor, but I tuck it up so the extra fabric loops over my belt. The collar is low and round, and Maeve helps me adjust the sleeves which drape nearly to my knees while Ailbe selects a fitted ionar carefully. This one is red and gold, reaching only to the elbow so my fancy sleeves swing freely, and lacing at the front—because my bust is more generous than Saba's, and her other ionar would not fit.

I cannot help but notice that Saba adjusts her belt a little higher, over the taut curve of an early pregnancy. This must be Oisín, then? She says nothing, and from their chatter I know that none of the other women are yet mothers. It is possible that no one else recognized her gesture, in the brief second before the folds of her léine obscures everything again.

***

The feast is everything I imagined, and more. Saba and I arrive hand in hand, and although the other ladies sit throughout the room, Saba keeps me at the honored place beside her. There are perhaps three or four dozen people seated at the trestle tables, in the space where my family spread comfortably, five children and I and our bowls of minestrone. The crowd's laughter bounces off the walls, and it makes me shiver in delight to recognize the same pale sandstone that I pass every day. I recognize the way that darker block abuts that redder one; these are the very walls where I live, too.

With a grand fanfare, Fionn mac Cumhaill enters with his retinue. Saba leaps to her feet, clapping her hands. She appears ready to dive into his arms, but he pauses a step away from the high table, gesturing broadly and beginning a speech in praise of her. I can feel Saba's moment of hesitation; in the flickering light I catch a fleeting expression of disappointment. But Fionn praises her extravagantly, bringing her out to stand beside him, and she is back to her usual vivacious self.

While the servants bring out dishes of salmon and venison, Saba murmurs something to her husband and he turns to me.

"Maura of Kilkenny." He sweeps a graceful bow. "We are honored by your presence at our humble feast. My beloved tells me that we are greatly in your debt, and I will promise you"—he flashes a smile that is almost predatory—"I never fail to honor a debt."

"Thank you, my lord," I reply, knowing the correct gesture even though I have never seen it. Something about Fionn makes me uncomfortable, but I suppose this whole world is strange.

Just imagine! Here I am! In the world where history and mythology join!

Throughout the evening, Saba and Fionn pass me choice morsels of meat, instruct the servants to give me the largest barley buns, and sip from the cup before passing me goblets of sparkling mead, assuring me that my wine is not poisoned. This is fascinating! I am thrilled!

I am thrilled in a different way by the warrior who takes the seat on my other side. He has broad shoulders and an easy smile, and introduces himself as Rian of Kilkirk. Now, it might be that for nine years, I've had no attention for any man but a handsome, cheating skink, but I am still a woman. I recognize perfectly well the way that Rian of Kilkirk is looking at me, and I intend to enjoy every minute of it.

I enjoy Rian's laughter and the brush of his knee against mine, and I enjoy the harp and the fife, and I enjoy the fowl cooked in clay and stuffed with green onions and herbs. The boar and juniper berries is a bit more of an acquired taste, and the barley buns are interesting for a few bites but then a little too heavy. As the night goes on, the Great Hall becomes heavy with smoke and human sweat, and I realize I'd better be careful with sipping this mead or I'm going to tumble onto Rian's lap. I might enjoy it, but I don't know what kind of message that would send. I giggle, and my shoulder lists against his sturdy arm. Oops.

Most of all, I enjoy being in the circle of Saba's enthusiasm and kindness. She asks my opinion and laughs at my jokes, and the way her smile meets mine I know this is not only loyalty...but also friendship.

The most precious of all.

Chapter 5

Queen Saba declares the next day is a festival as well, which I gather is partly to welcome home her husband and partly because it is time for the Mean Geimhreadh anyways. In this time, it is several days before Solstice—we have slipped a few centuries away, why not a few days to the side? Fionn is taking his wife and his court back to Dún Ailline tomorrow, so today the people will celebrate all together.

In the daylight, Fionn mac Cumhaill looks much like his son, with tight curls and a round face. I am watching him so closely, teasing out which features are Oisín's (the smile is Saba's, I am quite sure), and perhaps that is why I notice his skin. It is impossibly smooth, like a painting of a person instead of a real man. It reminds me of Saba and the other all-white people, although Fionn's skin is dark. Everything I have read about Fionn mac Cumhaill, he is a great warrior but not magical, but of course I wouldn't know anything.

But I am not the only one with questions. As we gather our cloaks to go outside, Ailbe glances at Saba.

"Our lord looks so perfect now," Ailbe says. "Didn't he have a scar just here? And laugh lines around his eyes."

Saba shrugs. "He has been to the druids. Perhaps they allowed him a sip of the Water of Youth."

"That seems likely," Ailbe agrees.

So that is how they look so strangely perfect—although I am becoming more accustomed to Saba.

Our cloaks are made of the furs of otters or foxes, sewn together with such skill that they appear to be all of one piece. We perch on benches in the courtyard while the warriors put on shows of strength and skill for our enjoyment. Of course Saba cheers for Fionn, and I believe the others let him win, but I notice that Maeve always claps for a particular gentleman as well. I raise my voice when Rian takes the field, and am rewarded by the flash of his brilliant grin.

Later, we all walk to the top of a hill to watch the setting sun, and Rian escorts me. I recognize the twist of streams and folds of land, although in my time there is a highway here and a McMansion over there.

"How fair is your face!" Rian says, watching me instead of the colors in the sky. "Your cheeks bloom like roses, and your eyes are full of many sparkling colors, like fine honey."

I cut him a teasing glance. "Are you sure that your lord didn't tell you to say that? Flatter the new lady, he says."

"I'll tell you who tells me to flatter the new lady." Rian pauses dramatically. "My own manly heart tells me to catch her eye."

I laugh with genuine joy. Since Oona was born, Roy has only told me that I'm too dour and too tired and too squashy about the middle, so I welcome the masculine flattery, even if I'm going home in a few days.

Perhaps leaving soon makes it easier to enjoy.

When we return to Saba's chamber, she is upset about something. I let the others flutter around her, bringing her tea and rubbing her back.

"Just think, you shall be at Dún Ailline and see your father soon," Maeve suggests.

"No, I shan't!" Saba bursts into speech. "That's what Fionn told me while we were walking. He's not taking me home after all."

That's too bad of Fionn, to disappoint his wife so soon after returning! And he went on about how he loved her more than the moon and stars.

"Where are we going?" Ailbe asks quietly.

"That's the other trouble." Saba squeezes Ailbe's hand. "Most of you are staying here. Fionn wants to travel quickly, and is only allowing me one of my ladies to care for my needs."

My heart swoops in fear. If Saba leaves me behind, I will be sickeningly alone in a strange land. And what about the best druids in the south of Ireland—they were going to help me return to my children.

The six ladies-in-waiting exchange looks, and all turn to me.

"You must take Maura, of course," Maeve says.

"Of course," the others murmur, eyes cast down.

Or perhaps I should stay with my own castle, and hope that one day I just walk through a door into my own rooms?

"There is something about the way she came to us," Ailbe says. "I believe there might be a reason for her presence just now."

"Besides"—Maeve drops her voice so only Saba and I can hear—"Maura is a mother herself, and our queen might need the advice of a married woman."

"Yes, indeed." Saba squeezes my hand, although her smile is tight. "I would like your advice, dear."

"Where are you going instead?" asks the youngest lady.

"An Cnoc Rúa," Saba answers. "My beloved wishes to see the magic of the sunlight returning at the ancient sacrificial stones."

Didn't she tell me that she had been to solstice at Knockroe? Perhaps we are about to make that very memory!—no, she had said that her father brought her there.

"Sunbeams are a poor substitute for being among your family," Ailbe mutters.

"He says that we will return to Kildare after the solstice, in time for the feasting," Saba says.

"That's in quite the opposite direction!" Maeve exclaims.

Saba sighs and turns away. "Never mind. Let us don our festive apparel and enjoy this night together, my dears."

I remember how difficult traveling was when I was early in a pregnancy, even in cars with fancy suspension and climate control. I am disappointed that for all his fine manners, Fionn is not treating his wife with care and respect. I wanted the greatest hero of Ireland to be a kinder man.

Tonight is about the merriment of song and story, rather than a formal feast at trestle tables. We each have trenchers of stew and gather close while the various people tell stories, and the bard plays his harp to accentuate the emotion in their tales. I try to soak it all up and remember every word. One of the white people transforms into a bird and sings so beautifully that the women weep, then transforms back to take his bow. Fionn tells a story of a victory in battle, although the details are rather flat. Rian recites a humorous poem, and after his applause he gestures to me.

I do not wish to take over something that is not meant for me, but clearly these people are excited for the possibility of a new story. I do like telling stories, even if it's usually just children listening. After some consideration, I tell a Finnish folk tale, and then one from northern Spain. I have a brief moment of fear that I am changing history and will confuse some poor dissertation student trying to figure out the route of Catalan stories into Ireland, but brush it aside. This is not history, this is not linear. Oisín is a pregnancy in this time, a child in my time, and in the middle years he becomes a bard and historian.

When I return to the jumble of listeners, I cannot find a place to sit. Rian smiles and lightly tugs my arm, inviting me into his lap.

I glance about. Maeve is sitting with her man, and I know by now that she is everything that is proper, and her father will arrange her marriage.

Rian smiles up at me.

I perch on his knees, his solid arm supports my back, and it feels good.

After another song, some of the people take up a chant of Queen Saba's name. She laughs, and takes Ailbe's hand and steps forward onto the little dias. Ailbe borrows the harp, and they begin what is clearly a well-rehearsed and much beloved performance.

"When I was but a maiden, I was gathering herbs by the stream near my father's castle. I had wandered far, because my littlest brother was ill, and only the lambs-foot could save him. It was the wrong time of year, but I thought I recalled seeing lambs-foot growing around the turn of the stream. Which turn? I wandered further to find it, meanwhile collecting the herbs that would heal and nurture my people."

Ailbe plays, queer ominous notes sneaking into her melody.

"My ladies were with me, sweet Ailbe among them. One moment we were talking, the next someone would spy a much-needed herb on the bark of a tree or hidden under a great stone. I believed that we were all together..."

"But an evil sorcerer had overtaken us," Ailbe continues, with a twang of the harp. "He is called The Dark Man, and his face is as white as snow. We were loyal to our princess, even at the cost of our own lives, but the Dark Man slipped behind us, laying his insidious magics so quietly that we could not feel him."

"First in the form of a fox," Saba says—

"And then a wren," Ailbe continues.

"The bird of the devil—"

"But most ordinary and unexceptional, when one is walking in the wood." Ailbe plays the trill of the wren. "He crept behind us, hidden under our very eyes. And one after another, he closed those eyes."

Ailbe's music becomes slow, monotonous, and I find my head drooping against Rian. He shakes me lightly, and I startle upright.

"Don't let it get to you," Rian whispers. "The music is strong tonight. Here, look at this while she is playing." He unclasps his brooch and passes it to me.

It is an intricate knot of silver, cool when it first touches my palm, warming with his hand and mine. I run my fingers across the fine smithwork, and he is right; it keeps me grounded. Saba's story becomes a story again, not something I am half-living.

When I glance back up, Ailbe has described each of the hand-maidens falling asleep.

"I spoke a name, and heard no reply," Saba says, as the harp music rushes. "I glanced forward and backwards, and realized I was alone. Then—lo! Before me, the Dark Man himself rose from the bushes, in his own true form, dressed in white robes and capes made of white feathers."

I had noticed, way back when I was a grad student, that the Irish have truly an odd thing going with their depiction of black and white. It is not making any more sense now.

"I took my deer form, that I might run the faster," Saba continues, and describes the chase, uphill and through dale, while Ailbe's harp flies up and down the scales. Eventually, the Dark Man strikes her with his willow wand. Saba escapes, but is trapped in her deer form. She wanders through Kildare for three years, lost and alone, knowing the Dark Man will find her if she attempts to return home.

Then—the music makes the call of a horn—hounds are chasing the poor enchanted princess. She outruns the pack, but cannot shake the last two dogs. Saba names Bran and Sceolaun, and a cheer goes up around the Great Hall.

"The druid foretold that if I was ever captured in my deer form, I could only escape in the palace of Fionn mac Cumhaill. No!" Saba holds up one finger, and everyone in the hall holds their breath, enraptured. "I could escape my deer form only if I am loved by Fionn mac Cumhaill."

They erupt in cheers, and I can't help but clap along.

I know this story, too. It is strange that I had forgotten it when I first recognized the name "Saba," because she is famous; it is even stranger that I did not encounter any version of this story when I was skimming through my books of mythology. Even now, I can easily remember the part that Saba is telling up and how she married Fionn mac Cumhaill, but I cannot recall the later parts of the tale. I don't know why she became trapped again as a deer, or when she bore Oisín. But I know how to drape the léine and how to greet a king; our knowledge shivers and shimmers, I suppose, as we exist in the different planes.

Bran and Sceolaun are the hounds of Finn mac Cumhaill, but they were born to his aunt when she was transformed, so they are human in some ways—more or less, depending on the story. The next part will be how the cousins/hounds brought Saba back to Fionn's castle, where she is able to reveal her human form. Like most of the others, my eyes go to the real Fionn mac Cumhaill, sitting with his knees spread on a grand chair in the corner.

Saba casts her husband an adoring glance, but there is something different in his expression. I think of how Saba described Aiden, the way that Aiden was holding his little sister (I really shouldn't have interfered; I squirm with guilt). Fionn's face bears no resemblance to the softness in Aiden's eyes, and watches Saba as though she is a possession. A victory.

Maeve has her hands clasped at her breast, and several women are weeping. Do none of them see how Fionn looks at her?

The harp tinkles behind Saba's exuberant voice as she tells her love story. Rian's brooch is smooth in my hands, and he smells of juniper and the particular salty warmth that I already know is himself. He has not attempted to fondle me or pull me closer; I want to think he is a good man, but panic is building in my stomach.

What if I am idealizing this culture, and their acceptance of torture and violence is going to harm me? I am not tough the way they have learned to be, or so comfortable with the idea of death.

What if Fionn is tired of his wife, and turns against Saba?

What if Saba abandons me?

What if my judgement is as bad as it always has been, and Rian will trap me and belittle me, and leave me with more children in this time and

I cannot ever get home to Oona and Oliver and Kaylee and Aiden... the children I love?

Chapter 6

We have some miles to go through the dense forest. Saba and I are pressed together, our backs against the front wall of a pony cart. This way we cannot fall out, but we can only see the path behind us, nothing ahead.

"If we were going to my father's house, we could take the Slighe Dala," Saba complains.

"What is that?" I just want to get her chattering, back to her normal self.

"One of the Great Roads, connecting Tara to Dún Ailline," Saba begins.

By the time she gets to how the Great Roads run as straight as the arrow flies and are paved with flat logs or stones, I am entirely convinced. We are wedged among bundles of tents and foodstuffs, and every jolt of the wheels sends us our jaws knocking. There are two chariots for the men, but they choose to walk while we are on the little lámraite roads through the woods. No wonder.

Fionn has brought a half-dozen warriors and another half-dozen servants. Saba and I are the only women, which flickers between helping me feel safe and making me feel threatened. At least Saba seems to want to stay as close to me as I want to stay close to her. I realize, today, that I have not seen Bran and Sceolaun at all, even though all the stories say they are always with Fionn. This journey is strange and physically uncomfortable, but my duty now is clearly to support Saba. My children are fine, because time is not passing in my world. I can remain with Saba until she is safely at her uncle's palace, then consult with the druids and go home.

Luckily, the hard frost means that the cart wheels do not sink too deeply into the dirt track, and Fionn is delighted with our speed. I expect him to try to get as far as we can today (isn't that what all men do?) but he calls a halt mid-afternoon. When Rian stops by to check on Saba and I, he explains that Fionn wants to arrive at an Cnoc Rúa the day before Solstice and no sooner. The druids will perform sacrifices at the holy site, Rian explains, and there will be a great feast in the night.

Fionn is a king, but he has brought no cattle to contribute to the ceremony. Perhaps my understanding is flawed, and he isn't expected to bring anything. A shiver of fear works along my spine, but surely some explanation will become clear.

The men erect a small tent for Saba and I, a small tent for Fionn, and a large tent where we will gather together and the rest of the men will sleep. Saba adjusts her léine, pinches color in her cheeks, dons her most charming smile, and slips off to talk with Fionn.

She comes back sulky. "He won't let me sleep with him."

"Perhaps he wants you to have the more private tent?"

"He didn't want me to stay with him in the castle, either. He has barely even kissed me since he has come home!" Saba shakes her head, annoyed. "I know I could ease all our troubles if only I could hold him in my arms. I do not know what is wrong."

I don't know what is wrong, either, but I don't trust Fionn mac Cumhaill.

***

That evening, Fionn seems determined to win us all over. There is mead and music, griddle-cakes and fire-roasted mussels as big as my hand. The inside of the tent is much larger than the outside, and the bundles squashed into the cart with us reveal pillows and fur blankets and goblets inlaid with jewels.

Yeah...When I get home, I'm not going to write this up into an academic paper about Late Iron Age Ireland. No one would believe me.

But Saba is cheerful, and Saba's joy is irresistible. She laughs and tells stories, then tucks up her léinte and dances down the center of the tent. She captures my hands and we dance together, then the warriors stamp their boots and chant to the music, Rian has my hands and we are lost in a swirl of eager, breathless, giddy bodies.

When Saba and I crawl into our nest of blankets and pillows, we are hot with exercise and bleary with exhaustion.

"Wasn't that lovely?" Saba mumbles.

"Mm, yes." I snuggle up, her back against mine. "I do love a good party now and then."

"Fionn does know how to throw a party."

I sigh with delight, already half asleep. "I haven't had this much fun since Roy first came to UCLA. He took me out all the time. New things. Dancing. Fun..."

***

By morning, Saba and I are stuffed back into our cart, and I have realized that comparing Saba's love affair to how Roy courted me is not a good sign. No way no how, definitely not good.

Saba wants to know about pregnancy and birth, and we wile away the jostling, uncomfortable hours while I tell her stories. I know that first-time mother wants to know about birth, but they need to know about newborns. I talk about sleep, and how often little babies need comfort or milk, and how their personality is vivid from the beginning but you don't know yet what it means. I tell her about little fingernails, and the panic when you almost trip and can't stop thinking about your baby's head splitting on the floor like a melon. As my stories go on, I realized I'm talking an awful lot about how to do it alone.

Funny thing, for a woman who raised newborns with her husband right there in the house with her. Eight weeks of paternity leave each time.

But I have the feeling that Saba might need to know how to do it alone, too.

During every break, I watch Rian suspiciously. I like him, but I don't trust my own judgement. Is this gesture like Roy, would Roy make that comment? If now is like the good side of Roy, that means that the other part is waiting in the shadows.

But I don't see it—yet. The most salient aspect of my early courtship with Roy was how quickly everything moved. I was so beautiful, I was so clever, he couldn't bear to be away from me. He'd fly down from Seattle after work with a return flight by midnight, and how can a girl say no when there's only a few thrilling hours to be together? Probably a wiser girl would have, but I felt so alone after leaving Boston, and Roy was my first lover.

I give Rian back his brooch, and he gives me cups of fresh water and an extra pillow for my back, but nothing extravagant. He goes right to work at every stop, putting his shoulder to the burden and following Fionn's instructions. That was the other thing about Roy; he always had an excuse for why other people should do his work. But whenever I think he might be different, I force myself to be skeptical. Just look at Fionn.

When we get back in the cart after lunch, I start telling Saba these stories. The Roy stories. Usually, I don't talk about myself much, but I am heavy with the awareness that I am the only source of wisdom in her world. Like me, she left her family to go live far away. Fionn—or her father—has "honored" her by giving her ladies-in-waiting who are young and beautiful, but that means she has no elder women to guide her.

As she draws the stories out of me, I see them in a new light, like pictures emerging from the random sprinkle of stars. I missed so many warning signs.

"Did he do that again after Oona was born?" she asks, or "how did he treat the other women at that party?"

Roy has always told me all the things I did to ruin our marriage, just like this week he's been telling me all the things I should have done to convince Kaylee to go home. I could do it if I tried, he said. But if Roy was the one to create the pattern, maybe I didn't have much to do with it at all.

Sitting in the cart, bracing my back against the rolls of tent, watching the bare branches of trees scroll out behind me against the backdrop of the white winter sky, I'm not sure why I even wanted to send Kaylee back to that mess. She deserves better.

All our quick progress is used up by the last mile of the day. Fionn has a way station in mind, nice and clear where the lámraite meets the larger ród. But we have to pass a low spot, and the coin-shaped cart wheels sink and the men's packs weigh them down. We're forced to walk, although it is a relief to move our bodies. One of the warriors pushes through the brush to see if there is a way through the higher ground, and returns to beckon to Saba and I. We pull our cloaks tight and trudge after him, thin branches whipping our faces, heavy droplets shaking down from the tree branches overhead. My thighs burn with the steep slope, and Saba stops often. I think at first that she needs to catch her breath because of the baby, but I realize that she is studying the terrain around us. I remember her story about leading the search for herbs; Saba herself is a mná feasa, a healer.

I smile in spite of my aches. We don't need those druids, those men.

***

That night we are all too tired for dancing. The servants cook up trout and watercress and wild onions, with more griddlecakes on the side. I pick at it, overwhelmed by the strong flavors and repelled by the char on the unleavened cakes. I just want a nice slice of toast, and some nice bland breaded chicken breast, and a slice of fluffy cake. Definitely I want some cake. "Maura and I thank you for your manly work on our behalf," Saba announces, her tone as smooth as butter. "Shall I tell a story, to enliven the dark evening?"

The men chorus their appreciation. Rian hands me a mug of tea, smelling of mint and honey, and settles on the pillows near me. Not quite touching. He has picked up on my hesitation, and part of me is disappointed, but a bigger part relieved. It's better this way.

Saba sips her mead, arranging the lamp so the light catches her bright hair and expressive mouth. "Sound of the wind in a branching wood, grey cloud; river-falls, cry of a swan--beautiful music... Wait, my darling, what is wrong?"

We all turn to where Fionn is sitting, arms crossed, separated from the rest of us. He purses his lips. "Nothing. Go on."

"I like that one," Rian says quietly, only for me. "I am impressed that she knows the epic poetry."

It sounds like he believes, like I do, that Fionn will soon make her stop.

Saba continues, but now there is hesitation in her voice. I am fascinated to hear the ancient style of verse as it was meant to be shared, but early Irish verse has no rhyme and not a great deal of reason. Now that Saba is losing her confidence, the meaning slips away too.

Fionn makes an impatient gesture, and Saba freezes like a deer in the grass.

"Perhaps you would prefer something else...?" Saba's voice is shaky.

One of the men chuckles nervously, quickly smothering the sound. Other men shift uncomfortably.

"A valiant tale of heroes and war?" Saba suggests.

Fionn waves his hand dismissively. "It doesn't matter," he says. "Sing what you want."

Saba's eyes flit to mine.

I shake my head. I'm no good with men like this, either.

"My lady, would you like the bodhran? I can play for you." One of the warriors reaches for his drum, starting the meandering sort of beat that fits epic poems. I am grateful to him. He is clearly one of the good ones.

Saba stumbles through another verse (or two? it's hard to tell), but keeps missing words. "Would you like a different tale?"

Fionn is still, gazing beyond her head. "It doesn't matter. It really doesn't matter at all."

Saba begins a humorous ballad, and the man with the bodhran joins in. She lets him take over, clapping and smiling in a way I am sure is false.

Rian turns away, his jaw tight. "That is not the way to treat a lady," he tells me. "Fionn has been rough with the men and strict in his demands, this trip, but I never thought he would go so far."

I just mumble in agreement, but I am confused. Rian spends all year with Fionn; wouldn't he know what his character is like?

***

Despite the furs, Saba and I are cold in our tent tonight. We huddle close. There is a rustle in the woods, and one of the hounds bays.

Saba leaps, then laughs weakly. "I always have the sensibilities of a deer. But in this form, the hounds are here to protect me."

"Would you ever go back to being a deer?"

I can feel Saba's shrug through the blankets. "My people can take our animal shape at will. But I always prefer to be a girl."

"I would too." I think about holding my children in bed, the soft tickle of their hair on my throat and the smell of baby soap, our bodies fitted together. I cannot imagine the pain of not being able to hold them close this way.

I said I could not imagine the pain if they didn't want to see me for Christmas. *I don't think it works like that*, Aiden told me, meaning Amber, and I turn over his words in my mind. Saba will raise her child in the form of a deer. Amber did...I don't even know what, but Kaylee keeps saying you don't understand and I finally do. Not all the journeys of motherhood look like mine.

***

On the day before the Solstice, Saba wakes me early. The servants are building the fires and filling the cauldron from the stream, but the king and his men are not yet stirring. The stars are still in the dim purple sky; it is probably half past seven. Saba finishes pinning up my hair, pulls the folds of her brat over her head, and takes up a basket.

"Where are we going?" I wait until we are well out of camp, down one of the paths leading into the thick forest. Fionn was right; this campsite is well beaten down, the stream dammed to make a pool for washing.

Saba touches one leaf, lifts a fallen stick to check underneath. "My husband has always liked poetry," she tells me, "and he has never passed up the opportunity to sleep with me. I am thinking of your stories about how your husband changed."

"Or...how he never was who I believed him to be."

"Mm. Our womanly hearts are so tender, and our womanly minds prefer to believe what our strong men tell us." She snaps off some leaves and puts them in her basket.

I would like to believe that a millennia or so of feminism has helped me grow beyond her simplistic view of romance, but I fear she is right. Roy's personality was strong, the attention felt good, and look at me now, single mother to four of his five children.

Saba kneels to carefully choose a few mushrooms, then turns to me. In the pre-dawn, with her fur cloak and pale léinte and serious eyes, she looks like a spectre. Or a goddess.

I am almost afraid.

Never mind. This whole thing is terrifying. I want to go home.

"If you could go back and speak to Young Maura"—Saba's voice fades into the forest mist—"perhaps that day of the folklore department holiday party, when Roy came in and everyone turned to look at him—if you could speak to that Maura, what would you say?"

The words spill out before I even think. "Run, Maura, run."

Saba smiles, but oddly. The gesture is tight, and there is something strange about her mouth. "The one thing about deer, Maura, is they are good at running."

***

The ród makes for much easier traveling. It is still mostly packed dirt, but the low places are filled, and the route was chosen to avoid the hills or bogs. I watch the furlongs creep behind us, and try to admire the brilliant engineering skills of our ancestors. Even in this time, these roads are ancient.

But I am too tired, too sore, and miss my children too much. I was just going to stay until Saba gets home, I remind myself. I can't leave her like this.

Fionn calls for a break, and Saba and I go a few yards into the woods to relieve ourselves.

"Look." As Saba stands, she removes a bundle of moss from under her léinte.

I touch it, unsure.

"It has the spirit of the forest and the deer," she tells me. "I have filled it with my essence, and now we must connect it to you. If I need to transform, it will bring you with me."

I am not sure I want to transform, ever, but I am even more sure that I do not want Saba to run and leave me with these men.

Saba turns the bundle over in her hands. "I am not sure of the next part. I have planned out the verse, but there is something else. Blood, perhaps?"

"Oh! It needs both of us?"

Saba nods.

"You have given the herbs and the verse. My...my magic is sewing." The words feel presumptuous, and my face heats.

"Of course!" Saba beams. "But not just any sewing. Your sewing makes the world more beautiful. Look, we can strip the fibers in that reed. And pick the embroidery off my ionar; I don't need it."

Before we get out of the cart for the next break, I slip scissors into my pocket. Out of sight of the men, we snip at the ionar and pull threads out of our hems. While we ride, Saba fiddles with the reeds, and I hold the bundle of colorful thread, planning something beautiful.

***

We camp tonight within two stones' throw of an Cnoc Rúa, the sacred stones. There are several groups in the area, and we find a clearing so small that the shaggy fingers of oak and maple meet overhead, mist clinging to the streambank. Saba and I huddle on a log while the men pitch the camp, winter's chill creeping under our robes and through our boots. I am stitching, and Saba is sitting in such a way that the men cannot see. I am not sure who it is that we do not trust. I am ready to fear all of them, but Saba keeps glancing at Fionn with longing in her eyes.

"Our camp is ready." Fionn stands in the clearing, hands on his hips. "There is still an hour of daylight and a long twilight. Call the hounds and we will hunt."

"No!" cries Saba, hand on her heart.

The men turn to look at her.

"I understand your other form is a deer, White Lady," one of the warriors says. "But you eat meat as well."

"I know." Saba is flustered, although her strange skin does not blush. "I understand the cycle of the woods, and how some animals must die. But hunt the boar who threatens our homes. Slaughter the cows who are old and weak. Catch the bird with swift sling or arrow. But please, my love, do not hunt the fox or deer for sport."

Fionn laughs, and there is a strange note to it.

I go still. This is the third time that the lovers want something of the other: Saba wished to share a bed, Fionn wished her to stop the poem, Saba wishes he will not hunt for sport. There is always magic in threes, and we do not need magic just now. We need to see the solstice and then get back to Saba's home, and thus get me back to mine. That's all. One of the servants emerges from the tent with his arms full of spears and weapons, but he pauses.

Everyone watches Fionn, his cloak billowing behind him in the chill breeze.

He smiles, slowly.

"But...of course, my love." Fionn's voice is too smooth, his smile too oily. "You do not like the chase. I live to please you."

Saba does not answer. She is stiff beside me.

"In fact"—Fionn throws up a hand—"I will never hunt again. I put my wishes aside to suit your desires." He takes two large steps towards us, bows deeply, and kisses both Saba's hands.

"Thank you, my darling! What a sacrifice you have made for me!" Saba steps closer to her husband.

Fionn avoids her embrace. "Of course, my dear. My wishes do not matter."

When I meet Rian's eyes he looks as skeptical as I feel.

Later, as Saba and I huddle by the fire, she asks my opinion and I try to explain.

"But why does it feel bad when Fionn says he will give me what I ask for?" Saba asks. "What is wrong?"

My words keep tangling over themselves as I sort through the years with Roy. When couples are trying to make a life together, they ask for what is important. When Roy said "it doesn't matter," he meant that he was not going to be around long enough to care. It meant that I no longer mattered to him.

I mention Aiden and Kaylee, who have changed even in the last few months.

"Aiden will be a good warrior," Saba agrees. "And a fine husband as well."

Aiden is a good example of non-toxic masculinity. I bite back the words, because explaining that to Saba really would put me in a pickle.

Chapter 7

I t is the longest night of the year; the same night when I left home. Tomorrow we will rise before dawn and watch the new sun's rays pierce the ancient stones, sending their beams through the passage tomb and onto the hillside beyond. Tonight, Fionn leads our group through the forest, the servants bowed over with food and drink, joining with others as we make our way to the clearing below an Cnoc Rúa. Saba and I have new decorations on our bodices, celestial patterns covering the enchanted deer-moss. Below the stones, there are bonfires and torches in the ground, the skirl of pipes and drums and the smell of roasting boar. Saba smiles, and in the flickering light I cannot tell if her usual enthusiasm is true.

As for me, I am suspicious of everyone, and I stay close to Saba like a tick on her hide. When men bring us goblets of mead, I accept only the ones from which they drink first. Saba and I listen to the bards together, we clap and sing together, we eat honey-soaked pastries together.

But I can hardly gainsay Fionn when he takes his own wife to dance. I glance around desperately, and Rian is by my side, leading me to the next place beside them.

"It is an unusual night," he tells me, leaning close so only I can hear. "The festivities are unusually bright."

"Do you come here often?" I ask.

He shakes his head. "Fionn usually goes to Dún Ailline. But my foster family lived near here and I attended several times during my training."

"Is Fionn acting like himself, lately?"

Rian pulls back to see my eyes and shakes his head. "Do not ask so many questions, Lady Maura."

But I think shaking his head might be in answer to what I asked.

Or it may just be a warning, like he said aloud.

I doubt and second guess myself. I wish I had not left my castle at all! Even stuck in the wrong time, that is where I belong, and where my magic is waiting. I do not know what will happen out here in the wild countryside, but I depend on Saba too much. I am telling myself that I am trying to keep Saba safe, but really, I need her a great deal more than she needs me. Her uncle is High King and she is a mná feasa, and I am a worn-out woman whose husband left her and who can't do anything practical.

Rian spins me back down the line.

A line of robed dancers cuts through the crowd, and the music changes to something eerie. These must be druids—I almost start forward, but Rian's arm holds me back like a fence.

He is right. This is not the time to bother them with my requests, no matter how desperately I want to be home. I watch as they chant and shake rattles of feather and bone, women in the crowd keening along. Someone throws himself on the ground, writhing, and one of the druids lays a bare foot on his head.

I am frightened. I draw closer to Rian, and his arm is comforting around me. I do not know if I can trust him, but he is warm and he is human and he has not hurt me yet. Maybe that is the best I deserve.

A man leads a calf into the clearing, and one of the druids pulls out a long knife. The crowd is pulsing and ululating, and the animal braces its knees and refuses to walk. Someone laughs and beats the calf with a switch. This is too terrible! I turn and press my forehead into Rian's shoulder.

"We do not need to stay," he says, stroking a slow circle on my back.

"Let's go! Now!"

He shifts, and with his bulk, is able to push through the throbbing crowd.

"The sacrifice from the King of Meath!" calls a powerful voice, and the people cheer. This must be the calf.

I must look around so I do not stumble, and I see an old horse being led forward. The poor beast!

"The sacrifice from the King of Connacht!"

I remember again that Fionn has brought no sacrifice. The horses for our carts are young and strong, as are his hounds, and the cattle are all still at the castle.

Does he mean to sacrifice a deer—a White Deer? Or perhaps the friend of the White Deer, a woman with no man to claim and protect her. I shiver and cling to Rian's ionar, but I do not dare ask him anything.

"The offering from the King of Bleadth!"

Finally, we are beyond the clearing and the press of people. I hurry into the trees and stumble. Rian catches me, but my cloak slides off my shoulder and I shiver.

His arms come around me and my mantle slides farther, the warmth of his palm sliding down my arm where my decorative sleeves split. My forehead brushes his cheek; he smells of mead and his own clean skin. Something warm and pleasant goes through my belly, and I lean into his embrace.

No! No, he is taking me away from the crowd to ravish me! If we go back to our camp alone he will have his manly way with me! I am not ready for a lover!

I push against his chest and try to run. My furs slide to the ground behind me and I shiver, wobbling from one tree to another, into a bush. The frosty air nips my elbow and throat and down my bodice. One of my feet slips into water, and I catch back a sob and lurch deeper into the woods.

"Maura!" Rian cries. "I am not trying to harm you. Stop, please! This is no place for a woman alone. Maura!"

I stumble on, crying now. I don't know where I am going, and Rian is physically powerful and could catch me easily. So could bears or wolves, I suppose, or druids with long knives in their hands. Worse and worse! I take one step after another, afraid to fall. My hand rests on one tree trunk until I have passed it, and I reach the other for the next trunk. One by one, I weave through the forest.

Through the tears in my eyes, a light shimmers ahead. We left a torch in our campsite, didn't we? Or perhaps it is another tent, perhaps an old woman inside, stirring the stew. Safety...

I take another few steps. The wind sighs down the hill, hitting me because...there are no trees any longer. My feet touch a depression, and I see a circle carved in the earth, reaching towards either side.

Where am I?

Slowly, I raise my head. In front of me is a group of standing stones, some nearly as tall as I am, some leaning towards each other. Torches flicker from every corner, making the carved spirals and waves seem to dance.

Standing by the first stone, white robes fluttering around her, is Saba. She is smiling.

I take a step closer. Then another.

This is her odd smile. Something is wrong in her face, around her mouth.

Her eyes are fixed on mine, strangely round and large. We are alone out here—are we? I can hear the celebration in the distance, drums and chanting and screeches.

She cocks her finger and I step closer again.

Saba is my friend. She helped my daughter sleep when she was scared. She is the one person I can trust in this eerie, ancient world... Right?

Saba's smile widens, showing her teeth. In the flickering fire light, they appear sharp and pointed, her posture shifting as though she is prepared to attack.

"Run, Maura," she murmurs. "Run."

Saba leaps towards me and I scream. She is a wolf—she will kill me! The smell of animal musk—a heavy blow hits my shoulder—I fall backwards, landing hard in the grass and stones.

Above me, a mighty crash of iron on stone.

I shove myself upright, scrabbling back with my feet. My legs are throbbing with strange pain.

There, in the center of the circle of stones, holding a heavy knife in his hands, stands Fionn mac Cumhaill. But now my sight is clear, and I see him two ways, the same way I could see both the deer and the deerhound who leapt down from Claire O'Connelly's van. It is the dark round face whom I have known these last few days, and he is also a man with skin as white as snow, beaked nose and twisted mouth. He wears a cloak made entirely from white feathers.

The Dark Man has been searching for Saba all this time. He shapeshifted into Fionn mac Cumhaill to trick the White Deer of Kildare to leave the castle where she was safe. He fooled us all.

All this happens in three beats of my racing heart.

Behind me, a crash in the bushes and the thud of bounding hooves. The Dark Man's gaze follows Saba, then turns to me wriggling on the ground.

"I will at least have this one," he says.

He seizes my ankle and pulls me towards the stones.

I thrash wildly and try to grab the grass, but it slides past my hands. I kick harder, pleased with the power of my blow, but his hand is like a manacle. My other foot makes contact with his body but he only laughs.

"This one will be excellent," he says, dragging me forward.

I can hardly breathe, the world blurry as I blink, sounds from the celebration too sharp. He drags and the standing stone scrapes against my thigh, my hip, my belly.

Suddenly, the Dark Man gasps and his hand falls from my ankle. I smell metallic blood and hear the wheeze of his every breath.

As I pull away from the stones, my head lifts and I am looking into the woods. I can see clearly. Rian is there, a second knife poised in his hand to throw.

"Run, Maura," he says. "Run."

I scrabble to my knees, hindquarters into the air. And I run, one giant bounding leap after another.

Chapter 8

The Dark Man is here and Saba has abandoned me! My deer-mind is blank with panic, and I stretch my legs in a giant leap. The woods is no longer dark and forbidding, but perfectly clear in different shades of gray. Around this tree! Over this boulder! This way! No, that way!

A sound startles me and I freeze, breathless.

It is a white deer. She watches me and tosses her chin, and I recognize her sound as comfort and encouragement.

I didn't want to be a deer! The Dark Man can trap Saba in her deer form, and now he will trap me too, and I will never get home to my children, and they will wake alone, and their hearts will break because the one adult who was there for them is now gone. Disaster!

Saba snorts and tosses her head, checking to make sure I follow.

I don't want to follow.

She waits.

Don't be a fool, Maura. Saba is not the one who betrayed me. Maybe I don't want to be a deer, but it was the one power that she could give me, and she gave it freely, that we might stay together.

I take a step forward, surprised how my body feels. When I think about it, I almost tumble.

Saba touches my nose with hers. Her ears flicker back towards the camp and the stones, and I can smell the fear on her. She really wants us to run. Wait, I can smell fear?

My Maura-self has all kinds of concerns, but my deer-self agrees entirely. Go! Go! Go!

We are leaping off together.

***

Once we are out of hearing distance of the celebration, we have to stop, our heads hanging while we catch our breath. After a little time, Saba shakes her head, and starts trotting again. My lungs burn and I feel strangely weak. Then I remember Aiden and Oliver having a discussion about how humans are endurance predators and can chase down almost anything if they just keep going, and I understand Saba's perspective. We must push our deer-bodies into something they are not made for. The Dark Man was hurt but not down, and with his powerful magic he will heal himself or shapeshift again or heaven even knows what. I am from the days of hospitals, not human sacrifices. I trot after Saba.

For the first half of the night, we bound for a little while, walk a bit, pause to munch leaves and slurp water from streams. As we go on, I get better at using this body.

I still don't like it, though. Ending up in this time was bad enough; I should have never left my castle. But I think of my children, and push forward.

We are taking a drink when we hear the first howl, and we both freeze. It is a wolf, but my sensitive ears understand a great deal more. It is precisely on the low hill behind us, and the deep timbre is both otherworldly and familiar. I have heard this voice all week, coming out of the shape of Fionn mac Cumhaill. This is the Dark Man, and he is chasing us.

Saba's ears flicker and she bounds into the woods, me on her heels.

We race.

We breathe.

We hear his howls, his scrabbling claws, his panting breath.

We race. We trot. We stop to breathe.

If the wolf kills me now, all of Maura will be dead. There is no second chance. My children! My children! I must go home to my children!

I can tell we are headed toward my castle, but Saba leads us on ever-widening zigzags, keeping to the hills and the deepest parts of the forest. Exhausted and new to this form, I would have no idea what to do, but human Maura can understand what she is doing. If we ever got to a straight run, the Dark Man would run us down; as a wolf he can keep steady. We have only desperate bursts of speed.

I trot and bound and stop to breathe, bound and trot and pant. I don't like this. I don't belong here, and I want no part in their mythological cycle of predator and prey, desire and beloved. One of my professors wrote a paper about that, and now it's so real that it could rip the skin off my haunches and puncture my lungs and I am not happy about this at all. Was Fionn always the Dark Man? Or is the real Fionn hidden someplace else—dead?—while the Dark Man takes his form?

But for now, there is nothing to do but trust Saba and go.

So I do.

***

Clouds passing the moon. Scent of ice.

Run. Pant. Trot. Drink.

Wolf close! Run!

***

We pace around a stand of berry bushes, sides heaving, hooves sinking into the boggy ground. We are only two hills and a valley away from the castle.

Two more steps, and Saba's white hide gleams bright and we blink in the moonlight.

On the far side of the clearing, one shadow detaches itself from the woods. It throws back its head and opens its jaws in wolfy laughter.

Saba spins and leaps into the dark woods, and I scrabble to follow her. The Dark Man howls as he breaks into a run, but we do not waste our breath. Saba darts, one way then the other, giant leaps through bracken, quick turns around trees. I try to stay close but my legs are burning and my lungs are weak, and my deer instincts remind me to dart in slightly different directions. Confuse the predator.

Maybe he only wants Saba?

I am trying to find the best place to clear this shrubbery, when the Dark Man's teeth snap at my ankle. Burning! Fear! I strike out with my hind feet, feel them connect, and push off in a mighty leap. The branches tangle around my head, but I land safely. Away! Run!

Ahead of me, Saba pauses. Behind me, the slap of bushes and sweep of wolf-feet. Together, we burst through the trees—smell of campfire, human, hound!

Hop—hop—spring—hop—Saba zig-zags across the camp, scattering live coals, knocking down tent poles, startling the hounds from sleep. Terrified, I cut through the edge of camp, knocking over a water barrel and heading straight towards my castle. The hounds bay—their teeth will close on my leg next!

Pell-mell we tumble into the next clearing. Saba halts and I collapse beside her, barely able to draw breath. They will kill me.

My children, my baby, my Oona. My head drops to the ground. Barking, yowling, growling. I shiver, bracing for teeth and claws.

Saba noses my neck. "I know. I know. Come, my dear."

I hear her voice as clearly as though we were both human, and it makes me jolt upright.

Awful sounds of fighting! They are almost on us!

Saba nudges me again. "Three wolf-hounds will slow him down for a few minutes. He cannot get away from them. Come. We are not far. I promise."

A man yells, then another voice. There is a thump, a yowl, and splashing.

Instinctively, my body starts trotting away. I sway and gasp, but Saba braces herself next to me. Together, we keep walking, our long legs eating up the yards while our ears flicker back to the terrible fight.

The dogs and the wolf. They are fighting each other, all too busy to chase after us.

I understand now. With the wolf too close to change course, Saba led him into camp and woke the hunters and dogs. They're in a bad mood and there's a wolf right there. Ha!

Saba takes us onto one of the paths leading to the castle. Now that our enemy is distracted, it is easier for us to walk here, too. One step after another. We still have to stop to hang our heads and breathe. Keep walking, keep going.

The dirt and log ramparts loom before us, darker in the dark of the night. Twenty paces to the right, a stream gurgles. Twenty paces to the left—safety. The gate.

We stop, blinking at each other, trying to breathe.

"Goodbye," Saba says.

Wait—what?

Saba nuzzles me. "The Dark Man will chase me until the end of the earth. Do you remember that first night, when you met the Dark Man masquerading as my husband? He said *I never fail to honor a debt.* Now I understand that it was a message to me. He was telling me that he had put on this entire trickery in order to catch me, because he once swore he would. Those words have been pounding in my mind this whole night."

"Don't leave." I want to speak so badly, I focus on my voice and my thoughts and it comes out. I can hear myself.

Saba glances back towards the woods, ears flickering. "The Dark Man will find me again. I would only lead him to you, and you must go home to your children."

I must. I must! If I can only save Saba or my children, the choice is clear. ...But impossible.

Saba tosses her head towards the creek. "You see that? That is the entrance to the Peaceful Valley. It only opens for me, and the Dark Man cannot harm me there. I will go there."

"Would I be safe there?"

"Of course. But you must go home to your children."

"How do I get home?"

"You will find it, Maura." Deer-Saba has no expression on her face, but her voice is kind. "I was wrong, trying to find the druids for you. Use your woman's power."

Sewing. Tea. Love for my children that will pull me through the veils; I think I understand, but I am sad.

"Do not worry about me, Maura. Perhaps one day, the real Fionn will find me again. He will disenchant me again, and we will live together in peace." She tosses her head, the deer equivalent to a smile.

I turn away, sorrow and anger closing my throat. I know that Fionn mac Cumhaill will marry again. His first love never comes back into the tales.

Saba nudges me. "You go first. I will make sure you are inside, and I can be over the stream in two bounds."

I cannot leave her like that. I nuzzle her back. "You—your child." The words are hard to find, my human self wavering with the intensity of my emotion. "He will...come to me. One day. If he is in need, I will protect him. My house is always his."

"Oh, Maura!" Saba's eyes sparkle as she tosses her head. "That is everything! I was afraid we would be doomed to be ever alone. But you will find my son?"

I nod. "I will feed him, and give him gifts for Solstice, and hold him in my arms as a little child needs."

"Oh!" Saba snorts and shakes her head, delighted. "I knew you were a good mother who always knows how to make her children feel safe and loved. I knew it! I can leave happy, now."

A sound—we both lift our heads. It is nothing but the breeze.

No, not the wolf. Not yet.

We touch noses, but there is nothing more to say. If Saba will not leave until I am safe, I should go.

It breaks my heart, but I turn to the left. One step after another.

I can hear her still. The rasp of her breath, one tap of a foot.

I am at the gate, and look back.

Saba is watching me.

I look up. I am not sure how to get through, really, and the people here eat venison. Will they help me or slaughter me? When do I return to my human shape? Can I bang with my hooves? My front feet do not reach out that way.

There is muffled shouting, and the gate scrapes open. Two grizzled men are staring at me, wrapped in heavy wool scarves and bear-skin cloaks.

Saba will not leave until I am safe. Terrified, I walk forward, waiting for their blows to fall.

But this is Saba's castle, and I suppose when a deer arrives at the gate it is not totally unexpected. The men step back to let me pass, and I stagger forward. I am stumbling—tired—such pain!

I fall, my knees hitting the earth and my hand scraping against a stone.

My hand!

"Lady Maura!" calls one of the guards at the same moment. "Call the castle! Bring the ladies! Ho, ho!"

I hear the scraping of the gate but wait! I must, I must—

I scramble to my feet, staggering with the change in balance. I run back to the gate, my skirts tangling around my legs. Leaning heavily on the edge of the door, I crane my head back towards the wood.

Saba is gone.

The stream is gone too.

Chapter 9

I wake in Saba's bed, the soot-soaked beams above me. I turn to the wall and sob. In the pain and haze of the last night, I had hoped so very much that I would awake in my own home. It seemed like I had done my part, had my adventure, and my arc was complete. The castle, however, does not appear to agree. Here I remain.

"Hush, darling, hush. You are safe." Ailbe's hands are soft on my arms. She helps me to sit, bracing pillows behind me and lifting a cup to my lips. It is some mix of terrible pungent herbs; I do not know which ones, but Saba would. I start to cry again.

"I know, I know. Hush. I know." Ailbe strokes my hair and makes me take another sip of tea.

I am a grown woman. I must get better so I am not a burden on Ailbe, removing her from her proper jobs.

I appreciate that she does not tell me that everything is fine. I think in this time, they have a deeper acceptance of tragedy. There is no sugar-coating here.

***

Despite my best intentions, I am unable to leave the queen's chambers. I am bruised and scraped, my legs like jelly, and my lungs sear with fire when I try to push myself forward. The women bring a tub, and although I protest that they need not carry water through the whole castle, they fill it for me. Ailbe throws in herbs, and I lay in the water until the heat takes away some of the pain.

The back of my calf is scored with a shallow, jagged, bite. I am terrified it will become infected, but when Ailbe wishes to pack the wound with herbs and moss, and what can I do but agree? Some form of treatment might be better than just leaving it open.

Over the course of the day, Ailbe eases the story out of me. I don't want to hold anything back, any hint or secret that might be useful to them here, so I share every detail that flashes into my mind. The other women come in and out, bringing tidbits to eat, stroking my forehead, sewing next to me

.

It is so much better, not being alone.

Saba, oh, Saba. I cry again, my gasping breath ripping at my lungs.

***

"Ailbe! Maura! Come look, oh come look!"

It is the third day. I am dressed and sitting by the window when Maeve bursts in. She is flushed and wide-eyed, fingers twitching anxiously.

"What happened?" Ailbe turns from where she was folding clothes.

"I hope it's not true! Perhaps we can see out the window."

Maeve races over and wrestles with the stiff window panes. It swings open and the room is washed with light and cold.

We join her, staring down at the front gates. A solitary traveler stands by the guards-men, gesticulating urgently. One of the men drops onto his knees. The traveler turns towards the castle, anger and despair written in every gesture.

He throws his hat to the ground in frustration, and we can see him clearly. Round, dark face. Tight curly hair. Two hounds at his feet, their faces full of human understanding.

Fionn mac Cumhaill is home.

***

He wants to see me, but I refuse until I have proof that he is who he says he is. I am not the only one. His favorite warriors and wife are gone, but one after another, the others who knew him best give him tests.

Yes, this Fionn remembers this particular moment from childhood.

Yes, this Fionn laughs uproariously at a joke.

Yes, this Fionn has the scrape from this battle, and the little mole on the back of his right pinky knuckle.

The only one that really convinces me is that Bran and Sceolaun are with him this time, and everyone is positive that the hounds are themselves.

"Now that you know who I am, I need to know what happened to my wife." Fionn folds his hands and studies me. "Don't worry, you will come to no harm."

We are ensconced in Fionn's chambers, beneath what will one day be the wing with my bedrooms. His space is hung with tapestries, deep with rugs, and bristling with weapons and gold. I wish Rian were back, but I do not even know if he is alive. He could be dying right now, infections festering in the wounds that the Dark Man surely gave him in punishment for helping me.

I squirm in the carved oak chair. I barely knew Rian, and he made such a sacrifice for me. I am consumed with guilt that I ran away, and that I am living in comfort while he could be dead or suffering. I spent so much time worrying about the things that he might do wrong to me, but truly I was the one who took his kindness for granted and gave nothing in return.

Since Rian is not here to protect me, two other warriors stand by the walls, as well as Ailbe and Maeve beside me.

"We thought you had come home from war," I tell Fionn. "If that was the Dark Man, then where were you?"

"He caught me on the road from Meath. He startled me at my meal, but I took out my—"

I clear my throat. I am not interested in blow by blows.

"—er—well, after a hard-fought battle, he bound me in strips of rawhide, flung me over his shoulder, and bore me away up the rocky mountainside. Up we climbed and higher, where the wind whips cold and the falcons soar in lonely circles."

The false Fionn mac Cumhaill stumbled through a paragraph and sighed when confronted with a metaphor. How was anyone fooled? The lack of poetry in his voice alone should have given the Dark Man away.

Fionn goes on to describe how he was imprisoned within the mountain itself, giving copious detail about the barricades around him. The Dark Man stole a lock of his hair and a drop of his blood, thus the capability of appearing as Fionn himself. He apparently went back to camp and fooled the warriors, but Bran and Sceolaun went looking for Fionn. It took Fionn a week to dismantle the entire mountain (so typical of him; changing the landscape willy-nilly), rock by rock, while his faithful hounds dropped partridges and nuts down the crack that served as a chimney.

Fine, fine, fine. He's such a hero. Mighty enough to move mountains—I get the point. But I still don't think I like this guy.

So, he didn't actually do any of the things that worried Saba and I during our journey. He didn't not actually disdain Saba's poetry, or refuse to touch her, or make that extravagant, resentful speech about giving up hunting for her sake. That was all the Dark Man, and the reason why Saba felt unsure of her husband's love was because the man giving her those slimy smiles was actually someone who hated her.

However.

If Fionn was a consistently kind and loving man, Saba would have known immediately that the petty jibes were not his true self. If his warriors trusted their leader in a personal way, they would have voiced the questions that Rian hinted at to me—and they would not be in his office now, ensuring that he does not lose his temper with a guest.

Saba was infatuated with her new husband, and I am (grudgingly) willing to admit that the real Fionn was probably infatuated with her too. But underneath her girlish enthusiasm, Saba has some wisdom about people. If she had trusted her own husband, she wouldn't have needed my stories about Roy. Instead, they gave her enough warning to make the spell with the moss, enough to be suspicious when he brought her to the stones.

***

I wake in the night. Two ladies-in-waiting are in Saba's bed with me, and the others and their personal servants nearby. What is that noise? I slip from under the corners, pausing to pull on a wool robe, and wend my way through the sleeping bodies on the floor.

Thumping and chanting. It grows more clear as I approach the window, but of course I can see nothing through the panels of horn.

I lift the latch and tug the pane aside, careful to not let a breeze into the room and chill the others.

Two dozen men are gathered in the courtyard below. Warriors are leaping around the fire, bare-chested despite the cold. Druids, beating drums or contorting in strange boneless dances. Fionn mac Cumhaill paces through the center, raising his fists and pounding his chest and accepting their obsequiousness.

"Saba!" he shouts, shaking his fists at the air.

"Sa-ba, Sa-ba," they chant.

"Revenge!" Fionn screams. "Sweet revenge will be ours!"

And now they erupt in exultation.

Men pound spears against the ground, then assume hunting positions as someone releases as small, dark, frantic, shape into the firelight. Whoops of anticipation—

And I close the window.

So that is what Saba meant to him. The excuse to make war, to pursue the pleasure of revenge, the thrill of battle. My professor was right—nothing more than the metaphorical cycle of predator and prey, desire and beloved.

To me, Saba meant a great deal more. She was joyful in the face of difficulty; she was resilient; she was loyal. She was creative, using her wits to overcome the limitations of her deer form. She was infinitely curious, infatuated but reasonably skeptical. She loved poetry, knew the forest, and had a heart that was exploding with love. She longed for a friend, but instead of keeping me with her, she told me to go home to my children.

My children.

I turn back towards the bed, and even in the dark a slight movement catches my eye. Something swinging from the rafter. I reach out my hand, and touch fuzzy balls of Red Lion wool.

"Saba, I will find you again," I say into the night.

I drop Kaylee's pompom chain over my head.

Chapter 10

S tiff. So stiff.

I force my back to uncurl and push my aching legs straight. One foot pops out from under the blanket and a draft slides up my leg. Brr!

Wait. These are not heavy blankets and furs.

I open my eyes, looking straight at my own familiar woodstove, sitting in the middle of a 17th-century marble fireplace with a very scrubby, very large Yule log. In the distance, there is the distinctive sound of Kaylee slamming the microwave, and the even more distinctive sound of Kaylee trying to light the stove and calling it stupid.

I swing my feet to the floor, rub my eyes, and smile. I adore my stupid gas range, and I adore my sweet grumpy Kaylee. Because she is mine. They all are. My children, my beloveds.

Aiden comes into the room, balancing a steaming Santa mug. "Merry Christmas, Mum. I mean, Happy Solstice. Or...um, something." He smiles, his face lighting up.

"Happy Solstice." I pat the couch next to me and take the mug.

Oooh, nice dark smoky Assam with milk and honey. A proper cup. I breathe in the steam and savor my first sip.

But I want something else even more—I set down the mug, turn, and wrap my arms around Aiden. He has never really seemed to care about physical affection, and he is stiff...then gradually relaxes, as though he has to tell each body part how to behave.

I hear the boys gallop into the kitchen.

"I'm ready to make the pancake batter!" Oliver shouts.

There's a clunk of a pan, and Kaylee answers. I can't make out her words, but her tone is satisfied, so I think she's going to fry them up.

Oona and Oisín cheer.

I pull back and look Aiden in the eyes. We both smile.

"You're going to be the right kind of warrior," I tell him, thinking of the man who offered to play the bodhran for Saba, the ones who stood in Fionn's office to protect me.

Okay, I'm thinking of Rian. I hope he's okay. I hope he understood that I couldn't stay.

"I'm not very brave, but I'll...be a warrior for you," Aiden answers. "If that's okay."

And he puts his arm around my shoulders and squeezes me close.

***

Sunset at an Cnoc Rúa is at 3:45, and we wanted to get there an hour beforehand. We leave the house at 2 o'clock.

It's only 27 kilometers. All that pain and discomfort, bouncing in the cart along the muddy lamráite and ród, my lungs searing as we raced back again, and Google Maps says it's 15 minutes away.

Oona sits on Kaylee's lap, all squeezed together in the back seat of the Peugeot, which is not really ideal but it's hard to worry about seatbelts just now. Bubbling over with togetherness, I start singing, drumming on the steering wheel, and they join in the carol. I like children, I like being surrounded with their bright voices and new thoughts, I like seeing them grow and change and become themselves. I'm happy to have Oisín among us, and whenever Saba makes it back, I am quite positive she will be a better co-parent than Amber and Roy.

This afternoon, filled with love and relief, I am sure that I will find Saba again. Somehow, some way; that was not our goodbye forever.

Once we reach the site, local volunteers direct me where to park, and the kids burst out of the car like popcorn. Aiden makes a game of catching the little kids, shoving hats on their heads so the hat covers their eyes and then pretending he can't find them, having the mittens munch up their hands.

For the first time, I don't offer to help. I don't feel guilty that he is doing my job, because this is my job too—raising a loving and confident man.

I follow the kids slowly towards the festive knot of people and tables. Hedgerows snake across the green fields, clumps of trees reaching dark branches towards the pale sky, but I recognize the shape of hill and horizon. The stones look nearly the same, although they are buried a little deeper in the earth.

There are no druids, no complaining cows, and no Dark Man waiting with a knife. That's good, I know...but as I watch my children in the distance, I feel particularly alone. In our culture today, this is the way it's supposed to be. Mothers raise their kids, holding up all the responsibilities for a house, just small talk with other moms at school events or the grocery store. Maybe you get one chance at a husband, but plenty of married women are as alone as I am. There was something good about sleeping with twelve women in the room, sharing the burden of household tasks.

Roy was always the social one, and when he left there was some relief to doing things my own quiet way. But now I'm ready for my own friendships.

Maybe a little bit of flirtation, if I ever find a good man—but I shy away from the thought. Today is enough.

I tuck my scarf closer and zip my coat to the top. I appreciate modern fabrics, but have to admit that the otter fur was warmer. It looks like someone is showing the kids around, pointing to something in the trees, Aiden asking questions. They'll be fine for another few minutes.

I take out my phone, but just stare at the lock screen.

Maybe I'll put off business till tomorrow, and keep today as a family day. That's what I told myself earlier.

I let my gaze blur, living the memories from the past few days. I thought that Saba deserved the best of me, whatever wisdom I had from raising children and falling out of love. It would have been more comfortable to just agree that Fionn was brave and handsome and full of compliments, which was true. I did something hard for Saba, and I can do it again.

I swipe open my mail app. I already drafted an email after talking with the older kids, one at a time—no, after listening to them. I grit my teeth, call upon my inner warrior, and open it. I change a word here, add a phrase here. I take out an explanation in three places; I don't need to justify myself. I check all the email addresses at the top; Amber, Roy, my lawyer, and everyone who has felt the need to text and email me about what the teens ought to be doing and what I have done wrong.

"Five minutes until the presentation starts!" someone calls through a megaphone, and the crowd starts to mill closer. My children are talking to the cows across the fence.

It doesn't matter. I don't need to hear the lecture about an Cnoc Rúa; I've been here before, and we'll be back next year. This is my home.

I read my letter one last time:

> To All Concerned:
> I, Maura O'Leary Robinson, have been assigned full custody of the minor children Aiden Robinson and Kaylee Robinson. I interpret my role as putting the needs of said Aiden and Kaylee above the wants of any other individual. Judge Clancy trusted the children to make their own decisions about their custody, and my role is to advise, nurture, and ultimately uphold the decisions that Aiden and Kaylee make for themselves.

In light of that, Aiden and Kaylee have made their needs clear that they do not wish to see their biological parents during this holiday vacation. Either in Florida or in Ireland either. If Amber wishes to come to Kilkenny, I personally will meet her at a public restaurant to share how the children have been doing this autumn. But the children have expressed that they will not come to this meeting and I will not pressure them against their will.

Neither non-custodial parent may come to my house without permission. That is expressly in the custody agreement. I have not invited anyone.

(I had to go back four times and remove extra apologies and explanations from that paragraph. It's very short now.)

I am not willing to continue this discussion any longer. We wish to enjoy our holidays together without dealing with arguments. Therefore, I have blocked everyone who isn't supporting the children's wishes from my text, email, Whatsapp, Facebook Messenger, and every other conceivable avenue of communication. Aiden and Kaylee have done this too. We will unblock them in one month, on 21st January.

If anyone wishes to express further concerns, they may express them to my lawyer.

Sincerely,
Maura O'Leary Robinson

I swipe up and down, biting my lip. Is it clear enough? Is it too rude? My lawyer promised that Roy couldn't take me to court and get custody of Oliver and Oona; I guess I just have to trust that he's right. That he's one of the good ones.

On the field below me, the professor waves her hands and everyone draws close. Aiden swings Oona onto his shoulders, while Oliver and Oisín hold Kaylee's hands.

Wait!

I go back to the email. After the last sentence and before the signature I add:

> And I think since Roy is expecting me to transport four of his children, he can provide a larger car than a Peugeot. I would accept a Citroen C4 Picasso.
>
> Thank you.

Before I can doubt myself again, I push send, the little sound swoops, and I start down the hill. I haven't actually blocked their emails yet; I'm too nervous about what they're going to say. But it's only 6am on the west coast so no one will—

Ding!

I can't help it. I stop and check.

And then I smile.

> As Maura's lawyer, I concur with everything she says. She is acting according to the spirit of the custody agreement, which is that Aiden and Kaylee make their own choices. I will handle all communication from here on out.

Ding!

Another email from my lawyer, directly to me this time.

> It's not your fault if Amber upset the kids so much they never
> want to see her again. Stop worrying.

> And I'll get you that Citroen. I checked the line item already,
> and a compact car is not "reasonable transportation" for a
> family of five.

> Now go actually block those numbers. I bet you haven't done
> it yet.   Enjoy your holidays. You've got great kids!

But it's almost sunset on Winter Solstice, and I don't want to mess with
blocking right now. I just power off the phone and walk down until I end
up between Aiden and Kaylee. I put an arm around both of them, patting
Oona's boot, rubbing Oliver's shoulder, moving forward to give Oisín a
special squeeze. He turns and grins up at me; Fionn's round face and Saba's
bright smile. I will make sure he is well loved.

The sun sinks lower and we all tramp over to the stones. People gather
round, laughing, pointing at the sun on the edge of the hills or the spirals
in the stones. Someone starts a Christmas carol.

Oisín leans with his back against me, and I let my arms loop around his
chest. Everyone is watching the sun, but I turn to the dark woods.

One shadow separates itself from the trees, watching us. Long legs,
graceful neck, flickering ears. In the twilight, I cannot tell if she is an
ordinary brown deer or something more.

I turn back when a cheer rises around me, and a thrill rises in my
chest—this magical place, this magical time.

"Look!" Oona cries. "The sunbeam on the grass!"

"The sunbeam!" Oisín shouts, bursting away from me.

"That's really amazing," Kaylee says. "Don't you think it's amazing? I'm glad I'm here."

"The stones look like they're made of gold," Oliver says.

Aiden just meets my eyes and smiles. We are all together, a family of six... and it is good.

Glossary and Pronunciation Guide

When pronunciations for multiple dialects were available, I chose the Munster dialect since our characters live in the south of Ireland.

Characters:

Oisín (oh-SHEEN) — Irish name meaning "little deer"

Fionn mac Cumhaill — Finn McCool or Finn MacCool. Most pronounce it just like it looks in English, but the southern Irish dialect says "f-yoon."

Ailbe — ancient version of the name Ailbhe (Al-vuh; the l is light so this is essentially the modern name Ava); meaning "white," and a famous female warrior of the Fianna (Fionn's band of warriors)

Rian — historical spelling of Ryan

Places:

an Cnoc Rúa (un ca-nook ROO-ah) — Knockroe Passage Tombs in modern Ireland; translates to "the Red Hill." Neolithic site dating from 3000 BC, with dual passages for the rising and setting sun on the days around the Winter Solstice. Stones are decorated with megalithic art such as spirals, cup marks, and zigzags.

Dún Ailline (doon AL-ih-nuh) — One of the Great Royal sites of early Ireland, ruled by the Kings of Leinster, located in the current County Kildare. Nearby is the Hill of Allen (Cnoc Alúine or Cnoc Almaine), which in Irish mythology becomes the seat of Fionn mac Cumhaill. My sources indicated that Saba was from one of these places, but their names are so similar and have been spelled so many ways, I chose to simplify the story by only mentioning Dún Ailline. I figured that the King of Leinster gave Fionn the land to make his castle after this story takes place.

Clothing:

Tunica — under garment

Léine (LAY-nuh) — close-fitting smock or long tunic, often with long loose sleeves, held in place by a belt. Worn by both men and women, it could vary between knee-length and 30 yards of material.

Ionar (ON-er) — short garment worn over the léine, like a jacket or vest. It often had short or split sleeves to allow the sleeves of the léine to swing freely, and could be laced in front.

brat (braht, pl brait) — cloak, circular or rectangular in cut, held in place with a brooch.□

Roads:

Slighe (slee) — the five main roads radiating out from the Hill of Tara, some of which define the routes for modern Irish highways. The southern slighe went to Dún Ailline, but not to an Cnoc Rúa.

Ród (road) — regional main road

Lámraite — connecting road (no pronunciation guide found)

Bóthar (BO-her) — cow road, still used for small roads in Ireland today

Solstice and more:

Grianstad an Gheimhridh — Irish term for Winter Solstice, translating to "the sun stop"

Mean Geimhreadh — midwinter

Mná feasa (mu-NAH FA-sa, with a as in apple) — wise woman or healer. The mná feasa used plant medicine, charms and rituals.

Author's Note

Saba's story is taken directly from Irish folklore and mythology. She appears in the Fenian Cycle, which places her life in approximately the 3rd century CE. I have also used the story collected by William Butler Yeats, "The Birth of Oisín," for more reference points. In these traditional stories, Saba is an important princess and sorceress/herb woman/??? with the power to transform into a deer. She appears breifly as someone who is pursued, rescued, and tricked, and then she escapes into Peaceful Valley in her deer form. Her son emerges years later, and Oisín becomes an important bard and warrior, but Saba is never mentioned again. I have enjoyed fleshing out her character and her existence after she disappears, but all the details of her life, especially with the Dark Man and Fionn, are taken faithfully from the available mythology.

Writing 3rd Century Ireland involves a great deal of creativity. We have contemporary sources from the Romans in England and the Celts on the continent (the Romans never conquered Ireland), and we have a wealth of historical information written by Irish monks in the 8th-11th centuries. The problem is that all of that is written by outsiders with a strong motivation to see the Irish as foreign and "barbaric," while the physical evidence left behind shows a culture that was warlike, but also sophisticated in terms of social structure, engineering, and trade routes.

My interpretation as a historian is to always take external narratives with a great deal of salt, especially when they look down on certain groups—monks have very specific ideas about women and traditional religion, and invading armies are pretty unreliable narrators, especially when they keep losing and are grumpy about it.

History, mythology...or both?

I admit that my historical specialty has not been ancient history. What I have found fascinating about Irish history is that we have so much written history, so early, but the way that written history includes gods, giant bulls, prophecies, and overlapping worlds right alongside technical details over who was ruling and what was the weather and politics.

Personally, I believe that maybe our current scientific observation doesn't explain everything. Maybe there is some magic in our real world, just like the early stories tell us.

Meanwhile, Fionn was very probably a real historical figure, as was Saba's father and other important leaders.

The way "the Veil" and time slipping is described in my stories is also set in Irish mythology. They believed that there was another world below ours (and sometimes one in the sky), which was essentially the same, where the Fae were going about their business. Both humans and Fae went back and forth, both deliberately and accidentally. There were certain places and times of year where it was easier for this to happen, but there weren't strong limits. There are frequent stories of coming out of the Fae world into a completely different time in the human world. Fae frequently had their own "homes" which they had particularly simple access to, so for instance Saba can get into the Peaceful Valley more easily than anyone else, although it still has a loose physical connection to her castle.

As you read my different stories in the "Castle in Kilkenny" series, my rules for slipping in and out of the Fae world (and different times) become more clear. Everything I have set up is based in Irish stories and mythology—and admittedly, their system is vague and constantly flexible. It comes down to accepting that our perspective on the world is not the only one, which has been the default in Ireland well into the 20th century—and many people accept it still, given that Ireland has an E.U. protected habitat for leprechauns.

Cultural & racial diversity

One important consideration of this time period was that the Celts were the third wave of population. Ireland is located along a nice ocean passageway around the edge of Europe, and long-range migrations washed up upon their shores. Irish mythology also accounts for several waves of migration, although of course the language is different and some of the people were gods. It seems as though these waves co-existed for decades or centuries, gradually becoming a more unified culture, but since much of Ireland was dense woods and steep hills, integration was slow. (The English found the same problem a couple thousand years later.)

The first documented wave was from North Africa, which I associate with the mythological "Nemed" people in these books. It is possible that by the 3rd century these peoples had been integrated into the population and were no longer visibly African...but it is also possible that they were still enclaves of specific cultures. In this story, Fionn is Nemed, which makes sense to me because a hero who is surrounded by so much prophecy would probably have long ties back into their culture and history.

The second wave was from the middle east or Turkiye, but a different ethnic group than the modern Turkish. From following different explanations and pictures, they probably looked similar to people who now live in east Asia or the Indian subcontinent. They had "long heads" (archeological evidence), medium-to-dark skin, and slanted eyes. I use "Fir Bolg" for this culture, which seems to be what they were probably called given the similarities between the mythology and the historical evidence. ("Fir" means men; there are multiple options for "bolg.") They were the majority race in Ireland for centuries around this period. In my story, most of the secondary characters around the castle were Fir Bolg, including Rian and Ailbe.

The last immigration wave in Heroic Ireland was the Celts (or Gauls) from France. In this period, they were spread widely across Europe, but eventually were defeated everywhere except enclaves in Ireland and Scotland. Their name from the mythological creation stories is the Milesians, and this almost certainly refers to the Celts. They were tall, fair-skinned, and the option of blonde hair seemed to be highly prized given the historical descriptions of beauty. The south of Ireland (where my stories are set) is by far the most geographically accessible, so it seems probable that by the 3rd century, the Celtic culture dominated the south and the coast closest to France, while the Fir Bolg were still the majority in the dense inland hills.

I assembled various hints and invented the White People. I don't know if the sorcerers or shape changers (who are prevalent in Irish history) had a distinct look to them or not. I did try to avoid names that have distinct racial connotations in modern English, but the primary sources are absolutely chock-full of White and Black, Above and Below, Peaceful Valley and Terrible Valley. I will point out that they do not always mean white=good and black=negative, and I deliberately made the White People both good (like Saba) and bad (like the Dark Man—also, Irish mythology is full of calling something one thing while it does the exact opposite, so a Dark Man who is physically white is absolutely in the right style).

BOOK 3

THE KNIGHT OF THE TERRIBLE VALLEY AND AIDEN OF FLORIDA

Dedication

To everyone who was not parented the way they needed, but is working to change those patterns in their own lives. The world needs more grace and kindness, and you are building it. It's your superpower.

Content and Trigger Warnings

This story contains memories of children who were neglected. On the page, no children are ever hurt, but the main character has deep misbeliefs about his intrinsic value.

Like always, I write happy endings, but I acknowledge it is impossible to solve problems of this scope within one novella.

Chapter 1

"C'mon, Oona-Baloona, can't we go inside?"

My little sister spins to look at me, and I hold up my hands as she teeters on the rock wall.

"No, Aiden!" She draws out my name in her piercing little five-year-old voice. "I'm a unicorn-pegasus! I'm flying and—"

She windmills her arms frantically and I catch her, then spin her around a couple times to make her giggle before putting her safely on the ground.

"Look, your mittens are all wet. How 'bout we go in." Besides, the damp February cold has long since gotten under my jacket and my feet are going numb.

"But a pegasus has got to fly!" Oona scrambles up a low rock, flapping her arms and making what she assures me are unicorn-pegasus noises.

"We could get some hot chocolate." What might distract a busy pegasus? Popcorn, or I'll promise to color in the Disney princess book with her. It's hard to think of anything besides a nice hot fire, when my phone buzzes.

I glance at Oona before checking my phone. Safe on the grass, no more flying off walls. I swipe the green icon.

"Hey, mate. How's it goin'?"

"Um...fine." The screen reads Dylan McFarlane. We text to decide where to meet for lunch at school, but he's never called before.

"I'm out with Arthur, and we're only a few minutes from your place."

We're half an hour from Kilkenny town, where most of the kids at my school live. "Um...what brings you out here?"

"We were dropping some stuff off for his mum, and we're just down the road from you. So we could swing by? Is that cool?"

"Oh...sure. If you're all the way out here." I guess they could just be taking a joy-ride in the country. We're all in the same grade, but Arthur just turned seventeen so he can drive now. "Do you need the post code for Google Maps?" We live between a cow field and a beetroot farm, with patches of trees and little streams making everything soggy. There are no street numbers.

Dylan laughs. "You're at the castle, bro. We know where it is."

"Um, yeah. I guess so." I haven't gotten used to living somewhere so distinctive.

"So, we'll be there in five?"

"Oh—wait. We're around the back." I'm thinking fast. "Just park in the gravel area and take the path around."

"Okayyyy." Dylan doesn't sound convinced.

I want them to like me, but no way am I letting a couple guys into my house with just my two sisters home with me. "Yeah. The main path goes to the old stable and stuff, but keep towards the castle side. We'll be directly in the back. It's open, you'll see us."

I hear Arthur's voice in the background, then Dylan comes back on. "Right, bro. Bye-bye-bye-bye-bye!"

"Uh...see ya." I'm trying to learn some Irish slang, but I just can't do that one.

Oona is still unicorn-pegasus-ing on solid ground, flapping her arms as she gallops around the wood pile. I guess she wins, and we'll stay outside for a while. I glance up at the castle—we're behind the part that's mostly ruined now—and back at my phone. I tap my other sister's picture, and wait for the European ring-tone. Six months in, and it still startles me every time.

"Yeah?"

"Hey, Kay-bear-baloney-girl."

"Hey." I hear the smile in her voice. She's thirteen but she still likes my silly names.

"I invited a couple guys over. From school. But don't worry, they'll stay out here with me."

"Oh great. I'm in my room now. Where are you gonna be?"

"In the back garden. Oona can play in the treehouse."

"Okay." There are thumps, the squeak of her heavy door. "I'll go sit in the library. Then I can watch you."

"That's good." It's not a real library, it's one of the extra bedrooms, which Maura set up mostly so Kaylee can see people in the garden and not feel alone. "How's your headache?"

"Mostly better. I was ready to get out of bed anyways."

"Good."

I put my phone away just in time to see Oona scrambling up again.

"Hey—no unicorn-pegasuses on the wall! It's too high for them."

"But I need to—"

"Down we go, Buffoona." I scoop her into my arms. "I know, do you want to go play in the labyrinth?"

"The labyrinth? Yay!"

No dangerous walls back there, and besides, it's kind of shielded from the wind. Man, it sure is cold out. I zip Oona's coat up to her chin since we're going to be out here a while, and I can't help but smile back at her. She's a silly pest, but I adore her.

"How is your skipping today?" I ask.

"I've been practicing," she tells me, totally serious. "Wanna see?"

"You bet."

She skips ahead, her dark head bobbing and lurching back and forth across the path. I wish we all looked alike, but Kaylee and I are blond like our biological mother, while Oliver and Oona have dark hair and blue eyes like Maura. We're the same through the jaw and all four of us have pinky fingers that turn in, like our dad, but people don't notice that stuff. And now Oisín is living with us, and he's Black. Saba brought him, because she was stuck as a deer. When people come out of fairy tales, apparently they just bring their paperwork or whatever they need with them, so I hope he stays forever. I like having little sibs around, and I like how Maura makes room for everyone.

But I do want all five of us kids to match. I want people to look at us and know we belong together.

Then maybe I'd feel like I belong here a little bit. Instead of just an almost-adult getting raised by his ex-step-mother.

"Oona, wait up—"

Oona spins around and runs back to me. Guess I knew she's gotten to the end of her invisible yo-yo string that keeps us together. She's afraid of being alone, like Kaylee. The little boys—nope, they'd run right off.

I scan the back garden as we enter together. The overgrown paths are in straight lines radiating out from thorny tangles of weeds (or roses, Maura says), but some mornings when I come out I can see something else instead. Radiating circles beat into the grass and scrubby gray-green herbs that smell like soap. That's why we call it the labyrinth, because hundreds of years ago that's what it was. Maura says the straight paths were planted in the eighteenth century. I like geometry and this is really cool; two patterns sitting on top of each other.

However, I don't like how this castle shimmers between one thing and another. I'm glad Oisín is here, but we don't need any more time slip nonsense. It's behaving properly today, so I let Oona run ahead.

My phone buzzes with Kaylee's text pattern. *???* I glance up along the stone wall, find the sixth window over, and wave. *At least you're warm,* I text, and she does the haha on my message. She's fine. I just have to take care of Oona today.

***

"Hey, Robinson, yoo-hoo?"

"Are you back here or are you lost in the brambles?"

The guys come around the corner of the castle, laughing and elbowing each other. They both have hurley sticks over their shoulders and Dylan is tossing the sliotar ball. Dang—I should have gotten out my hurley! How could I forget? I'm never going to fit in here if I can't play, but it's super hard. They use the hurley—which is like an upside-down hockey stick, with the flat part in the air instead of on the ground—to jab, poke, roll, and flick the ball, which they can also kick or pass from one sweaty teammate to another. The guys who have lived here their whole lives can run full tilt while bouncing the sliotar on the end of their hurley, which is about a bazillion times trickier than dribbling a basketball or soccer ball. Both of which I could do just fine, back in Florida, but the hurley won't behave for m e.

"Hey, guys." I put out my hand and we slap and punch each other.

"Let's go inside," Dylan suggests.

"Yeah, you want to show us around the castle?" Eagerness is evident in Arthur's voice.

"Uh, maybe in a bit." Are they just hanging out with me so they can see the house? "My sister's still playing. See?"

We all turn to watch Oona, who is singing while she collects things in a clay pot.

"Cute," Dylan says.

My heart swells with pride.

"Stuck on babysitting duty?" Arthur laughs. "Sucker."

My inflated heart plunges into the mud. It shouldn't be a crime to enjoy hanging out with your sister.

Dylan fills the awkward pause with complaining about one of our teachers. And soon we're joking around and it's kind of fun. Well, they mostly joke and I laugh along. Dylan and Arthur aren't the most popular boys at school or anything, but they're right in the middle of things and they're very Irish.

I check on Oona, climbing down from the treehouse. Still safe.

And if I'm kind of cool at school, things will be a million times easier for all my sibs. Making their social lives easier is the least I can do for Maura, so I laugh at Arthur's jokes. Even when they aren't very funny. Besides, this feels kind of good. Hanging out with guys, acting like a kid with no worries. I actually like Dylan.

"Aiden, put this on the fort for me!" Oona waves a giant branch, almost tipping herself over backwards.

Arthur rolls his eyes.

I flush, but I go help Oona. I wish she could just take care of herself for a few minutes. Dylan shouts, and there's the smack of the hurleys, laughter. I'm missing out on everything fun while Oona gives me a long list of instructions. I shove the branch in any which way, make sure it won't fall and hurt her, and turn back to the boys.

"Can you do this stick too?" Oona asks.

I pretend not to hear her. "Go get some flowers. You can decorate the tree house, won't that be fun?"

"There isn't any flowers, it's Feb-boo-berry! Please can—"

"How about pretty rocks?"

Oona stares at me, dark eyes wide as plates. Behind us, Dylan and Arthur smack the sliotar and laugh.

I attempt a smile for Oona. "I saw a bunch of pretty stones by the old greenhouse."

She turns to look through the trees, her eyebrows furrowing. She doesn't move.

I can see the swoop of the greenhouse roof across the stream. "I'll be along in just a sec," I promise her. For just a moment, I'm frustrated. I've spent my whole life with a sister clinging to my coat. "It's not very far."

"Okayyyy," Oona says, and then she flashes her bright smile. "I'll go really fast."

She scampers off and I trudge back to the boys, my stomach twisting with guilt. I didn't mean it. I just sometimes wish...

I don't know. It's just the way things are.

"Who are you asking to the Valentine's dance?" Dylan asks, tossing the sliotar at me.

I dodge and the boys laugh.

"Maybe..." I mumble a vaguely feminine name, glancing at the castle. The back wall looms above us, and the little windows look like they're squinting in disapproval.

But wait—the castle wall looks brighter than usual, and there's a noise behind me.

"Who's that?" Arthur snaps at the same time.

I spin around, and clock that he's staring towards the greenhouse. Towards Oona!

"It's him!" Dylan starts to run and we're both just a pace after. My feet hit the ground—faster, faster!—and my heart threatens to beat out of my chest.

"Stop, thief!" Arthur yells from behind me.

I don't know why Arthur thinks this guy is a thief, but it's hard to see much while dodging through the trees. Down into the gulley, branches whipping my face. Dylan leaps over the stream rather than slow down for the log bridge and I follow, my sneakers slipping in the mud. We scramble up the bank and can see. The stranger is dressed in some sort of wildly colorful patchwork robe, leaning over to talk to my sister, who is holding up a flower. He's not doing anything wrong, I guess, but the whole situation is bizarre.

"Stop!" Arthur yells again.

The man raises his head. Dylan is only ten paces away and me a little behind that, there's no way the guy can—

The patchwork man snatches Oona like she's nothing more than a muffin and flees. But he doesn't run like a person, it's like he's got a motorcycle under those robes of his. But it doesn't make noise. He just....zooms. And normally this is a little clearing and then a few more trees, and if you go right it's the Farland's cow pasture and if you go left you get to the groomed lawns of the McMansion. But today, soggy green lawns spread out as far as we can see, criss-crossed with muddy gravel pathways.

Shocked, I check around the greenhouse. No clues, but Oona dropped her mitten, and I shove it in my pocket and take off after her. Dylan stretches out and sprints. He's young and hurley-field fast, but he might as well be a one-legged man chasing a giraffe.

Arthur shouts again and his footsteps pound after us. I got going first with a burst of speed, but it doesn't close the distance with the Patchwork Man, and I can't keep sprinting. Arthur glares at me as he draws up, getting ready to pass.

Well, dammit. If Arthur can keep running, so can I. I squeeze the mitten in my pocket and settle into my own long-distance pace. Maura knit these mittens herself. She's going to be home soon, and I can't just lose her daughter!

I should be holding my sister's hand, not her mitten. Oh god.

Each step makes my stomach hurt worse. I got impatient with Oona instead of keeping her close, and now she got snatched.

My feet pound on the path. Thump. Thump. Thump.

I thought it would be easier, taking care of Oona than it was with Kaylee. But I failed. One job, and I failed. *Again*.

How long have we been running? These paths go on forever, twisting and turning. I'm too tired to avoid the puddles, and my feet get soaked and my pants splashed with mud. I have to concentrate, making my legs keep going, reaching with each step. The horizon is flat and gray-green. Dylan is way up ahead, and he gestures or points a couple of times so I get the impression he knows where he's going and trusts we'll follow.

I squeeze Oona's mitten, feet pounding. I've got to get her back! I suck so bad.

Dylan has stopped in some trees ahead, and with my lungs burning, I slog through the last few puddles to meet him. Dylan paces to cool down but Arthur half-collapses against a tree, head sagging.

I'm super glad they're helping with Oona, but I'm braced for their accusations. Like *what is wrong with your house, Robinson?* And then I'll explain about Maura and Kaylee, and the strange horned women they saw, and the labyrinth that flutters into another era—but I'm not going to mention any of the stuff with my Oisín, who was born a thousand years ago but arrived in our time and he's a kid who needs a home and I'm not giving away his secrets and—

"Did you see that?" Dylan exclaims, exultant. "That's *definitely* the Patchwork Man."

"Were his—knees out of his—trousers and his—elbows—?" Arthur gasps.

"Definitely through his clothing," Dylan gloats.

What the heck? What does "knees out of his trousers" even mean?

"That was a good guess about the castle," Dylan says. "I didn't expect to find him the first time we went over."

My house. I thought it was odd they wanted to visit. I should know better than to try to make friends; it never works out. It would be easier for Oliver and Oisín, if I could teach them hurley, take them guy places. It would be easier for Kaylee if her big brother were popular. I just wanted to be a good brother. I press my back against a tree, dizzy and sick.

"Strange things—always—castle—" Arthur pants.

Dylan shoves him, chuckling. "You haven't been training enough."

"You ran—fast! Taller!"

"Who's the Patchwork Man?" I've got to know.

Then turn, as though they had forgotten I'm here.

"Don't you hear the stories?" Dylan asks. "He keeps bugging people around here. Stealing things and stuff. But not like, regular thief things."

Like people's little sisters?!?

"So Council—offered reward," Arthur adds. "Pay for—"

College, I expect him to say.

"A house!" Dylan rubs his hands together. "Three beds and a garden!"

Oh yeah. Over here, college doesn't sink young people into lifelong debt, but housing is really unaffordable for locals. People like my dad ruin it, sweeping in with American dollars and paying cash for the castle. A bribe—oh, I mean a settlement—so he can be done with Maura, and all us kids too. Now he's moved on to his third wife. Already has a new baby.

Arthur straightens up, shaking out his hands.

"You ready?" Dylan asks him.

"Did you see—where he went?"

Dylan gestures into the woods. "I kinda lost him here. But with the mud, we ought to be able to figure it out. His tracks are fresh, and there's no one else out here."

Wherever "here" is, because it's not the farms that usually fill this area between County Tipperary and County Kilkenny.

We slog through the woods, only to find more grassy area, more paths, more woods in the distance. It's hilly now, and my thighs burn.

I glance back and forth between the other boys, waiting them for be weirded out. I would sure be weirded out, except my sister and Maura have had these adventures when the castle slips back a few centuries before it remembers what year it's supposed to be. Apparently this time, the whole county slipped. But the other two march on, faces set in determination, only stopping to check for footprints.

We get to the far side of the grassy hill and it starts to drizzle. Dylan zips up his coat and Arthur pulls his hat down over his forehead. It's one of those caps that is wool and kind of flat on top with a little brim, which I thought was old-man-ish until I moved here, at which point I realized they probably do a good job keeping the rain off your face. I don't know, I don't have any kind of hat. I'm just wet.

"You don't have to come." Arthur spins to me, his mouth twisted down. "You're not even Irish! You can just go home."

I hunch my shoulders and stare at my sopping sneakers. I don't know if he means home to the castle or back to Florida. Maybe all of it.

"Unless you don't know how to get back?" Arthur taunts.

"We studied the Patchwork Man," Dylan explains, apologetically. "We know what we're in for. It's gonna be...um, kind of confusing for you."

"And we're not sharing the reward," Arthur adds. "It doesn't matter if you go along."

"Okay. Um, okay." I feel like I'm going to throw up. "You can keep the reward. But that patchwork guy, you know...he's got my sister."

"When *we* catch him, we'll get your *sister* back." Arthur speaks slowly and loudly, like I'm an idiot.

"I can't go away and leave her." Poor Oona! It took a whole month before she went to school without crying. Every extra minute that I can be with her is one minute she doesn't need to be afraid. I'm not like her mother or something good, but she's my baby sister and I love her like crazy cakes.

"Just go home." Arthur pushes my shoulder.

I keep my hands in my pockets and my eyes on my toes, but I don't budge. I might not play hurley, but we're all about the same height and they're not any more filled out than I am. They can't send me home.

"Aw, let him alone." Dylan turns and moves on. "He already said we can keep the reward, and maybe it'll be easier with three."

"Fine." Arthur spins and stomps after Dylan. "It's not the plan, though."

"It is his sister," Dylan shrugs. "No one planned for her to get involved."

"I guess it was good she tempted the Patchwork Man to come close," Arthur admits. "What was the description in the story? That does look like her!"

Her name is Oona, and she's not bait.

She's the only one who ever mattered at all.

Chapter 2

The three of us keep trudging for the rest of the afternoon. They go back to talking about school and their plan. It's not so bad, if I'm not thinking about how I'm the worst brother in the history of brothers. At least I don't have to worry about Kaylee. She's okay now that we're living with Maura.

And I paid Maura back by losing her own kid. Great.

It's getting dark by the time we smell woodsmoke and dinner. The boys go charging into the clearing, excited because this was in their stories, and I'm just relieved to see any sign of human habitation at all.

The cabin door opens and an old woman steps onto the stones in front. She's wearing some kind of robe and a cape. Yup, we're definitely somewhere different now.

"Welcome, young heroes," she says.

Dylan and Arthur make low bows, and Arthur starts a speech. I pause and lower my head, not wanting to get in the way but not wanting to insult her, either. Besides, she couldn't mean me. I'm not a hero.

"Can we assist you with anything, honored grandmother?" Dylan asks.

"Come inside," the woman says. "I could use your strong arms and cheerful company, and I have dinner and bed to repay you."

They bow again and go into the house. The woman waits at the door, looking at me.

Oh, so I guess I'm supposed to go too.

"Um, thanks so much. Really." I try to bow, but I've never done it before.

"Welcome to my home, Aiden Robinson."

My head snaps up. That's funny—but the boys must have mentioned who I was.

She smiles encouragingly, and I almost do a double take. She's dressed in something really old fashioned, loops and drapes all over the place, but her face is familiar. So is her voice.

She looks just like Mrs Morrisy, our literature teacher at Kilkenny Boys Secondary.

***

The three of us are standing by a shed where apparently someone dumped pieces of a tree, which we've got to carry and stack up by the house.

Arthur puts his hands on his hips. "Dylan did the sprinting, so he's worn out. I'll do the chopping. You carry the wood."

"Okay. Great." I mean, it's not great. After a few minutes inside, I've realized just how chilled I am, and my feet are wet and throbbing. But I've listened to Maura telling fairy tales to the kids, and I've got the gist. We'll help Mrs Morrisy (she's not, really, but I'm going to call her that in my head), and then she'll give us advice, and we'll be closer to Oona. I'll carry wood all night if it gets me closer to Oona. I

There's small branches scattered around, so I start to gather those. Arthur fetches the ax and gets a big round log all set up on the chopping block. By the time I get back, Arthur is balancing the log yet again, and it's got a few nicks out of it.

"Try a different one," Dylan suggests.

When I get back from the third armful, Arthur is leaning on the ax, breathing hard.

"You can take these now," he tells me, pointing at a few chopped pieces scattered on the muddy ground.

It's barely half an armload. My chest feels like a punching bag, my left arm is trembling, and I'm just so dang cold.

"My turn to chop," Dylan says, like it's something exciting.

***

Our second task is the stable. There's barely enough light to see, and the horse I'm trying to feed is....really big. I'm afraid he's going to step on my toe. Or she? Who knows.

"Keep your hand on them when you have to walk behind them!" Arthur orders. "Then the horses know where you are and won't kick."

Kick?! I shoot out my hand and the horse's fur twitches. I jump. These things are creepy.

"How do I get him to move so I can get to the food bin thing?" Dylan calls.

"Maybe clap?"

Judging from the sounds in the stall next to me, that doesn't work, but eventually there's the swish of pouring grain, and his horse joins mine in noisy chomping. Arthur has done all the research for this, and that's cool and all, but we'd get done faster if he actually helped.

I bend and scoop, bend and scoop. Half the straw falls right back off my pitchfork, so I just go slow and steady. According to Arthur, this was going to be like the Augean Stables, where we have to clean up years of horse poo. But this just seems to be an ordinary stable, and we're just doing the daily chores. My stomach is stabbing with hunger, but at least it's warm in here. And Mrs Morrisy said that if the Patchwork Man wanted Oona, I couldn't have done a single thing about it, and promised that he'll take her to his place and treat her like a little princess. I know that Oona will be too scared to sleep and she always hates new places, but at least she'll be fed and bathed and warm. That's important. Bend and scoop, bend and scoop. I pause to stretch my back, pleased that the wheelbarrow is almost full.

"Good work, men!" Arthur says. "Those stalls are looking ready for the fresh straw. Then we fill the water barrel, and on to the third task!"

"You could fill the water barrel, ya thick eejit," Dylan says. The insult is playful, but his tone has an edge to it.

Arthur hems and haws, but eventually we hear the clank of the wooden buckets and feel the draft from the barn door opening.

"Almost to the third task, right," Dylan says.

He must be talking to me. "Right."

"Then dinner. Oh god, this is harder than I thought it would be!" Dylan sighs.

I grunt in agreement, but this could be worse. The rhythm of cleaning the stall has given me time to think, and secretly...this is kind of a relief. Because it's simple.

My sister is in trouble—but there are rules to this whole thing. We find the Wise Woman (aka Mrs Morrisy), we do three tasks, and then she repays us with magical advice. We do everything she says, and we'll get Oona.

I like knowing how to do something. If I'd had a list like this when we moved to Florida, I would have done a lot fewer dumb things. I guess Kaylee turned out fine, but I was hungry a lot back then. The worst was when I'd been storing up all the extra packets of crackers and fruit gummies and stuff, and then our housekeeper thought it was trash and threw it all out while we were at school. I don't even like to think about how awful that day was, me picking up my T-shirts and finding nothing underneath, and Kaylee was already crying. Mom was having one of her "sleeping" days. Later, I took a bunch of pamphlets when I was at the school nurse's office and found out that little kids can't even survive on graham crackers and fruit gummies. Who knew? Kaylee perked right up once I started sneaking packets of tuna fish and peanut butter, and I made her eat two fruits every day at school lunch. No one told me those things beforehand.

I didn't steal the tuna fish, since they put out food every Tuesday at Warren Park. I just wore cargo pants and took more than my fair share. Well, my fair share was nothing, because we lived in a big house and Mom drove—I mean, Kaylee's and my biological mother—and I don't care what she drove. We've moved on.

I push the wheelbarrow out towards the compost heap, passing Arthur coming back with one bucket of water.

"One?" Dylan says, grunting behind his own wheelbarrow. They're solid wood, including the wheels, and super heavy.

"It's splashing all over!" Arthur says. "It's getting my trousers wet, and I'm feckin' freezing."

Ignoring Arthur, I offer to dump Dylan's wheelbarrow if he can get the fresh straw. It's almost dark, so we should be efficient.

When I get back, Arthur is sulking on the bench, rubbing his palms, and Dylan's voice comes from the loft.

"Dude, we need to hurry. We've got one more task before dinner."

"I think I've got blisters." Arthur's voice is whiny, but also exhausted.

"So do we all. C'mon, man, don't you think Aiden and I are worn to the bone too?"

"Aiden's not even s'posed to be here!" Arthur glares at me, his face boiling with hatred.

I get it. They had a plan. I don't belong, although I don't know why I'm hurting him. I'm doing more than my share of work.

I hunch my shoulders, getting the barrows back in place. "I'll spread the straw if you push it out," I say to Dylan.

"Okay. I'm just shoving it over."

Arthur slumps out with the buckets, and Dylan and I work on the straw.

"He's thinking about the Council reward." Dylan waits until Arthur is outside. "You said you didn't even want the house...?"

"I don't care about the house! I just want Oona back."

"Yeah." Dylan waits while Arthur dumps the buckets and goes back out again. "He's not really an arsehole. He just...really needs...yeah, the house would change everything."

Arthur comes back. He nods at me before heading for the next load, and I think that's kind of an apology.

"What about you?" I ask Dylan. "Why do you need a house?" I thought they were out for an adventure, but I'm beginning to guess these boys are desperate, too.

"Done with the straw." Dylan swings down. "Now this leather stuff, and we can ask about the third chore."

"Tack," corrects Arthur with the next load of water. "I figured out if I only fill the buckets part-way, they don't splash and they're not too heavy. It'll just take a lot of trips. Unless..."

"We're doing the tack," Dylan says firmly.

He and I both take a rag, and Arthur sighs and heads back out.

"You know Hannah Rowland?" Dylan looks at me.

"Yeah." I'm surprised he would ask. "You're dating."

Dylan shrugs. "Kind of. I mean, we are, but it's more than that."

We work in silence. Arthur dumps another load of water. The ointment we're using smells tangy, mixed with the scent of straw and the whuffles and shuffles of the horses. It's kind of cozy.

"We were neighbors until the Rowlands moved to the country. Hannah and I have always known...I don't know, it's stupid to say."

"Try me." I can tell it's important to him, and important stuff is never stupid.

"We've always known we're, like, soulmates." Dylan sighs, anxious. "Everyone says it's too young, but we're gonna get married. As soon as we both get our Leaving Certs. I'll go full-time at my uncle's store and make enough for the bills, but never enough for a proper house. But her parents would never let her go somewhere that's shite, so we've got to get..."

"A proper house," I agree. "Well, don't worry. I don't have any use for a house in Kilkenny."

"Naw." There's raw envy in Dylan's voice. "You could bring home a wife and have a dozen kiddies, and there'd still be room in that place of your mum's."

"I suppose I could." I like how easily he calls Maura my mum, but I always feel guilty when other kids talk about my house. The one in Florida or this one. "It needs fixing up, though. We live in the only bit that doesn't have leaks and mice and stuff."

"I could fix it up for you!" Arthur is back. He dumps the buckets and leans back, hands on hips. "I'm gonna be in construction worker with a specialty in masonwork. I could come work on it, so you've got a place to live too."

"That's...great! Thanks." Arthur actually sounds excited, so I won't mention that Maura has guys to come and work on it, paid for out of her divorce settlement—and my dad owes her a whole boat-load more than some masonry.

We put away the tools and discuss if there's anything else we need to do. "I'm not just some dope," Arthur tells me, as we plod back to the cottage.

"I figured you need the house too," I say.

Arthur sighs.

"His da lost too much on the races," Dylan says quietly. "And his mum's been sick a long time."

"Yeah. My two brothers still live at home." Arthur kicks a stone. "All of us in one bedroom. We can't pay our mum's bills if we move out."

"But if we get the house, Arthur can fix up one part for a bed-sit," Dylan says.

"Or build a place in the yard. It's not urgent 'till Hannah wants babies."

"The place the Council is offering is big enough to divide."

"In two. I get it." There's no room for me.

"Welcome back, lads," Mrs Morrisy calls from the doorway.

We greet her and stop to take off our shoes.

"That, or I'm sleeping in a bunk bed in a top-floor tenement 'til I'm forty," Arthur mutters.

I know that kids from school see my clothes and my headphones and think I've had everything easy, but they don't know why I was so desperate to get out of that fancy house in Florida. If I were Arthur, I'd be mean to me too.

Chapter 3

F airy-tale-Mrs Morrisy insists that there is no third task, so the boys and I wash up in a basin while she sets the table.

But I'm starting to have second thoughts.

I shake the wood chips and straw out of my jacket outside, chewing my lip and thinking. Arthur's research has been wrong a couple times already, and what if this is more like a Persephone thing? There's a bunch of stories like that. If you eat something, then you're stuck in that place.

Arthur and Dylan slide onto the bench while I fiddle with hanging my jacket by the fire and focus on what I know for certain. We're in some kind of ancient time, either the Heroic Ages or the Dark Ages maybe. There's a stone fireplace that takes up one wall with just a hole in the roof so the house is smoky, and we boys have to duck our heads to avoid the strings of hams and green stuff hanging from the beams. There's a sort of floor-to-ceiling cupboard with bunkbeds built into it, and a shallow loft where I'm going to sleep. The walls are super thick, and I think they're made of stacked up dirt. It sounds weird, but it's nice and warm in here.

Mrs Morrisy brings over a big pot of soup, a round dark loaf of bread like they have at the farmers' market where I carry Maura's basket, and unwraps two white-ish balls which I think are butter and cheese. Even though I'm used to being hungry, it smells so good I think I might pass out. I perch on the edge of the bench across from Dylan and don't eat.

The other two heap their wooden plates and bury Mrs Morrisy in compliments.

"Are you sure there isn't anything more we can do for you?" Dylan asks.

Mrs Morrisy settles herself next to me. "Well, after supper we'll tell stories. I'm greatly looking forward to hearing some new tales, living out here by myself."

"Of course!" Arthur mumbles through that fragrant, crumbly, tender-looking bread. "Sounds fun!"

Mrs Morrisy ladles her soup and raises one eyebrow. Dylan freezes and I catch his eye. Yup, this is the third task.

"I've heard in your time, you know the story of Shylock and Portia and the Duke of Venice. And I do love a poem—perhaps you could recite Kavanagh or Yeats? And I wouldn't expect you to have memorized the whole of An Triail, of course, but surely you could tell me the significance of the laundries and the role of the church in 20th-century Ireland, hm?"

We all freeze. This is precisely our fall curriculum in the real Mrs Morrisy's class, and those are the exact questions on the essay that is due next Monday.

"Feckin' bloody hell with a—"

I speak quickly to cover up Dylan's muttering. "Of course we can! Those are great stories. Um, really great!" I smile weakly at the other boys. It's weird, but it should be easy, right? We just read this stuff.

Dylan and Arthur wear matching expressions of horror. Arthur drops his head to his bowl, not meeting anyone's eyes.

"Aiden's the best story-teller of us," Dylan says, weakly. "We'll let him do all that, right?"

"Right," I say. Guess they didn't do the homework.

"Let me serve you some soup, boy." Mrs Morrisy takes my bowl.

I have to sit on my hands. I want it so bad. "Thanks a lot, ma'am. But I'm not, um, very hungry. Mostly tired." I make a big show of yawning.

They all stare at me. Dylan tears a piece of bread and deliberately thunks it onto my plate.

I get the feeling I'm not fooling anyone.

"She's eating the same food as us," Arthur says.

"How long are you gonna wait to see if we die?" Dylan grins and kicks me under the table.

"I'm not worried about dying," I mutter. The bread smells so good. "But what if—I've got to leave here and get my sister tomorrow. That's all. I have to."

"Jaysus Christ, you don't trust anyone," Arthur says, and there's respect in his voice.

"You can eat the food, lad," Mrs Morrisy says.

She nudges my bowl, so the soup sloshes and the scent rushes up to my nose.

"Thanks," I repeat. I'm still sitting on my hands, shoulders pulled in. My lower lip is raw from where I've been biting it.

"Aiden Robinson." There is a command in Mrs Morrisy's voice, and I look up, startled. Her eyes are very blue through the steam of the soup. "It is obvious that sometimes when we trust too much, it opens our lives for someone to hurt us. But have you ever had a time in your life when you pulled away and did something all yourself, when that person could have helped you—and your sister, too?"

I stare into my soup, and am hurtled back into a memory so clear that I can smell coconut shampoo and feel the shag under my bare feet. It's the condo Dad rented in Hawaii the first time we came to visit him after my parents divorced, where the bathroom had a fluffy mint-green carpet and a big pink tub. I am eight, Kaylee is five, and Maura is big and round with a child that Mom despises with every ounce in her body. My biological mother prepared us for this trip by telling me over and over how terrible Maura is and how terrible this baby is, and somehow I am both that little boy who believes that Maura is going to be like the witch in Hansel and

Gretel and also the grownup boy who understands that the pain of getting left for a new woman and a new baby was what unhinged my mom, and also that it was Dad's fault. Not Maura. Not the baby's.

I am squashed in behind the vanity pretending to read a comic book, but really making sure that our evil stepmother doesn't do anything to hurt Kaylee while she's in the tub. I know about sexual abuse. So far, Maura is making crown sculptures in Kaylee's shampooed up hair, and Kaylee is giggling like she's never watched Snow White or anything.

Once she's all rinsed off, I reach for the towel but Maura already has it. Kaylee's kind of stumbly for a kindergartener, and I usually help her with baths because by herself she gets the water too hot and has soap in her hair and stuff. Here in the mint-green bathroom, Maura wraps Kaylee all up in the towel and her arms, and Kaylee giggles more. I keep a close watch on Maura's hands, but they rub Kaylee down just as no-nonsense as I do. Maura has Kaylee sit on the toilet—which is also covered with a green fuzzy thing—and she dries behind her knees and around her belly carefully.

"You've got quite a rash here," Maura says.

"Yup," Kaylee answers cheerfully. "I'm a good girl and don't scratch it."

I hold my breath, knowing I've failed at something but not sure what.

"Do you have the cream in your bag?" Maura asks.

Cream?

"Maybe your mom forgot to pack it. It's okay." Maura pats Kaylee's bony knee and pushes herself to her feet.

What sort of cream is Kaylee supposed to have? Did I need to take her to the doctor? How do I get my mom to make a doctor's appointment?

Maura opens the medicine cabinet while Kaylee watches with her little mouth pinched up. "We'll use some Vaseline tonight, okay, honey? I'll stop by the store in the morning and get some hydrocortisone cream, and then it won't itch so much."

Kaylee darts a wobbly smile at me.

Hy-dro-cor-ti-sone, I whisper to myself. Over and over, so I don't forget. If it's at the regular store, I can drop it my mom's basket when she's not looking. She often stops to buy a lipstick and some barrettes for Kaylee or something.

Maura kneels back down and dabs the Vaseline carefully onto Kaylee's tummy, and Kaylee holds out her inner arm and stretches out her leg so Maura can get those too. I know the itching drives my sister nuts. I tried to keep it clean. I did the best I could. We even have Vaseline at home, but I never thought to use it, and my chest closes in with shame.

The minutes pass. The bathroom smells nice, everything is green and fuzzy, and the mirror is foggy and dreamy.

"Kaylee?" Maura looks up at my little sister. "Is there anything else bothering you? Any other owies? Maybe I can help."

Kaylee looks over at me, eyes wide.

I clear my throat, which has gotten all tight. I know about evil stepmothers. I know about abuse. I know how to keep my sister safe.

"There's nothing," I say. "Mom just forgot to pack the hydrocortisone. We're fine."

"We'll pick some up tomorrow," Maura said, and that's the end of it.

I tumble from green fuzzy carpet onto the hard wooden bench in a mud cottage. Except I remember how the rash started to go away as soon as Maura bought the cream, and I convinced Mo—our biological mother—to keep some on hand and it helps whenever Kaylee gets a rash, which is often.

And I'm sixteen years old and know that Maura was never evil. She would have just said something to our dad, and our dad is a pretty sucky husband but he's always been a responsible father. He would have—

I can't think about it. I can't think about what could have been different.

I clear my throat, which is tight in real life too.

"No," I tell Mrs Morrisy, trying to be casual. "You can never be too careful about people."

But I start eating the soup. It seems like a worse risk to refuse.

***

I'm halfway through telling "The Merchant of Venice," and I'm actually having fun. I started with "An Triail," which is the most depressing play ever but Mrs Morrisy asked some good questions which got me thinking, and even Arthur perked up. I only memorized one poem in the car on the way to school on the day I had to recite, so of course it's un-memorized already, but I figure if I do a really great job with "The Merchant of Venice" then maybe Mrs Morrisy won't get around to asking for Yeats. I make different voices for the different characters, and growl and squeal at the right times. Dylan gets into it and adds some sound effects, and with the flickering lantern and the smoke it's pretty cool.

At first I think Dylan is thumping to add drama, but then Mrs Morrisy puts down her sewing and goes to the door, brows furrowed.

A cold blast sweeps over us.

"Dear child!" Mrs Morrisy cries, and someone lands in her arms.

Blond hair. Blue jacket.

"Kaylee!" I'm shouting. "Kay-bear baby-bear—"

Kaylee throws herself in my arms, and she's shivering but she holds me tight. Her flashlight hits the ground at our feet.

"You're fine," I murmur to her hair. "You're safe now, I've got you, I've got you."

"What are you doing here?" Arthur demands, but he's holding up a blanket to wrap around us both.

"Let's get her dry first," Mrs Morrisy says. "Arthur, build up the fire. Dylan, get her some soup and bread. Aiden, get the wet jacket off her. I'll get new clothes."

Half an hour later, Kaylee is dry and fed and sitting by the fire wrapped in a bunch of cloth held together with a belt and brooch.

"I saw the guy take Oona," Kaylee says, blowing on her tea, "and you ran off."

"You should have stayed home where you're safe," I scold.

"You ran off!" Kaylee insists.

"You were safe with Maura," I say.

"I'm not letting you go." Kaylee bumps her forehead against my shoulder. "Never again."

"This was different," I say, but I squeeze her tight. "No one was dragging me," I murmur, for her ears alone. "I left you with safe people. I promised."

"Still," Kaylee says.

"You could have gotten lost trying to follow us," Arthur says. He's been kind of a jerk to me, but there's real concern for Kaylee.

"We would have stopped and waited if we knew," Dylan adds. "Your brother's right, you shouldn't have come. But we would have waited for you."

"It's no place for a girl to be out alone," Arthur says.

"Well, no harm done," Mrs Morrisy says. "She'll go with you heroes tomorrow. You boys will take good care of her, and I'm sure she'll be able to help with something important."

Dylan and Arthur exchange a speaking look.

"I think tomorrow Aiden had better take her home," Arthur says.

Mrs Morrisy chuckles. "You're all here, so you'll all go on together. That's the way it works."

She's the Wise Woman, so none of us are going to argue. Arthur looks stormy and Dylan turns away and I know what they're thinking. It's one thing to just make out that I was tagging along, but now half our party is Robinsons, and Mrs Morrisy just predicted that Kaylee is going to do something important.

It gets worse, because once her tea is done, Mrs Morrisy bundles Kaylee up in the top cupboard-bed and takes the other one herself. Arthur and Dylan were going to get the beds, but now they're relegated to the loft with me. We only have worn furs and prickly wool blankets, the floor is hard wood, and we're squashed up between wooden boxes and bundles of food. It smells like onions and smoke and teenage boy sweat.

Dylan and Arthur aren't talking to me anymore.

Chapter 4

In the morning, Mrs Morrisy gives us a whole lecture about our quest. I memorize each step, determined to do it right. "In your world," she explains, "he disguises himself with patchwork, with his—"

"Knees out of his trousers and elbows through his clothing," Dylan and Arthur chorus.

Kaylee looks as confused as I was yesterday.

Mrs Morrisy nods. "But in his own world, he is called the Green Knight, and he is the lord of the Terrible Valley."

Terrible? I wish I didn't have to take Kaylee into it, in order to get Oona out of it.

"I've heard of that!" Arthur bolts upright. "We need the Sword of Daylight, and—"

Mrs Morrisy is waving her finger. "Patience, child. We will see if you have earned it."

The boys immediately retreat into respectful and attentive silence, and Mrs Morrisy explains how we are supposed to get to Terrible Valley. They perk up when she mentions magical gifts. I can practically see the thought bubble over Arthur's head, imagining himself holding up a gleaming sword. I tuck the thought away to make Kaylee smile later.

"What happens when we get there? What makes it terrible?" Dylan leans forward, expression intent.

But Mrs Morrisy shakes her head. "My lads, I cannot tell you that. But I can tell you what must happen when you return home."

"How we prove to the Council that we completed the quest?" Dylan leans closer.

"You must bring back the fair lady that the Green Knight stole; her skin as white as snow, lips as red as blood, and hair as dark as ebony. Ha! That's your sister, lad."

Arthur snaps his fingers. "I should have thought of that when I first saw Oona!"

I don't like this talk, like my kindergarten sister is an object of beauty. "She's just a kid," I mutter.

"I don't know why he selected a child," Mrs Morrisy says, "but she is the fair princess, now."

But Kaylee has followed my thinking. "It's just the way people talk about girls." She elbows me. "They always mention my hair, too."

"You must return to your Council with the fair princess, and with the heart of the Green Knight."

"The heart?" Dylan sounds as confused as I am. "Like...a heart shaped...thing?"

Mrs Morrisy pounds both palms onto her own chest. "His heart, my young heroes."

I recoil and Dylan goes a little green, but Arthur looks ready to dive right in. For that matter, so does Kaylee.

"Thank you, honored grandmother." Dylan stands and bows. "And now..."

"Now we finish the morning chores."

Mrs Morrisy is old-fashioned—no wonder, given that we've slipped back a thousand years or so—and sends us boys to do the outdoor work, while she hands Kaylee a broom. Good thing we've been living with Maura; six months ago Kaylee couldn't have swept a floor if it got down on its knees and begged her to.

When we think we're ready for the gifts, Mrs Morrisy makes us wash all the breakfast dishes. And put them away. And refill the water. And stoke the fire, which looked perfectly fine. I can feel Arthur and Dylan twitching with impatience, and I'm sure Mrs Morrisy does too. She has a little smile, like when the real Mrs Morrisy gets ready to hand back our tests but spends a while tapping them on her desk and talking about metaphors.

"Thank you for your assistance, young heroes." Mrs Morrisy smiles at each of us, even Kaylee, arranged on the benches in front of her. She glances at me. "And your trust. Arthur, you are the eldest. Go and bring the ebony chest from beneath the bed."

Arthur leaps to his feet, puffing as he carries the box back to the fireplace.

Mrs Morrisy pours us all a cup of herbal tea, but Kaylee is the only one to sip it.

"By the power vested in me," Mrs Morrisy says, "this chest contains a tool that will help each of you achieve your greatest desire...whatever has been weighing upon your heart as you sleep under my roof and drink my tea."

Both boys slurp their tea immediately.

I scoot farther out of the light, tucking my hands between my knees. Arthur and Dylan will get the magic sword to capture the Patchwork Man, and that's enough for me. I don't need to mess around with magical gifts. With Kaylee here, I'm even more anxious to rescue Oona and get them back home.

"But I will warn you"—another one of those annoying smiles—"you cannot share nor give away your tool. For anyone who has not completed the magic circle of giving, receiving, and hoping, the tool will just be as any item wrought of iron or wood."

"Yes, honored grandmother," Arthur says. One hand still rests on the lid of the box, almost twitching.

"Go ahead, my boy."

Arthur fumbles with the clasp and the box creaks open. He stares in, then shuffles around, then stares again.

"What is it?" Dylan asks, leaning closer. "Is it the sword?"

Arthur turns away. "Look."

He holds up...a pie server? And a...?

"How am I supposed to defeat the Patchwork Man with a *chisel*?" Arthur wails.

Mrs Morrisy shrugs. "With those tools, you will be the finest mason in the county. You will never be without work, and people will pay well and well again for your services. Is that not your desire?"

"But that's years away! I'm still in school and right now—"

Mrs Morrisy raises her eyebrows. "So you have a promise for years away. Is that not your desire?"

Arthur just stares at the pie server, which is probably not a pie server.

"Me next?" Dylan asks.

Mrs Morrisy waves him on, turning away from Arthur's stormy face.

Kaylee nudges closer to me. "I can't think of what my heart's desire is, can you?"

"I don't have one," I answer. "I just want Oona back."

And you, I think. I've spent my life wanting Kaylee to be safe, and here she is in trouble again.

Dylan gapes at the open box in his lap, his mouth gaping. "It's empty!"

Empty? Poor Dylan, to get so close and—

"Check carefully, my boy."

Dylan flops his hand around inside. After a moment, he comes out with something very small and sparkling. "A...ring? What do I do with a ring?"

"Don't you have a girl to give it to?" Mrs Morrisy smiles, completely placid.

"Well yes—but—"

"That is a very valuable ring, my lad. I've only seen it come out of the chest once before, so you must have a truly loving and selfless heart. That ring gives you a lifetime of loyalty, and when you die you will love each other a hundredfold beyond what you can even imagine today. Lovely, isn't it?"

"Yes—that's nice and all"—Dylan slides the ring onto his littlest finger and closes his fist, holding it tight—"but I need a house first. And to get that, I need the Patchwork Man!"

Mrs Morrisy shrugs. "Lad, youth always wants a dozen things and a dozen more. The magic is for your heart's desire."

Dylan spreads his fingers and stares at the ring on his pinky.

"And you, lad." Mrs Morrisy waves me forward.

Arthur glares at me, and I hunch even smaller. But if that's the job, I'll obey Mrs Morrisy. The latch is kind of confusing, but I try to open it quickly and not make noise.

There's a hand-sized hook of blond wood, looking like it's growing from the bottom of the box.

"Is it a sword?" Dylan asks. "One of us needs to get the sword."

Arthur swears under his breath.

"No," I say quickly, but at the same time—

"Sure and it is!" crows Mrs Morrisy. "I can feel the bravery just shining out!"

"I'm not brave," I mutter. I pull on the handle, and it keeps coming, and coming and coming. The top of the stick is above my head when, with one last pull, the round paddle at the base comes out of the box.

"Since when was your heart's desire to play hurley?" Dylan asks.

"Sure, and you want to be the hero in Kilkenny?" Arthur mocks.

"I thought you weren't one of those boys!" Kaylee cries.

"I couldn't care less about hitting a stupid ball with a stupid stick!" I'm so upset, the words burst out of me. "I just want Oona!"

"Boys, boys, calm down." Mrs Morrisy cocks her head. "That's the Sword of Daylight, sure as mutton is mutton. I don't know why it's choosing to appear as a polished stick today, but you appear to recognize what this is? A hur-ley? Well then. You'd better swing it like a hurley, Aiden Robinson, or poke it like a hurley, or whatever boys do with those things. The Sword of Daylight goes through everything in The Terrible Valley like a hot knife through butter, whether it is in the mood to look like a glaive or a rapier. Or apparently, today it is in the mood to look like..."

"A hurley."

We all say it together, with equal degrees of misery, but for different reasons. Dylan and Arthur each wanted the sword themselves and Kaylee has told me a hundred times that hurley is "dumb." As for me, I'm not a hero, I don't want to mess around with some silly game, I just want—

"The Green Knight is faster than a deer, stronger than any man, and has more lives than a field has buttercups. But he cannot stand against the Sword of Daylight, in any of its forms."

"So wait—I need this to get Oona back?"

She nods.

"Then I—well I—I mean, of course I'll play hurley if it gets Oona home!" I jump to my feet, reach for my jacket.

"Check for the sliotar," Dylan says quietly.

Good thing, because the ball's in the corner of the box.

"Shall we go?" I say. My voice sounds too eager; I don't want to make them mad. "I know I need you guys. We're not gonna get there if we don't work together." But did that sound like I'm trying to be the leader? "Mrs Mor—I mean, honored grandmother, do you know how we get to the Terrible Valley?"

"But what about me?" Kaylee cries. "I want to open the box too!"

Arthur snaps, "But you're not a—"

"Of course, my dear." Mrs Morrisy nudges my sister forward. "See what you shall find."

But Kaylee really does find the box empty. She looks three times, and touches all the corners, and shows me and Mrs Morrisy. I'm braced for Kaylee to either cry or start a tantrum, but she seems only perplexed.

Mrs Morrisy puts her hands on either side of Kaylee's face, looking into her eyes. "My dear...what I can see is that you have had a dream, something you have wanted very much for a very long time. But my box cannot give it to you, because you already have it."

"I have it?" Kaylee smiles, slowly. "I *have* that?"

Mrs Morrisy pats her cheek. "Yes, my dear. I can't see your heart's desire, but I can see that it is within you."

"But don't we want something new, as soon as we get what we wanted?" asks Dylan.

Mrs Morrisy nods. "But Kaylee has just gotten this thing. Within weeks, or a few months. She has not even truly believed that it has happened, and she has not believed—until now, I think—that it belongs to her. It will not vanish again, just like your skill will not vanish, young Arthur; or you, lad, and your steadfast love."

Dylan sucks in his breath and closes his hand over the ring again.

Love for your whole life. Imagine that. He created it with Hannah, and now he's holding it in his hand. Unlike me, who loses love right and left.

"Let's go," I say. "We've got to get to the Terrible Valley."

And I turn for the door.

I'm outside before anyone has realized that I'm really leaving. I lean on the corner of the cottage and squeeze the knitted mitten in my pocket. I know Kaylee will need a minute with tying her shoes and fussing with her scarf, and I need a minute without Kaylee.

Because I know what her heart's desire must have been, and it means that I failed her. What happened a few months ago? We moved in with Maura. Kaylee spent weeks being prickly, inventing arguments to see if Maura would send her home. It's just been a little while since Kaylee started trusting that everything isn't going to vanish—just like Mrs Morrisy said.

She wanted a home. Or she wanted to be safe. Or, like Dylan, she wanted to love and be loved.

And apparently, I never did any of those things for her. I should have just told Maura to do it eight years ago, because I've never made my sister happy at all.

***

The cart is already hitched up, and the animal in the traces is not a mule, not a horse, but a real live freaking deer. Of course. I'm too hurting and angry and lonely to even care about one more stupid mix-up in this stupid mixed-up world. Let's just go to the Terrible Valley (what a stupid name) and whack people with my stupid hurley stick and get Oona and go home. To the home that was always Kaylee's heart's desire. Not me.

The others follow me. Arthur is holding a bag that smells like bread and bacon, Dylan's arms are full of blankets, and Kaylee has my hurley stick.

"Is it Saba?" she whispers to me, pointing at the deer and meaning our other-worldly Solstice visitor. Saba and Kaylee worked together a lot, even though Saba was enchanted and couldn't even talk.

I shrug. Yet another friend. Someone wonderful who is not me.

Kaylee goes up to the deer, cooing and chattering, while the boys fool around with climbing into the cart and pushing each other out again. How stupid. Mrs Morrisy gives me careful instructions and I do pay attention. I'm not going to make another mistake and screw up Oona's life, too.

"It's not Saba," Kaylee whispers on her way back. "But I think she's a *wise* deer. I bet she *knows* Saba."

"Okay." I try to smile at her. "Now get on in, Kay-bear."

But the problem is that there's no more "in." The cart has this thing kind of like a bar stool sticking off the front for the driver, and that's me because I have the Daylight Whatever. The back is a little wooden box, with barely enough room for Arthur and Dylan crammed together.

Kaylee starts to climb up but get stuck on Dylan's feet poking out the back, and the boys laugh uproariously.

"I'm not leaving without my sister," I snap.

"She doesn't fit," Arthur says. "We'll come back for—"

"If she doesn't get in, then you get out." I've been polite and all, but if it comes down to it, I'm the one with the sword and I'm the one with the reins. And you know why? Because I'm the only one who really wants to get Oona. They can suck it.

"There's room," Dylan says. "Kaylee, can you sit on my lap? Look, I'll make a space for you like this."

I turn and glare at them, because I know how my sister feels about boys. But Arthur is arranging the blankets and Dylan is showing Kaylee how she can pull herself up, and I guess he's in love with Hannah so he's not going to do anything to my sister. I'll let him help her.

"All right," Arthur calls. "We're ready."

"Readyyyyyy!" Kaylee squeals, and dissolves into giggles.

I guess she's happy, because she's finally got someone to take care of her. A proper someone. Someone besides me.

"North to the stars, south to the sun, and onwards to the Terrible Valley," I say to the deer.

She springs forward and we mount into the air, which means we could plummet hundreds of feet at any moment.

Great. Just great. Maybe it's just as well that Kaylee is squashed in like a sardine.

Chapter 5

The deer trots above the treetops. There's a little rail thing in front of me, and I hold tight to that, and tight to the reins, and keep my hurley tucked under my knees. Although it's not dark, the stars wheel in the sky overhead, and below us pass rivers and ponds and trees. Sometimes I can see the surf pounding against the rocky coastline, and sometimes we skirt around little towns with puffs of woodsmoke coming out of squat little mud and thatch houses. Then we go past these beehive houses, and I'm curious enough to forget how cold I am. I lean out to watch boys herding cows and a girl with her arms full of greenery, but I never forget my goal or slow the deer down.

As the hours pass, my frustration and anger fall away from me. There's no point in holding on to it. After all, Maura is a real mother with plenty of practice and a proper mother of her own. No wonder I can't do as much for Kaylee. A real household was all I wanted, back a year ago when Maura was divorcing my dad and he sent us for six sessions with a psychologist. I planned it all out on post-it notes, exactly how much I would say to her. Exactly what I would say in court. All I was thinking was how to get Kaylee out of that house in Florida, but not so much that Mom—I mean, my biological mother—would actually get in trouble. She wasn't a bad mother. She never hurt us or anything. She just got kind of...tired of how every-day children are.

It doesn't matter now. Oona matters now. Getting both my sisters home safely matters now.

I stretch my neck to see what we're coming up on next, and glimpse a bunch of boats on the flat gray ocean. Before I can decide if it would be scary or cool to watch a Norman invasion, I figure out that they're fishing boats. We glide above the sea, past low islands dotting out of the water, then back over green hills.

It's almost noon when the deer trots in an ever-descending circle, and finally stops in a meadow. She hangs her head, panting.

"Wait!" I remind the others. I crawl down, my legs so stiff that I almost trip. There's a little box fastened below the driver's seat, and Mrs Morrisy told me there's a knife inside. Here it is; made of black stone. Interesting.

"Bread, please." I put my hand into the cart, and Kaylee solemnly hands me a small bun and apple, which I give the deer, and I bow and thank her with the exact words Mrs Morrisy told me. While the deer stands chewing, I squat down by her front legs, and cut a square of the turf beneath her right hoof. I have to tug and pry to get it out, and then it comes so fast I fall backwards.

The deer twitches away from me, shaking her head. The little hole that I just pulled grows wider and wider, stretching like a rip in tights. When it's done, I creep forward on hands and knees and peer down.

Just like Mrs Morrisy told us, there's a whole other world down there. Rolling green hills, little streams, stands of trees in the distance. It looks just like Ireland; I guess druidic folklore never imagined anything like the Everglades or Miami. But the leaves are on the trees and the grass is greener, so maybe it's not the middle of the bleeping winter down there. If Oona's stuck there, it's just as well. She gets cold so fast, and besides, I have one of her mittens.

"Okay, you're good now!" I call to the others, and hear them tumble down, laughing and chatting. I work on unhooking the deer so she can graze or take a nap or whatever she likes. Kaylee and Arthur go into the nearby trees, looking for the supplies that Mrs Morrisy told us to find, while Dylan unpacks the cart.

An hour or so later, we've got a little fire roaring. Kaylee serves the food, while Arthur fiddles with the reeds and sticks and rope from the woods. We're supposed to turn it into a person-sized basket, which we can lower down the hole into the Terrible Valley. Arthur apparently read a book on basket weaving just in case he encountered this particular obstacle.

"C'mon," Dylan says to me. "If you've got to use a hurley stick to defeat the most dangerous knight in the history of Kilkenny, you'd better practice some hurley."

We head out into the meadow. Dylan saved a fat stick from the fire-making that works okay for demonstration purposes. He throws the sliotar, tells me where and how to run, adjusts my grip on the hurley. I always played sports at home, but it's hard to practice hurley when all the other boys are so much more advanced than I am. Dylan is patient, today, and the fourth time he moves my hands slightly and makes me lift the end higher, I suddenly get it. This is where the balance is, how it moves! I get a lot better all of a sudden.

When we're both sweaty and tired, we head back to the fire to check on the others. Kaylee is huddled over the fire, reading a book on her phone. (There's no internet in wherever we are, obviously, but also for some reason our phone batteries don't seem to run down.) Arthur is a little ways away, and even though his back is to us his movements are so jagged and angry that I don't want to disturb him.

Dylan goes over. Their voices quickly grow loud and sharp, so I put some more wood on the fire and ask Kaylee about her book. She's reading *All Creatures Wise and Wonderful* and is full of stories about meandering cats and sheep with temperatures of 104.

It's cute. I like seeing her excited about something, and I like that she's enjoying books about sheep instead of worrying about makeup and guys.

It was good getting her out of Florida, even if it means she doesn't need me anymore.

Arthur yells, and Dylan stomps back to the fire.

"Hey," he says to us. "Either of you know anything about basket weaving? We can't get it to work."

"I *know* how to make it work!" Arthur shouts.

Kaylee looks at me for permission, then shrugs. "Maura has showed me how to use a frame loom and an inkle loom. Is it like that?"

"That's cool," Dylan says. "Your mum's really good at making things. Why don't you come try?"

They chat as they head towards the giant basket, and I trail behind them. It hurts both when Kaylee says "Maura" and also when Dylan calls her our mum. I don't know why my brain is so illogical about it. When we moved to Ireland, I decided to start saying "Mum" instead of "Maura," to show the world that we belong together. I like how they say it here, a little flip of the mouth, like it's the simplest word there is. But it's not, because I can't teach myself to use it in my own thoughts, and apparently Kaylee still can't say it at all.

"Fine!" Arthur yells. "Ye want to do it yourselves, do it all, ye buggers!" He storms into the woods.

"I'm sorry..." Kaylee bites her lip.

Dylan turns to smile carefully at Kaylee. "An inkle loom, eh? So where would be the loom shaft? What would be the shuttle?" He picks up one of the straight sticks, half as tall as he is. "You just tell us where to go, and Aiden and I will hold the bits and bobs for you."

Kaylee twists at the waist so her whole head is sideways. I've seen her and Maura work, and I know what she's doing, because the loom pegs stick out horizontal and now they are sticking up vertical. It does look kind of similar though. Kaylee has to walk around it a couple times, and she gets flustered and apologizes, but Dylan brushes off her worries.

He treats her patiently. Like a little sister, not like a pretty blonde with curves under her T-shirt. He's going to make a good dad someday.

Him and Hannah, and love that is a hundredfold more than they could imagine today. Geez. I would take one person who loves me one-fold.

But Oona's more important. It's okay.

I've got plenty of time to stew it over, holding one pole in place and then another. Kaylee gets in a rhythm, and Dylan and I just do what we're told, which leaves me too much time to think about love. Isn't there attachment theory and stuff, that proves if your parents don't love you right when you're little that you'll never be able to love properly again? I mean, I guess my parents were fine when I was really little. My dad worked a lot, but he spent time with us when he was home. I remember snuggling in bed reading dump truck books with him, but also he made me clean up my toys and put me in time out when I refused. We had a housekeeper and a nanny and went to preschool. I guess my mom was pretty normal when she was married to Dad.

That's why I hated Maura so much at first. Because I'd had a family and then it was gone. Just me and Kaylee in that huge house, and Mo—our biological mother staring into space all day and going out with her friends at night.

"Done!" chirps Kaylee. "Do you think it will work?"

"We'd better make sure the stakes are solid so the base can support the weight of the load," Arthur warns.

Apparently he has reappeared, complete with a book's-worth of basket making vocabulary. I'm fiercely proud of Maura and Kaylee, who actually make things instead of just talking about them.

We push the basket. We lean on it. We tie it to the hemp rope (thank heavens we didn't have to weave that!) and lower the empty basket into the hole, just to test. Good thing, because we quickly realize we need additional mechanics to control the descent. But it isn't hard; I think about my physics textbook and come up with some logs that work kind of like a pulley. The deer comes back, nosing at the rope curiously, and perfectly willing to be put into her harness to pull the far end. It's strong enough to hold one person, we agree.

"Me first!"

Arthur is brave; I've got to give him that.

The basket swings wildly as we figure out how to get Arthur from the regular ground without dumping him to the bottom. I put my jacket sleeves over my hands to protect them and guide the rope through the proto-pulley, Dylan walks the deer slowly forward, and Kaylee lays on her belly watching the basket and shouting out progress updates.

This is kind of cool! We started with a pile of willows and now we're getting a whole human being down a giant hole. Way better than eighth grade physical science, when we dropped eggs off the balcony wrapped in popsicle sticks and Kleenex boxes.

Arthur yells, muffled.

"Pull him up!" Kaylee cries. "Hurry, hurry! He can't stand it!"

"Let's go!" Dylan urges the deer forward, I shuffle the pulley wheels, while Kaylee yells encouragement both down the hole and up. Now I can hear Arthur yelling, the deer strains harder, and I rush to help Kaylee pull the basket over the edge.

Arthur lays on the grass, moaning. "The little people...like tin cans...so sharp..."

Dylan and I exchange horrified glances. This isn't going according to plan.

"Lovely, lovely..." Dylan rubs his hands together. "I'll go down, then. You each can follow, maybe Arthur last. We'll go together. All together, right then!"

But Dylan doesn't make it even as far as Arthur, and we yank him up just as incoherent. He staggers back and forth across the clearing, raking his hands through his hair.

"You've got...Sword of Daylight...you're...go..."

I shove my hands deeper into my jacket pockets, flushed and hot despite the cold. I'm not a hero from a fairy tale. I'm just a stupid high school kid, only good enough for JV basketball. Now I'm supposed to face scary people dressed in tin cans? With nothing but a hurley stick?

"Okay," I say to Dylan, but I don't mean it. If they can't do it, I probably can't either.

I'm doing a breathing exercise the psychologist taught me when I meet Kaylee's eyes. She is watching me with a faint smile, head cocked like a little bird.

"Okay," I say. To Kaylee this time.

She's been looking at me like this for years. I never know what to do, but I keep going anyways. Because she's my sister, and I'm all she's got—and I'm all Oona's got out here, too.

"Arthur, get up off the ground." My voice comes out curt. "You've got to steady the basket then manage the pulley. Get over here so I can show you. Dylan! Come back and hold the deer, she's eating twigs. You know how to take off her harness when we're done? Kay-bear-baloney, go get your stuff. You and I are going down together."

"Together?" asks Dylan. "Is it strong enough?"

"It's gonna have to be," I answer, because I'm sure as heck not leaving Kaylee. Ever again.

***

The Terrible Valley isn't really so bad, it just goes on forever.

Kaylee and I walk and walk, on paths that go across fields and through trees, over the occasional stream, that kind of stuff. The weather is mild and summery. Kaylee chatters, and I ask enough questions to keep her going, make enough jokes to keep her laughing.

"We've walked a lot of places together, haven't we, Aiden?" She loops her pinky through mine and swings our hands. "Remember that park with the giant rocket ship? It was a long ways from our house."

Yeah, where they had free vision and hearing clinics in June, and flu shots in September. I always put fake names so they couldn't track it back to Mom, but now I don't remember why I bothered.

A few times, we pass little square huts made of mud with thatched roofs, like the one we stayed in last night. Other times, we hear the sound of clanking in the distance, and catch sight of something shiny and sharp over the gentle crest of a hill. I go hot and sweaty because it's probably the tin can men who scared Arthur and Dylan and whoever named this place.

I grip Kaylee's hand and my hurley stick. "If they come any closer, you get in a tree, okay?"

"A tree? Why?" Kaylee looks around. "I'm not sure I could climb one of those."

"You need to. You have to stay safe."

"I'm not worried," Kaylee protests. "Nothing ever hurts me when you're around."

But it's not true.

The tin can armies start getting closer to us. One is in the forest right ahead, and we turn sharply. A whole group of them comes marching down a streambank while we're in the same meadow. I put Kaylee behind me, breathing tight and watching closely, but they keep marching straight and don't come towards us.

Each one is about half my size. They're basically person-shaped, with arms and legs and head, but awkward and uneven, like Oliver drew a person. Each part of them looks like tin cans stacked together: thin tin cans for the arms, a big tin can for the head, flat tin cans for their feet. I can't tell if this is armor and there's something living inside, or they're just like giant walking toy soldiers. Even though they're little, they're creepier than if they were human.

They carry spears over their shoulders, or swords in their hands, or these long knives on sticks. Glaives; I remember reading the word for Oliver at one of the museums. He thought the weapons were cool, but they're not any more. I can't stop imagining them stabbing into Kaylee's flesh, or these freaky monsters guarding Oona's room while she weeps inside.

I'm scared. I want to run back to the basket and do three pulls on the rope and tell the deer to bring us home again.

But I don't. I look at the sun and which way the streams are flowing and I try to head farther into the Terrible Valley, because that must be where Oona is.

We're both getting tired and Kaylee is chattering less. We see the tin men more often, although they still ignore us.

The path goes right in front of one of the little huts.

"Welcome, Kaylee and Aiden!" calls a gentle voice. "Come in and rest."

I put my hand on Kaylee's back, making her run towards the cover of the trees.

"What's the matter?" she asks. "Let's stop! I'm getting tired."

"Let's get to Oona tonight," I say, not mentioning how creeped out I am. I'm not taking my sister into some dark talking house!

"Yeah. Despite what the nice old lady said, I want to see her myself. That'll be better." Kaylee's steps drag to a walk, and we pop out of the little forest.

There's a whole tin man army right here! Looking right at us! They turn towards us, raising swords and spears and other sharp pokey things that are way definitely gonna hurt!

"Tree! Kaylee! Now!" I manage to shout. Drat! I didn't find a branch for her!

Kaylee darts back into the woods, and I grip my hurley with both hands. I'd hide in a tree myself, but what if they followed us? What if they poked those things at Kaylee? I crouch down and brace myself, but I can't stop the tears from burning my eyes.

They march closer. All together.

Really shiny. Really pokey.

"Yayyy, Aiden!"

I am incredibly relieved that Kaylee's voice comes from behind and above, along with the sound of rattling leaves. She starts one of the cheers from our old school, and I grip my hurley and adjust my stance.

The tin can men get closer. Fourteen. I count them.

My breath is shaking and I can barely see from the tears. This is gonna hurt. So bad.

My baby sister is going to watch me die.

The first five raise their swords all together, and I shift my grip and swing the hurley stick the way Dylan taught me. Whoosh!

There's a huge clatter, but not the solid resistance I expected on my stick. I have to blink because there's also no one where I expected to see—

Oh.

They're all cut off, somewhere between the shoulders and the hips, in a smooth arc like the scoop of a knife through butter. Tin arms and heads scatter the grass around us. They make no sound and there's nothing inside them.

And then the next five are on me, knocking over their team-mates' legs as they advance with their swords raised. They're short, so my hurley stick has a longer reach than their weapons. Hurley sticks aren't as long as hockey sticks, though, so I've got to swing fast and again and again, keep it going before the next wave gets to me. My chest heaves and sweat prickles my armpits and rolls down my neck. I've lost whatever rhythm I had with Dylan and am just heaving that thing as fast as I can. Swing! Backstroke! Swing!

The last few have spears instead of swords. Those are longer, and I haven't got the rhythm of getting from the right to the left fast enough. One catches my arm, and he's going for my chest but I manage a throat-catching jab and he goes down. Ha! I've admired that move for months!

I'm swirling from the thrill of my fancy move when I realize it's over. All the tin men are in pieces at my feet, and the last pair of empty legs is rocking and finally tumbles over with a clatter.

I lean on my hurley stick.

Oh gosh.

Even though there's no blood, I'm gonna be sick.

"Wow!" Kaylee rustles in the tree, a thump as she hits the ground. "That was..."

Kaylee throws her skinny arms around me. She rests her head against my back, and I put my free hand over her clasped hands.

"That was weird," Kaylee mumbles against my jacket.

I smile as I pull her around into a hug. I swallow down my bile, because we've got to keep going. I'm no kind of hero, but I've got the Hurley Stick of Daylight and two sisters. Here I go.

Chapter 6

The third time we pass a talking house, I'm tempted to stop. Kaylee's definitely tired—okay, so am I—and we're not getting any closer to Oona. I make a mark for the position of the sun and the top of a hill, just in case we're going in circles. There's danger if we go inside, but it's dangerous to spend the night outside, too. I've chopped up one more group of tin can soldiers, plus a pair that were on their own, and my shoulders are aching. If we're in a hut, then something bad could trap us in the corner. But if we're out in the open, then something bad could surround us.

"I'm hungry," Kaylee says.

"You're fine," I tell her, but I've never been able to stop worrying about Kaylee being hungry. My resistance is crumbling.

Like feta cheese. Or shrimp tacos. Or sugar cookies—the ones Maura makes. Yum.

"Aiden and Kaylee Robinson, welcome to the Friendly House. The table is laid for your pleasure."

I stop in my tracks, blinking.

"Oh Aiden!" Kaylee squeezes my arm. "This one has got to be good! That's a *person* talking to us!"

She pulls me forward, and I don't resist as hard as I should.

"Welcome in," the woman says, opening the door and making a sweeping gesture inside.

"We even *know* her," Kaylee whispers, not very quietly. "She's *nice!*"

Wait a minute, we do! We knew someone who looked just like this back when in Florida. I stop, Kaylee pulls. I try to brace my feet, but Kaylee pulls harder.

"Let's go!" she hisses. "I'm hungry! It smells good!"

So we go in the house. It's too weird, but I guess when I was with the boys I found someone from secondary school, and now with Kaylee here's someone back from our elementary school days. I bob a thank you to the woman at the door, very upright and smiling and way too young to call 'honored grandmother.' Instead of jeans like the regular-life version of herself, she wears the drapes and sashes like the other women we've seen here, but she still wears her hijab.

Nisha shows us around the cottage. The table is set with thick brown dishes and bowls of berries, there's a stew bubbling over the fireplace and flatbread warming in a little nook in the chimney. She shows us where the "white food" is kept (whatever that is?) for breakfast, and the little cupboard room with two beds piled high with brightly dyed wool blankets. She pulls back a curtain, showing a steaming big wooden barrel. I think the thing next to it is, um, a potty.

"A bath for your tired limbs," Nisha says, smiling.

"Awesome!" Kaylee cheers.

Nisha raises her eyebrows at Kaylee. "There are greens in the bowl on the window. Make sure you eat a whole serving. No sweets until you do!"

This is so weird. So familiar. So weird!

"*Are* there sweets?" Kaylee asks.

Nisha just smiles. "If you eat your greens, you might find some."

"Are you leaving?" I need to know what's going on. "Will you be back?"

"If you need my advice, you can call for me," Nisha answers, and she hands me a little bundle. "Toss the leaves in a fire and say my name three times, and I can find you anywhere in the Terrible Valley. Now I am off to serve dinner to my nephews."

We used to meet those nephews in the park, and Kaylee helped them climb the big tower while Nisha and I did homework at the picnic table. She was in college, but that was a few years ago—or a thousand years in the future? This makes no sense, and it makes me angry and unsettled.

When Nisha leaves, the house seems eerie and empty. I know what needs doing, though, so I go out to fill the woodpile and the water buckets before dark. At least I know how to manage these cottages by now; it's just like Mrs Morrisy's.

Gosh. I'm so tired. My arms and shoulders don't want to pick up anything more.

By the time I'm finished, Kaylee is out of the bath and she scoops soup into our bowls, only spilling a little. "Isn't this great? It smells so good!"

"I'm not sure we can trust the food here." I wipe up the drops of soup.

"But Nisha's always done nice things for us."

"She's just a grocery store clerk in Tallahassee." Well, I guess that sounds classist, but I just mean she wasn't important to us. Our family. Kaylee and me. "Although she is really nice and all."

"She told us how to find the summer lunch program." Kaylee slurps her soup.

I bump my bowl and almost spill it myself. I thought I'd figured out how to get to the summer lunch program. Myself.

"And she gave us a ride home when it was raining. Remember? That storm came up with no warning, and she had to go ask her boss for a break."

I put down my spoon without eating. Of course I remember that day. I'm hot, and cold, and those stupid tears are threatening again. Just like when I was a stupid kid, and I knew the hurricane was due but thought we could get to the grocery store and back before it got bad. Kaylee didn't want to go so I made a game of stomping in the puddles on the way there, but Kaylee got water in her rain boots and got cold and whiney. So doing the shopping took longer and longer, and I could hear the wind building up the whole time.

"That was just the once," I said, like it didn't matter. Like I hadn't been scared.

Kaylee giggles. "We opened the door and the trees were whipping back and forth! Like this!" She waves her hands. "Then Nisha came up and said she would drive us."

"Because she was due for a break anyways."

"No, she went to ask her boss. I remember."

I don't say anything, because maybe Kaylee is right. Maybe I screwed everything up.

Kaylee is already scraping the bottom of her bowl. "Yum. This is good! Do you want more?" She serves herself a second bowl.

I take a bite, and three more. I'm so hungry. "I never made you anything this good," I admit.

"You made like...chicken patties and Ben's minute rice. And Nisha made us get frozen vegetables too." Kaylee laughs.

Yeah, Nisha did everything and all I could manage was microwave rice. I try to keep my tone light. "You remember that? I thought you'd be upset."

Kaylee laughs again. "Oh, all kids think Kit-Kats are more fun than broccoli. It doesn't mean anything."

I stare at the bottom of my bowl, and it's almost like the picture of my memory is floating in the cracked glaze. When I was nine, Dad got me a Greenlight debit card and put thirty dollars on it every week. He told me that I could get as many toys as I wanted, just always buy a book first. Sometimes I did get a book, but when Mom was having one of her spells, I figured out that I could walk to the Aldi's down by 113th. Of course, I had to take Kaylee with me, which made it take longer, but thirty dollars could get a few meals for a couple kids. Then usually Mom would be back to normal.

The night Kaylee had a tantrum about the vegetables, it was a Friday. Mom had just left with her new boyfriend. We had half a box of Indian take-out in the fridge and a bag of cornflakes in the cupboard, and I was freaking out. Kaylee was tired and just wanted the chicken korma, but I wanted to get to Aldi's before it got dark, so I bribed her with the promise of KitKats.

I'd forgotten how badly I'd messed up that night. I thought I was clever for taking care of Kaylee, but I wasn't. I was such a stupid kid.

I was flustered and making dumb mistakes, and I got to the register with too much stuff. We always went to Nisha's register—why? maybe that's another thing I've forgotten?—and I watched the numbers go up and up. When they got past thirty, I started taking stuff out again.

"Not the grapes!" Kaylee whined. "Not the ice cream!"

Usually I would have listened to her, but Mom had packed her little red suitcase and I was afraid she would be gone the whole weekend. We could get breakfast and lunch at school, but weekends were just hard. I was trying to count out meals while Nisha rang stuff up, and I was telling her to take stuff off so she rang it the other way, so I ignored Kaylee. I was getting hotter and more flustered, and Kaylee was getting louder and complaining and stomping her feet.

"You promised me KitKats!" she screamed, and hit me.

The whole store turned and looked at us. It was my worst nightmare.

I waited for the police to come. Hit me with a bully club for pretending to be a grownup. Take Kaylee away and give her to another family.

Nisha's laugh broke the tension. "Let's get this all sorted out before your mama gets back, shall we?" she said, putting her "closed" sign on the conveyor belt. That was always what I said, that my mom was picking up something on the other side of the store. Nisha knew perfectly well that my mom never showed up, but the strangers around us didn't. The people who had been watching us in line grumbled and rolled their carts away. No one was calling the police; no one even cared.

"Look, sweetie," Nisha said to Kaylee. "Don't you want to do well at school? You've got to eat your vegetables so your brain is nice and strong!" Nisha kept chatting to Kaylee, sorting through everything on the belt. She made little piles for each meal, doing the math in her head while she talked. "You've got to get the meat and vegetables on your shopping list before you can do treats," she told Kaylee, who was nodding along by then. "That's what I have to do, too. Last week I wanted a cake but I had to put it back so I could get a pot roast instead."

"So your nephews can do good in school?" Kaylee asked, completely entranced.

Nisha nods. "Good grades are much sweeter than candy, I promise." She looked at me. "Honey, if you go grab the pack of chicken thighs, they're on sale this week. You can get two of those for the price of this one." She handed me the packet of chicken breasts and I raced off to the back of the store.

"Good grades are sweeter than candy," Kaylee mumbled to herself as we walked home, loaded down with grocery bags. Now that I think of it, I never taught her that. I didn't bother. She learned better life lessons from a grocery store clerk than from me.

"Here you go-ooo," Kaylee sings, putting a scoop of greens into my bowl and her own. "It will make your muscles big."

I swallow the first bite of greens, but they're really strong and I almost gag on the next mouthful.

I shove the rest of the greens in my mouth and force myself to swallow. Now that I think of it, I never added the amount up myself. Now that I think of it, we often managed to afford enough food at Nisha's checkstand. I wonder how much she was adding from her own paycheck.

I am sick with guilt, and now here she is helping us again.

***

I let Kaylee have first pick of the cupboard beds, and she wanted the upper bunk. Now that I'm laying down and warm, all the aches from the day are throbbing in my muscles. I can feel all the unaccustomed swinging in my shoulders, and a trembling in my elbows from the jolting of the hurley stick hitting those tin can men, which in the dark seems creepier than it did when I was all stoked up with adrenaline. It's darker than it ever has been at home, smells of wool and wood smoke, and the wind is making the trees groan outside.

"Aiden?" Kaylee says.

"Yes, Kaylee-did Bug?"

"Why didn't Dad give us more money? He has lots, why did he only give us thirty dollars a week for groceries?"

I'm half-asleep and answer without thinking. "He didn't know it was groceries. He thought I was buying add-ons for Minecraft and stuff."

"Wait."

Something in Kaylee's voice stabs me awake.

"Didn't you tell Dad about us?"

"Tell Dad what? What about us?" The old anger is trying to surface, the bile I have tried so hard to ignore pushing into the back of my throat. I swallow it down. Because if there's anything I've learned in my life it's how to stop wasting energy on the battles you can't win, and I know this anger is never going to get me anywhere.

Kaylee sighs, all dramatic thirteen-year-old again. "Oh, how about how sometimes Mom was really sweet and loving, and *sometimes* she'd just go to bed and not bother to do anything for a *week* at a time?"

Does Kaylee honestly still think that Mom was just sleeping? I guess I never let Kaylee go in there. Mom's skin would go gray and clammy and her eyes were weird, and I didn't want Kaylee to be upset.

Kaylee sighs even more gustily. "How about how we walked to the Aldi by *ourselves* because Mom *forgot* to get groceries half the time? And what about when Mom started to go away for—for the. Whole. Weekend." There's a lonely hiccup under Kaylee's theatrical tone. "Like going to concerts and stuff. And we never knew when she would be back. Didn't Dad know about all that?"

"I—I don't know. Maybe. He should have." The anger is burning, burning, hot in my throat and stinging my eyes.

"But did he *know?*"

"I kept you safe, didn't I?" I need her to agree.

"It was still scary!"

So I failed her.

"Did you *tell* him? Did you *talk* about it?"

"I didn't!" I don't have the strength left to control my words. "Dad *should* have figured it out! He said that he cared. He should have noticed that Mom wasn't there in our video calls! He should have surprised Mom with a visit some time and seen what it was like when she didn't have a chance to pretty everything up! He should have noticed"—what you were like when we visited him, I think, but I stop myself from saying something hurtful. She always acted way out when we had our visits with Dad and Maura. Any sensible person would know that something was wrong. "It wasn't like you had to be Sherlock Holmes," I finish, my voice ragged and sharp in my throat. "He just never bothered to look, so no, he didn't know any of that."

"He didn't *know?*" Kaylee is almost crying now. "He *didn't* even *know?*"

I am totally flustered. "It doesn't change anything!"

"All this time"—Kaylee swings around so her head is upside-down over the top bunk, a dark shadow looking into the darkness—"all this time I thought he knew what Mom was like and he just didn't *care*. I thought he knew we were alone at night and missing doctor's appointments and stuff but he didn't want us messing up his perfect life with Maura. I thought he hated us!"

My head is pounding and I can't think. I'm not sure what Kaylee means, what changed, but her raw emotion cuts me apart.

For me, her pain is a more brutal knife than the tin men's swords.

Kaylee swings back into her bunk.

She gulps one sob, then another. I know she is waiting to hear what I say. She always does.

I could say *Dad always loved you. He wanted you to be happy.* That would make Kaylee feel better, and it's probably true in a way, but that would exonerate my dad. The anger is still pounding in me, like waves sloshing against my skull and my ribcage.

I can't say it.

"That's why I was so bitchy with him all the time." Kaylee's voice is tiny. "I thought he knew and didn't *care*."

I turn and bury my face in my pillow so Kaylee can't hear if a sob bursts out. It's not her job to take care of my feelings. All the literature about raising children says that.

"It would have changed *everything* if I knew that he just didn't *know*," Kaylee wails. "He wasn't a bad dad if he just didn't *know*."

I can't stand how easily she would forgive him. He *should* have known, he *should* have known, he *should* have! I *hate* him!

The sheer raw ugliness of that shocks me, and I'm swamped with guilt. So I say the thing I didn't want to, and I do it for *her*. So she doesn't have to feel this pain.

"He loved you, Kaylee," I rasp. "He just couldn't...he didn't mean to." As though not meaning to is enough. I hold my breath as though it will hold in my anger as well. "But he always loved you."

"Oh," Kaylee says.

It's still a little whimpery sound, but I know it's what she wanted to hear. Maybe it's enough. Her breathing gets a little easier.

Not me. I still have to suck in a big breath and hold it tight while my chest tries to spasm. When the sob passes, I blow out through pursed lips and suck in fast before the next one hits. That usually helps.

"But I don't under*stand*," Kaylee says. "Why didn't you *tell* him? Why didn't you explain?"

I don't know why. I never thought of it, honestly. I blow out and suck fast. When I was a kid, it just seemed...clear to me. Or it hurt too much to think about. But Dad changed the custody agreement once I finally asked, so why didn't I ask earlier? Did I just put Kaylee through years of uncertainty for nothing?

I wish there were ibuprofen in this world. My whole body is so sore. And sleeping pills; I'd take one of those too. Just escape it all for a few hours.

"*Aiden*. Why didn't you *tell* him?"

Something inside me breaks, and I snap. "Why didn't you?"

Kaylee sighs, a long fluttering sigh that rips my heart to shreds. "Because you took care of things. I *trusted* you."

My heart breaks. Flays into a thousand pieces, throbbing, sliced with blunt swords and beaten with hurley sticks.

My sister trusted me, and I didn't help her.

I'm just as bad as my father.

Chapter 7

The next morning, I ache so badly that I can hardly walk, and my heart aches so badly that I can't talk at all. I manage to get the fire going, grateful I brought in plenty of wood last night. Kaylee sets the table and fills the kettle, and even though she splashes water everywhere, her lower lip is a little bit pushed out in that way I know she's feeling stubborn and hurt.

We've never talked about Da—either of our biological parents. We've heard the stories in school about bad things happening to kids and how to say no, but none of it ever seemed to fit our situation. I don't have words for all this mess inside of me, and I guess Kaylee doesn't either.

I lower myself onto the bench in increments, like an old man. Kaylee thumps the bowl with the "white foods" on the table and takes off the lid, peering in curiously. There are four balls wrapped in waxed cloth and a little jar of preserved berries.

Butter, it turns out. And cheese. And...another cheese? Cheesy butter? Doesn't matter; my stomach growls in anticipation. Normally, I would get back up to fetch the bread, but my joints really don't want to move. I pick off bits of cheese with my fingers while Kaylee warms the flatbread over the fire. It's made of a grain that is dark and heavy—Maura would know what kind—and it's pretty hard to eat when it's cold.

Without talking, we eat bread and cheese and butter and jam, and toasted bread and cheese, and cheese and jam without bread, and the last of the soup with bread. And cheese. I guess we were hungry.

By then, the iron kettle finally boils. I force my body to get it, because I'm proud that Kaylee is helping, but I don't want her to spill boiling water on herself. She spoons herbs into cups and sighs dramatically as I pour.

Good. I want regular old theatrical Kaylee back.

"Nisha says this is supposed to be good for our aches and give us energy and stuff, but it smells like mushrooms!" She wrinkles her nose. "And spaghetti sauce!"

I think she means it smells like herbs, and that makes me smile, which I hide while taking a grateful sip of anything that might help with aches.

We finish drinking and still don't have any energy. I'm pretty sure coffee and tea don't get to Europe for another few centuries or so. How did they make it through? Kaylee sighs and stomps over to put the white food away.

"Oh, look at this!" For the first time, Kaylee's voice is animated. "The cubby was empty when I got the breakfast, but now... Yum!"

"What is it?" I try to sound attentive.

She plonks her finds on the table and I am definitely interested.

"Nisha left us a present! It's even her stationery, don't you remember?"

It's a note on paper with beagle puppies, a half-used box of Taylor's & Harrogate English Breakfast, and two Kit-Kat bars.

Nisha to the rescue. Again.

***

Clankity bang! Clankity clunk!

The tin men fall to the ground, and I stagger backwards. I rebalance my hurley stick and push my hair of my damp forehead. These tin can men are more of an annoyance than anything, but—

"Aiden!" Kaylee screams. "Turn!"

There's a whoosh as I spin, and a sharp whack on my back before my hurley makes contact and slices right on through. The soldier falls into pieces at my feet, but I'm swinging forward off balance and trip over its arms and legs. My palms hit the grass and my shin bangs something hard and clanking.

Oof.

"They're gone!" Kaylee cries. "You've made it!"

I'm not injured—I don't think—but I let my head hang for a minute. I've always thought mind over body, don't think, just keep going. But my body is tired, and nothing is going right. Kaylee is still mad at me. We're making the same endless loops on the same endless pathways. The Green Knight has Oona and I can't get her back.

"Are you okay? Aiden? Are you?" Kaylee clatters over the broken tin limbs and pats my shoulder, as though I were a large dog.

"I'm fine. Just a sec." I push myself back onto my knees, try to get a deep breath and make my face smile reassuringly. I've done it a million times, but I'm having trouble today.

"Did he slice your back?" Kaylee circles me. "No, looks like it just got your jacket. Good thing it's thick, but Maura's gonna have to get you a new one when we get home."

Great. Yet another burden on Maura. She fulfills my sister's dreams, and in return I lose her real daughter and mess up my expensive coat. I push myself to my feet, one uncooperative leg at a time.

"Wait!" Kaylee pounces on something. "What's this?"

"What?"

Kaylee dangles a small red mitten.

"It's Oona's." It must have fallen out of my pocket when I was swinging and turning.

"Obviously," Kaylee snaps. "But where'd you get it? Back in our world? Did Maura make it?"

My brain is slow and wooden. I reach out my hand and Kaylee throws the mitten at my head. I ignore her frustration and finger the yarn, looking at it closely for the first time. It used to be neat rows of little knitted V's, but after a couple days in my pocket, it's squeezed and misshapen and all fuzzy where I keep rubbing it. "She dropped it when the Patchwork Man grabbed her," I say. "I made sure she was wearing all her warm clothes in the garden. I zipped her coat up to her chin and pulled her mittens on, but then she was playing"—and I wasn't paying attention to her—"and it must have gotten loose. Of course Maura made it."

Kaylee snatches the mitten back. "We've just been walking in circles, haven't you noticed?"

"I tried to—"

"Oh, be quiet." Kaylee turns away from me. "We need something to break the cycle, and Maura's things are *special*. This is Maura's, and it's Oona's, and maybe..."

Kaylee spins in a slow circle, the mitten held on both hands like a platter in front of her. Not satisfied, she holds it like a steering wheel and makes a slow loop around the field.

I watch her. She's right, I'm not getting us anywhere and we need to think of something new.

She works a thread loose from the edge of the mitten and holds it up. It spins slowly, and just when it seems like it's just any mitten hanging by any string, it stops. Absolutely frozen in the air, pointing the way.

Kaylee glances at me, triumphant.

"Good job," I say. "Let's go."

I let her choose, like always, and she follows the thumb. Seems reasonable. I pick up our bundle of food and blanket that we borrowed from Nisha's cottage, and head off after Kaylee and the mitten.

***

We pass a craggy hill we have never seen before. Take a bridge over a river larger than the ones we passed yesterday. Every little while, Kaylee holds up the mitten and we wait for it to stop spinning. Every little while, I have to chop up a band of tin soldiers. We stop to rest our legs, eat flatbread and cheese, and wash down the sourness with a canteen of lukewarm English Breakfast tea.

Nalgene has collapsible canteens. Totally normal. Not thinking at all about what these ones are made of, nope.

Kaylee does her part, and carries our bundle half the time, and divides the bread and tea evenly. She warns me when she sees tin armies and whether I've gotten them all, and checks me for injuries, every single time.

But sometimes when I catch a glimpse of her, her lip is out and her brow is furrowed. She doesn't chatter. And Kaylee isn't a talker, not really, not one of those girls who talks to everyone. But when she's comfortable, she's always thinking out loud, she's always finding something funny, she always has questions.

A little after lunch, the mitten thumb points towards an area where the trees seem dark, and as we get a little closer we can tell it's because there are buildings inside, with a pokey roof or a turret thing way back in the trees.

Gosh, my legs are so heavy, and my shoulders feel like someone was chopping wood on my back. I hope we don't meet many more tin can men, because one of these times I'm not going to be able to lift the hurley.

Oh no! When we get to that castle, that's where the Knight of the Terrible Valley lives. I'm going to have to fight him, and I'm going to have to win. Crap.

I try rolling my shoulders as we walk, tilting my neck to the side to stretch it. What else can I do? I see worse and worse visions in my head, of what the Green Knight might be like, how badly he's going to beat me up. I see Kaylee and Oona watching from the side, their eyes wide with horror—aaghh! No! When I fight the Terrible Knight, I'll make them go somewhere else. I'll lock them up if I have to! It would be really bad trauma to watch their brother get killed right in front of them.

Kaylee stops and I almost bump into her. She doesn't meet my eyes.

"Look." She points. "Like the story. It's the beautiful maiden, with lips as red as blood, skin as white as snow, and hair as black as ebony."

I shake my head and notice where we are. We're in a little stream valley, there are a ridiculous number of butterflies, and it smells like flowers. And there, in a pure white dress on a pure white blanket, dipping her toes in the water...there's Oona. I guess she does look a little like the fairy tales, now that I think about it, although I usually think about how mischievous her smile is, and her sticky little hand in mine, and whatever story she's telling me.

I am hit by a wave of love that's stronger than all the tin can men together. I hold a tree so it doesn't knock me off my feet; looking at the butterflies and the sparkling stream and the beautiful girl—my beautiful sisters, blonde and dark, both perfect.

This is the fairy tale, I think, like the words in my mind are coming from a long way away. This is the part where the hero falls in love with the maiden. It's something the fairy tale is doing to me.

But no fairy tale can falsify the blood pounding in my body. I do love these girls. This is what love is...both the tender new sweetness I have with Oona and my long tangled history with Kaylee. No mythical valley can make my love any bigger, because it already fills all of me. I've had some crummy times in my life, but I'm lucky to have them. This is enough.

"Oona!" Kaylee calls out, and goes running down the path.

Oona looks up, joy all over her little face. She opens up her arms, and Kaylee leaps over the stream and scoops her up and spins her around and around, and they are both laughing.

I follow, more slowly. I check our surroundings. No tin can men, but I do notice a woman sitting up by the trees. She has a picnic and stuff beside her, and the way she's watching Oona I know she's there to take care of her. Clearly, Oona is just fine, not hurt or in a dungeon or anything. We're all fine. We'll get out. They're safe.

Oona's face lights up and she runs over to me. I crouch down and she throws her skinny little arms around my neck, and for a little while, I just let everything else fall away and enjoy her. The smell of her hair, her short breaths, her little fingers squeezing my shoulders, and most of all, best of all, the familiar sweet weight of her. This is exactly Oona. This is exactly how she feels in my arms.

Then Kaylee is chit-chattering, and Oona turns to her, and I pat Oona's back and push onto my feet. Kaylee goes through everything we've seen in the Terrible Valley, and although her story is all out of order Oona doesn't seem to mind at all, and asks questions nearly as fast as Kaylee answers different ones.

"Thank you for coming to get me," Oona says, smiling shyly. "It's nice here, but I missed you."

She's still looking at Kaylee, I guess because they've been talking, but I feel a pang like she's leaving me out on purpose. Maybe she is. I'm the one who lost her, after all.

Oona looks over at me. "And thank you, too, Aiden."

She's so polite it's almost worse.

Kaylee looks at her feet and pushes out her lower lip, and doesn't say anything to me.

"It was Kaylee who did everything, not me," I say. "Kaylee who made the basket. Kaylee who figured out the magic to get to you. I'm just like...a big dumb puppy dog who follows along." When Oona smiles, I put out my tongue and goggle my eyes and pant like a puppy dog, and she laughs all the way. I goggle harder and make her laugh more, and I should feel good. But I don't. Maybe I don't deserve to.

"Come on," says Oona. "We've got to go back to my room. I'll show you."

She takes Kaylee's hand, and I don't feel good at all.

The nurse gathers up her things and follows my sisters, and she's half-turned away but for a moment I think I recognize her. I can't think about that right now. I go back for our sorry little bundle and trudge after, my sisters' bright chatter drifting back to me.

What is wrong with me? I dreamed over and over how good it would feel to be together with Oona again. I imagined that when I rescued her, then she would see how much I love her. I'd be special to her. Maybe I messed up, but I've been working super hard these last few days and that's what kept me going, imagining the look on her face. Imagining the way she'd look at me.

And instead, I gave it away. I ruined all that specialness by being silly. Kaylee did important stuff, but I know I did too. But for some reason, I told Oona I didn't.

I don't understand anything, even my own self, but I feel like scum.

***

Oona's nurse announces that we have to stay in the castle tonight. I know her, but I'm pretending I don't. She's a Black woman, taller than me, gray hair in tiny braids like a crown, and she gives me a lecture when the girls stop to look at the flower garden. It's too late to take a little girl out into Terrible Valley, and I'm too sore. The Green Knight has gone hunting for several days, so there's no reason to rush. Every night there's a feast on his magical table, so we might as well eat it, and she's going to give me herbs and treat my injuries. This is the nicest place in Terrible Valley, she tells me, and since we're Oona's guests then no one will bother us.

"Who is Oona?" I ask warily. "To them, I mean."

Nurse raises one eyebrow at me. "The Knight has declared his everlasting love for her, and announced that he will marry her when she turns sixteen. I don't think you need to be in any rush, young man. She's got a little while still to go."

"But we need to get home. Her mother will worry." I turn and follow my sisters, who are holding hands as they walk up the pathway, leaving me behind.

"Time doesn't pass the same in your home. Don't you know that by now?"

"You mean we could get back and seven years have gone by? Or everyone's old men, or dead?" I've heard fairy tales like that.

"You always think the worst, don't you." Nurse raises both eyebrows at me. "It might be a few minutes, or a few hours. That's all. The castle knows how to put you in the same place that you left."

Besides, as soon as I saw her face, I knew who this is and why she's fussing about my cuts. Of course. Nurse Raymond was the substitute nurse at our elementary school, and when we were little Mom hired her to take care of us sometimes, and she was really nice and I thought she actually liked Kaylee and me.

Until that day when I was almost fourteen, and she betrayed us.

Chapter 8

I have soaked in a bath filled with green stuff, submitted to Nurse rubbing me with oily green stuff—but only the parts I couldn't reach myself—and drank at least a gallon of yet more green stuff. We went to this big fancy room for dinner, with a long table filled with empty platters and bowls, until the sun set and they all magically filled themselves.

I wasn't impressed.

Oona's room is larger than both the cottages we've stayed in put together. It has white beds and pretty dresses, and an eclectic assortment of toys. The hoop and balls look right, but I'm pretty sure rocking horses weren't invented in the third century, and I'm quite sure the rainbow top and ceramic-headed dolls were later. Whatever; as long as it makes Oona happy.

Nurse Raymond is sewing, and I am lying next to her on this couch-without-a-back thing with poultices on my chest, watching my sisters. They're playing with jewelry and ignoring me. I'm not sure if it's because Kaylee is mad at me, or Oona is mad at me, or just I smell bad from all that green stuff.

I could ask Nurse what we're supposed to do next, or ask if Oona stayed up every night crying.

But I don't. Nurse Raymond might be smart with herbs, but I don't trust her with my thoughts, and not with my family.

"We leave in the morning," I tell her. I sound curt. Manly.

"Do you know how to get home?"

"I can manage."

"With the Sword of Daylight and your own true heart, you can defeat the Knight of Terrible Valley. Don't you want to know how?"

"We're just going to leave. My sisters and I. Together."

"There are rules of this place, Aiden Robinson. You can't just leave."

I turn away. Kaylee is combing Oona's hair and they are both giggling.

"I told you. I can manage." My throat clenches.

Nurse Raymond sighs. "You don't have to manage everything alone, Aiden Robinson."

Oh *right*. Fat lot she knows.

Or maybe she doesn't. I wonder if this world is populated by my memory, or if the people are truly the same. If we are traveling back and forth together.

"You never did," she adds quietly.

"Never?" I swing around, on my feet as quickly as if a tin can army were marching in the door. So she does remember my world!

Nurse Raymond shakes her head sadly. "Not in Florida, not here. You could—"

"No!" My hand is raised, one finger pointing at her like the ghost of my hurley. "No. You don't understand. You don't understand anything!"

"Aiden, I had to—"

"And stay away from my sister!"

Both Kaylee and Oona turn to stare at us.

"Both of them! Don't touch them!"

Oona starts to cry, every sob like shards of glass rubbing against my soul. But with someone like Nurse Raymond, it's better to have it over with now.

"Aiden, I only—"

"And don't you fill Oona's head with lies, like you did with Kaylee! Go, I tell you, go!"

Kaylee has that particular blank smile that she has when things get scary. Oona tries to cuddle into her lap but Kaylee ignores her, frozen.

Nurse Raymond watches me a moment longer, then shakes her head, gathers her sewing, and shuffles out of the room.

"She was nice!" Oona wails.

"Not really," I say, and she cries harder.

It's better to stop dreaming rather than watch your dreams destroyed.

***

In the morning, the three of us are bundled up with plenty of food for the journey. The servants washed our regular clothes, but my jacket and Kaylee's shoes are done for, so now we have ancient versions. The fur cloak is heavier than I expect, but warmer than my North Face. Maybe I'll just wear this to school and let Maura keep the child support payments for something she needs. Unlike my biological parents, Maura wasn't ever rich.

The sunshine and butterflies are gone, replaced by wind and spitting rain. Either because Irish summers switch around like that, or because this place is some eerie reflection of not only my memories, but my mood.

No wonder it's a Terrible Valley.

Nurse Raymond is just one more face among a dozen servants who stand at the front gate of the castle and wave goodbye. All of them women, and all of them asked me, or warned me, to stay and fight the Green Knight. They have no loyalty, apparently.

I mark where the sun is, note which way each stream runs, and point this out to both girls. Kaylee nods solemnly, and I see her making her own calculations when we reach turning points. No circles this time. I carry the bigger pack over one shoulder and the hurley in my other hand, although my palms are sore where I've been gripping it, so I keep fiddling to hold it some different way. Oona starts out skipping along, running ahead and darting back. I don't want her to get worn out, so I offer to tell her a story if she'll hold my hand, juggling everything unevenly to the other side. That keeps her walking more steadily for a while.

When I finish a really detailed version of *The Wizard of Oz*, Oona is sagging and I decide we can stop for lunch. Or—I check my phone, which weirdly still has power—elevensies. Early elevensies.

"Are we almost there?" Oona asks.

"Half-way," I reply with a confidence that I do not feel.

Kaylee spreads the blanket from her bundle, and it's a relief to lean back against a tree and stretch out my legs. I take off my tennis shoes to rub my feet and—

What's that, through the trees? I dip my head to find a clear spot and—no.

Kaylee caught my gesture and is already going around the corner, peering in the same direction. "It *is*," she says. "Oh my *god* it is, and we've been going for *hours*."

It's a turret. Next to another familiar turret. It's that stupid castle, no farther than a few hundred yards away.

"What did the Cowardly Lion do next?" Oona mumbles, cheerfully cramming a mouthful of egg.

When we finish our snack, Kaylee holds up the mitten, but when it stops spinning, the thumb just points to Oona. We try again, and the same thing. Right at Oona.

"Now go back to Maura, you stupid mitten," Kaylee mutters. "Wait—I've got an idea. I'll say a poem like Maura did that time. You go ahead."

She's scowling at the mitten now, not me. Our mutual fear about being stuck in this valley forever is washing away the resentment between us.

I try to keep Miss Draggy Feet going with Narnia, but Oona keeps correcting what is supposed to happen next. Normally we call this co-telling a story and I think it's cute. But right now I'm too anxious to keep track of one story, let alone try to organize something in my own head along with Oona's avalanche of slightly nonsensical suggestions. I am positive we don't have the pool of gold in the same story with everlasting winter, but Oona gets screechier and whinier, so I try to stick them both together, and then I can't make any sense of my own story.

Kaylee hurries up from behind us. "Let's stop for another snack!" She's slightly breathless.

Oona flops onto the blanket like a boneless puddle of five-year-old.

"Well, the good news"—Kaylee turns to me with an over-bright smile that means there is no good news—"it's not going to be a long walk if we have to go back to the Terrible Castle."

"I have princess rooms," Oona mumbles, face in the blanket. "With lots of toys. And a nice nurse who does puppet shows."

Kaylee sighs, watching to see what I'll do next. We're back to normal.

"Your real room at home would be even nicer," I tell Oona.

All day, I've been waiting for Kaylee to say the same thing she did about Nisha. I'm waiting for Kaylee to remind me about all the nice things Nurse Raymond did, that she cooked us shrimp gumbo, and wiped Kaylee's fevered face, and sang us songs while she drove us to appointments.

"If you want puppet shows, I'll do that for you," Kaylee says, her voice steel. "We don't need to go back to Nurse."

So apparently, this time she remembers the same thing that I do.

When we start up again, Kaylee takes both our packs so I can carry Oona on my back and pretend to be a horsie. I am the world's most floppy, ploddy, miserable horsie. Oona screeches with laughter and hits me to make me go faster, which *is. Not. Funny.*

"Tin can men!" Kaylee squeals.

I drop Oona too fast, trying to get the proper grip on the hurley. Kaylee grabs Oona and pulls her away, which makes Oona cry, but I'm too busy to care. Whap, slam, clankity clank! My shoulders scream in pain, refusing to make the same difficult moves for the third day in a row. Too bad! I've got to get those buggers! Swing! Rebalance, swing again.

It's only a dozen or so men. I can do it! I swing and swing, blinded by sweat or tears. By the time they're all on the ground, I hurt so badly I can't tell if any of them got me.

Kaylee checks me, while I wipe my face.

"You're fine. No marks." But for the first time, Kaylee brushes my cheek and tucks my hair behind my ear. "Do we keep going?"

I look ahead. "One more time. Let's just keep checking and keep the turrets behind us." I don't want to deal with the Knight, but I really don't want to go back to Nurse Raymond. She feels more real.

I do some stretches, and then just sink onto the ground for a minute, while Kaylee gives Oona a snack and a pep talk. We set off again. We let Oona pick a number between ten and forty, and count it off with her, then turn around, find the turrets, and adjust so they're behind us.

"Tin men!" Oona claps. "Goooo, Aiden!"

It's only six of them. I can do this. I adjust the hurley, but my balance is off for the first swing and I barely ding the first guy. I have to pause to adjust my grip, and something gets me from the side.

"Turn! Down lo—" Kaylee cuts herself off as I hack at it.

It's just as well; I can barely focus and her voice pulls at my attention. My shoulder spasms as I try to swing and I switch tactics, just beating and chopping every which way. But just cutting off an empty-tin-can-arm doesn't stop anything but that arm, and I've got to keep whacking the same dude until he falls apart. Something sharp comes at my face and I push it away, whack in that direction. It's only four of them. Only three. Almost done.

They've fallen.

The meadow is quiet.

Actually, I can hear my breath, ragged and harsh. I drop my hurley and it clatters on the tin at my feet, and I wipe both palms over my face. My hair is drenched with sweat as I push it off my forehead.

Her leather shoes are silent, but I can feel Kaylee coming up behind me. She turns me towards her, away from the fallen tin can bodies. She dabs a wet rag on my face—I didn't think he got me—and then turns my left hand palm up.

Oh. When I pushed the sword away it must have sliced my hand. Just a little.

I mean, hands bleed a lot. It doesn't mean much.

Kaylee ties up my palm, and places her hand on my cheek. I put a little effort in, and focus on her eyes.

"I'm okay." I manage to smile.

"We're going back." Kaylee doesn't smile.

"We could just—"

"We're going back," Kaylee repeats. "Period."

So we do.

***

Back in the princess rooms, I drop onto the couch and don't wake until nightfall. There's Kaylee and Oona, playing on the floor near me. They saved some food from the magical dinner. I take another bath, and this time Kaylee rubs green stuff on the places I can't reach.

I am watching the two of them dressing a doll, ribbon flickering in the candlelight.

Then it's morning.

I still hurt.

***

We have to wait for the Knight of Terrible Valley to come home, the women say. If I defeat him, then I win Oona back. With the Sword of Daylight, I can win the battle.

Although it does look a little funny, the women agree. They've never seen it quite like this before.

Kaylee and I talk to them one by one. We are trying to avoid Nurse Raymond, but the dairy maids and kitchen maids and sweeping maids all tell us that she has the answers. She will tell me how to defeat the Green Knight.

At first, I am braced for another vision like I had in the first two houses, because I don't want to go back to that part in my life, no way no how. I am careful not to glance at myself in shiny surfaces or look at the bottom of my bowl, but after the second day passes, and the third, I relax a little bit. It helps that my sisters aren't mad at me anymore. Maybe I kind of screwed up, but that's the thing about siblings. You see each other when you aren't perfect, and you love each other anyways.

"Why don't you like Nursey?" Oona asks, while Kaylee is fixing her hair to go down to dinner.

Last night, Kaylee told me she prepared an answer. "We used to know her, back when I was your age. She was the nurse at our school, and then our mom—you know, Amber—hired her to take care of us when we were sick. Our mom, Amber, um, explained that she had to go to work and would Nurse stay with us if we had to stay home. So Nurse would come on the days we couldn't go to school, and she took us to the doctor if we had an ear infection or something. Well, it was me, mostly. Aiden was basically never sick."

Kaylee glances over, checking in with me, and I nod. That's an appropriate way to tell it. The thing is, it was egregiously inappropriate of my mom to have ever asked her. We had actual nannies when my parents were married, but when she moved to Florida my mom stopped volunteering and working out and never got us a new one. I assume the first time the school called and told her to pick up a sick Kaylee, my mom arrived at the school office and then looked around with that blank stare she had when reality slapped her hard enough.

And my mom is a Southern belle through and through, debutante ball and Kappa Kappa Gamma and everything. So I bet she looked at Nurse Raymond's round brown face and assumed that she would come stay with her sick child if she just offered enough money. And she probably started too low.

If I were her, I would hate us too.

"So why don't you like her?" Oona insists.

I do like her. I like her a lot. I just don't trust her.

Luckily, Kaylee has prepared a better answer than that. I think it is entirely made up, but it makes sense to a kindergartener.

"Aiden," Kaylee asks as we go down the stairs, "what do you do with a five-year-old? What did you used to play with me?"

I think about it. "You had dolls, and I had a bunch of stuffed dinosaurs. We had them be families, with a mommy and daddy and two kids in each one. We drew pictures of the things they ate for dinner, and sometimes we cut the pictures out."

Kaylee giggles. "Oh, I remember. We were very inclusive. Wasn't it usually a dinosaur daddy and a doll mommy?"

"Always. Apparently all dinosaurs are male. No wonder they died out."

We are both laughing as we get to the dining room. I help Oona fill her plate and climb up into the big red chair at the foot of the table ("because I'm the princess") before I lower my voice to ask why Kaylee needed to know.

She dabs a piece of meat in sauce and considers her answer. "Because outside, we build things and play unicorn-pegasus and stuff. But I'm not sure how to play with Oona inside."

"But you've been doing it!" I'm surprised. "The two of you have been so busy together!"

Kaylee wipes up the sauce with her bread, brow furrowed. She eats a roasted parsnip and pulls apart another piece of bread before she answers. "Yeah. We have. But I realized...I've been playing like Mom always played with me. I loved it when she came into my room and combed my hair and fussed over me. It was nice."

"Yeah. I know." I'm surprised it still hurts. I've known my whole entire life that Mom wanted a girl, and I was just an unfortunate side effect.

"But now that we're in this castle? And everything's fair princess this and beautiful princess that?" Kaylee pushes the bread mess off her plate, chooses a roasted plum, and glares at it. "I actually realized that everything Mom used to do was about making me pretty. She made me feel like wearing makeup and perfume was the biggest treat in the world. And you know what? That's pretty messed up, actually."

I link my pinky with hers, and she squeezes mine hard.

"I think," I say, stumbling over the words, "it wasn't the makeup that was a problem. It was how...that was the only way she..." Loved you, I think. "Said anything nice."

"Yeah, well." Kaylee thumps our hands together on the table, and stands up so fast her chair bangs. "I'm trying to do something different with Oona. That's all."

When we get back upstairs, there are bookshelves under the window, filled with everything from eighteenth century illustrated alphabet books to Mo Willems.

And on the bottom shelf, six stuffed dinosaurs. Good thing they've arrived at a house with plenty of dolls, seeing that all dinosaurs are male. Every one of them.

I smile as I watch my sisters play.

Chapter 9

The Knight of the Terrible Valley is home.

We watched out Oona's window, and he was pretty boring, really. No fanfare, no parade. Ten guys or so trudging home, and they were muddy and carrying all these dead animals. Gross.

And me? I'm great. Ten days of R&R—hot baths, herbal teas, picnics for lunch and feasts every night. Kaylee has some yoga videos downloaded on her phone, so we've all been doing yoga twice a day, and I go practice in the sword yard every afternoon. I've got the Hurley Stick of Daylight and Oona is pure of heart, so I'm going to win the boss battle. The Green Knight won't know what hit him.

Oona bangs the door, racing back into the princess room. "There's no point hiding," she announces. "He's got a brass gargoyle that tells him everything that happen—"

"Watch out!" Kaylee takes a running dive and knocks Oona onto the backless couch, right as the first tin can man marches in. The girls aren't very protected, but it doesn't matter because an entire wave comes straight at me like I'm a giant tin can magnet.

Oona cheers.

Ha! Let them come, I'm ready!

I swing my hurley and wade into the morass of little tin men. There's more of them but they're flatter, almost like these ones were packed up in the basement. My hurley is like a hot knife through butter, and my shoulders swing free and strong. Swoosh! Pow! Clang!

It takes a long time, lots of swinging, lots of focus. When they're finally done, my shirt is drenched with sweat. (Actually, it's called a léine; I can't just wear my regular clothes over and over.) All those workouts paid off, and I'm feeling okay. I check the hallways—empty, safe—and flex my hands.

Oona pops up over the pillows. "That was a lot of tin guys!"

"Three hundred," Kaylee adds. "They came in by twenties, and I was counting."

"Wow!" Oona laughs. "You're really good, Aiden!"

But what if I get worn out? Nope, not gonna worry about that. I laugh and scoop up Oona in my arms. She tries to tickle me, which is so not-even-kind-of-ticklish that it makes me laugh more, and I blow a raspberry in the general vicinity of her belly. She squeals and I drop her on the bed and collapse next to her, and Kaylee climbs over and tickles us both.

"You stink!" Oona giggles against my chest.

"He smells of *vic*-toryyyy!" Kaylee retorts. They both dissolve in giggles and I tussle their hair, dark on one side and golden on the other.

This is my magic power, I think. Right here. This joy.

***

We have swept up all the body parts and are playing a game of dominoes when Nurse Raymond enters, carrying a pitcher, white cloths over her arm.

"Are you well, Aiden Robinson?" She pours a mug of something steaming.

"I'm fine." I almost stretch and show off my biceps, but that feels a little silly so I don't. I'm not that kind of guy.

"You don't need these, then?" She sets down the bandages, placing two jars from her pocket on top. "They're here just in case, Miss Kaylee."

"I'm fine." I'm embarrassed that she calls my sister that.

"Are there gonna be more soldiers?" Oona asks.

Nurse Raymond turns to me. Her expression is grim and closed, like it has been since I told her to leave us alone. She has been doing her jobs around the princess room, and Kaylee and I have been polite to her, but that's it.

"The rule of three," she tells me.

I turn my face away, burning with guilt though I don't even know why. "Thanks." I sound gruff. "I know about that stuff. I do"—I take a risk and just say it—"I do have a folklorist for a mother. Now."

I'm hot all over and sure Nurse Raymond can see my blush. My sisters are watching me, quiet. I'm not sure I've ever claimed Maura like this before, but I want Nurse to know.

I want her to know that what she saw wasn't the end of our story.

***

I start to feel it in the middle of the second three hundred. Each swing jolts through my shoulder bones; the hurley grates the new callouses on my palms. My adrenaline fades, or at least settles to a dull march. But all that practice kicks in, the new muscle memory I have built, and my arms protest but settle into the routine of swing and backswing, block and swing.

"Here's three hundred," Kaylee says when the last set enters.

I grit my teeth and swing again. Each blow hurts; I lift the hurley and it feels like a hundred pounds. It's hard to keep breathing. This might be the last set, but twenty tin men is still a lot when they're all pointing sharp things at me. Twenty is more than any of the groups I fought the first few days.

It's less than twenty now. I breathe deep and swing hard. Sweat is stinging my eyes, but now there's a lot less. One more less. Ow! One more.

"Done," Kaylee says.

I drop to my knees and let my head sink, panting. I don't even double check that they're gone.

"Oh, Aidey," she says. "I wish I could help."

She hands me a glass and I make myself drink, but not too fast. We tried it one afternoon, just a little ways from the castle where they travel in small groups. Kaylee took my hurley and I stood right next to her. It hit the first tin shoulder with a thunk, barely leaving a dent. Kaylee screamed but as soon as my hands touched the handle, it went back to doing its job. Through them like butter.

She wipes my face with a cool cloth.

"You *are* helping," I mumble, but then I realize it's true. Something in our relationship has changed.

I have a few cuts and bruises this time, and we all know another set is coming sooner or later. Oona feeds me bread and cheese and willow bark tea, and Kaylee puts on a restorative yoga video. I do it in front of the fire, super slow, so my muscles don't seize up.

Then I lean back against the pillows and snuggle Oona. I close my eyes and rest my cheek against her hair, and she pats my arm.

"I have an idea," she says. "But I'm still thinking."

"Okay," I mumble. "I can't wait to hear it."

Maybe I doze, just a little bit.

"It's getting dusk," Kaylee warns.

There's clanking in the hall and I set Oona down gently.

This time it's just grim. So many of them. So tired. So many.

Keep swinging.

Keep going.

"Down lower," Kaylee calls. "They're getting smaller."

I push sweat out of my eyes and realize she's right, that's why I've been missing more often and swinging more frantically. They're thigh level, and then knee level, and they're less dangerous but it sure hurts my back to bend over like that. It takes two or three blows, sometimes, because my hands don't know where to find them and I can't focus my eyes.

"Three more sets! You're almost there!"

Sixty men, oh god. I pull in deep breaths and wipe my hands on my shirt. "Keep talking, it helps."

The next twenty march through the door. I adjust my grip, palms stinging.

"Alligators, alligators, go-go-go!" Kaylee starts, and then she goes through the whole cheer routine, clapping and all. Oona yells "go alligators!" whenever there's a pause, and the whole thing is so ridiculous that it does actually help. I match my swings to their rhythm, and since they don't stop I keep going too.

But then twenty more come in.

My left arms seizes up and I gasp, pulling it against my chest and staggering back.

"Go Aidennnnn!" Oona screams. "You can dooooo it!"

So I can. I swing one-handed until my elbow unfreezes. My heart is going to pound out of my chest, I might die, but I'm going down swinging that damn hurley. Another. Just swing. I grip with both hands and whack blindly.

"Done!" Kaylee yells. "Three hundred! You made it! Come here, come here!"

She guides me onto the bed as pain hits me so bad I can't even tell what's hurting. Oh god. Oh god.

"Oh, you're bleeding all over your legs!" Oona cries.

I retch. Nothing comes up but my stomach won't stop spasming, over and over. Dry and bile and I'm sobbing, too. Finally it stops. I lay still, breathing as shallow as I can.

It hurts. It *hurts*.

Kaylee says something, but my pulse is pounding so hard I can't make out her words.

I feel her hand on my hair. Then Oona's little one on my shoulder.

I'm not dead.

I guess.

Chapter 10

R ule of threes be damned. I still sleep with my bed in front of the door and my hurley stick under my fingers. Every time I wake, muscles cramping or nightmares swirling, I check to make sure it's not tangled in the blankets. I make myself walk to the window, check on my sisters, take a drink of cold herbal tea, and then I allow myself back in bed. The first couple times, I could barely drag my leg across the floor and I threw up again, but it gets better as the night goes on.

This is not fun. But I have to make my body work, or my sisters can't get home.

I hear them getting up and dressed, and Kaylee puts a hot poultice on my back. That feels so good that I guess I have one more sleep despite the sun pouring in the windows.

There's—something!

My hand clenches on the hurley! My eyes spring open!

Oona is standing approximately eight inches from my nose, completely still.

I roll onto my back, shake my head, and take a slow breath which is supposed to help with the racing heart thing. "Good afternoona, Oona-the-Loona." I catch a sidelong glance—yup, that worried face is melting into a smile. "Oona wearing pantaloonas, with a silver teaspoona."

Her nose scrunches up as she dissolves in giggles. "It's not afternoon, we just had breakfast. Do one more."

"Oona-the-Baboon-a, playing the bassoon-a under the big blue moon-a."

More giggles, and my arms work well enough to pull her in for a wiggly hug.

"Let Aiden up," Kaylee says.

Oona giggles and rolls on top of me more. I groan (but happily) and ruffle her hair.

Kaylee sighs, and then tries a deliberately encouraging tone. "Oona, remember we brought Aiden some treats from breakfast? Why don't you—"

"I hid them *in my pockets!*" Oona rockets off my bed.

I slept in my clothes, just in case. But I really need to use the outhouse-in-the-wall thing, and it feels good to wash up. By then, Oona has set up breakfast in the shape of a smiley face, and is presiding over it in her white léine like a mini Greek goddess.

"I have my plan ready," she announces. "I'm gonna tell you—"

"Let him eat first," Kaylee interrupts, and I know I'm not going to like whatever they've dreamed up. But she finds another box of sugar cubes and English Breakfast (seriously, what the hell is up with this place?) and I definitely feel better when I'm drinking something other than green sludge.

"I got the Green Knight to talk," Oona announces. "He likes me."

I don't like that Oona is learning how to charm bullies.

"He likes Kaylee, too," Oona adds. "She's pretty."

Kaylee casts me a worried glance; she knows how I feel about that. "The Green Knight thinks you're dead," she says quickly. "He can't figure out why his minions aren't coming back to him, but says they're probably having fun up here or something."

"You're talking!" Oona waves her hands. "It's my idea!"

"Okay, okay! You talk!"

"It's fine. I can listen to you both." I take another sip of tea. Delicious. "Kay-bear, is there more of this?"

"He has more names for me than he does for you!" Oona crows.

"What's your idea, Racoona?"

As soon as I say it, she looks so self-satisfied that I suspect I have walked into a trap.

"Well...this is a fairy tale, right? I know lots of fairy tales. And I've decided, you need to ask Nurse Raymond for her advice."

I try not to react, but Oona shakes her head and lets out a Kaylee-worthy sigh. "I knew you were gonna be like that! You don't like her. But listen. This is always the way fairy tales are. There's someone with advice, and if the hero follows it, then he wins. If he doesn't listen, then he gets lost somewhere. Aiden!" Oona puts her hand on mine. "I don't want you stuck on an island somewhere, with lots of plums but you can't get back to us."

I remember that one too. "We're in a valley, not an ocean, Oona-Typhoona."

"I just don't want to lose you!"

Oona's eyes fill with tears, and suddenly, I get it. I've spent all this time worrying about losing her, and it didn't occur to me that...

Actually, that's scary to even think to myself. Scary that Oona thinks I am...

I shake my head. I can't.

"Okay, baby, you're right. The—guy"—I can't call myself a hero—"has to follow the directions to win, so I'll ask Nurse Raymond. Don't worry, Oona, we met another old lady and I did everything—"

"Nisha!" Kaylee cries. "She said you could call on her. And you haven't."

"The rule of three!" Oona claps. "Three advice ladies!"

I hold up my hands in surrender, but it's worse than they thought.

The hero is supposed to take advice, but also, he's supposed to change. He's supposed to get over his worst flaw.

Whatever mine is, I don't know if I can do that.

***

Nurse Raymond enters the princess room with her head held high, braids shimmering in the morning sunlight.

"I have forgiven you, Aiden Robinson," she says. "When I was a child, I thought as a child, I understood as a child. I am now a woman grown, who need not resent a child for thinking such."

I'm not a child. This confuses me so much that I almost forget to wonder what she is forgiving me for.

"You wanted my advice?" She scoops up the skirts of her léine and sits across from me.

"Yes, please, ma'am." This I can manage.

She raises an eyebrow. "Awfully polite all of a sudden, aren't we?"

This is stupid. "It's for Oona and Kaylee. You'd be surprised what I can do for them—or my brothers, too, if they were here. Any of them."

Nurse sighs. "I wouldn't, actually, Aiden. But let's get started."

"Yes, please."

She points out the window. "There is a pole in the forecourt yonder. At noon, the Green Knight will call his men to him, and when they do not come he will know you have defeated them and that you live yet. He will strike the pole of combat to call you to battle. If he strikes first, he will win the battle. If you strike first, you will win—if you do what I tell you. Understand?"

"Yes, ma'am."

"And girls—I know you're listening. Your encouragement is his power, do you understand? The princess is the apex of the story, not the afterthought. Your praise and love does not just help the victor, it determines the victor. Do you understand?"

"Yes, ma'am," Kaylee answers immediately.

"What do I do? I'm the princess!" Oona chirps, and they mutter together.

Nurse Raymond turns back to me. "When yourself and himself are going out to fight, cut a sod a perch long; you'll leave the sod on the next hillock you meet."

"What's a perch long?"

"A perch is a fish. About yay big." She holds out her hands.

Oh, like I did under the deer's foot. I nod my understanding.

"The Green Knight has so much enchantment on him that if he sees the battle going against him, he'll rise like a fog in the air, come down in the same form, strike you, and make a green stone out of you. When the Knight is coming down and is ready to strike, give him a blow with the sod. You'll make a green stone of him, instead."

"Okay. Okay. But for the rest of the battle, my hurley stick will work?"

Nurse Raymond pinches her lips. "Your extremely inelegant and peurile Sword of Daylight, yes. It should work."

"Okay."

"Once he is a stone, you are unable to cut out his heart to prove your victory—"

I shudder.

"—but the essence of his heart will be contained in a ring. Place this ring on the finger of the princess—"

"That's me!"

Even Nurse Raymond smiles at Oona's enthusiasm. "It is, my chick. Aiden, once the ring is on her finger, no one but yourself can remove it. The princess and the heart. It is the proof of the quest that you must bring home."

To the Council, I remember. "How do I get home?"

Nurse shrugs. "You should have met a guide; call her, and she will lead you back to the basket where you entered the Terrible Valley."

"Nisha. Yeah, okay." I wipe my hands down my thighs, thinking hard. "Could I have called her any time?" Was it that easy?

Nurse nods. "At any time, your guide could have taken you anywhere you wished to go within the Terrible Valley. However, you cannot remove Oona from the park around the castle until you defeat the Green Knight. I suspect that is what you were really asking."

"Yeah. Okay. I understand." Good thing Kaylee made us go back before we got any more worn out. "Is there anything else I need to know?"

Nurse Raymond watches me for a long moment.

"Aiden Robinson..." She shakes her head. "You are almost to the end of your adventure in the Terrible Valley. I have no doubt that you will hold your sword correctly and cut the sod correctly. But I have known you for many years, and just listen..."

I don't want to listen to the Nurse Raymond from regular life. I was lulled along by her rhythmic speech, but now her Southern vowels slap me into attention. I stare at my lap, feeling my jaw go tight even though I don't want it to.

Nurse puts her hands on her knees and leans forward. "All these years, you have been thinking about yourself and Kaylee. This is what I mean, you think like a child. You have put her at the center of the universe and forget everyone else. That is the way a child thinks."

Of course I put Kaylee at the center of the universe. No one else did.

"You push everyone else away, as if by ignoring them we cannot see the two of you, either. You *matter* to people, Aiden Robinson."

We were alone in every way it mattered. From the moment my parents divorced until we flew to Ireland in economy class with Maura and her kids, Kaylee and I were alone.

Nurse Raymond leans forward farther. "We saw that serious little boy with the gaunt face, and the way his sister hid behind him. We saw that your hair was too long and shaggy, but Kaylee's was always neatly combed. We saw that you wore hundred-dollar shoes and fell asleep in the library."

"I figured out how to cut my hair! It wasn't so ugly!" And now I can't stop. "I learned how to braid Kaylee's hair from YouTube videos. The first ones were kind of wonky, but then I learned to do French braids and stuff. She looked fine!"

Nurse Raymond shakes her head sadly. "You were the best hair-braider at Larkin Elementary, except for the Black girls. But don't you understand? People noticed you. You were special, both because of who you each are, and because every child is special."

"Yeah. Okay." But it's not. The heat and anger blaze through me, and I'm tired of it. I jump to my feet, almost welcoming the distracting burn in my thighs. "Thanks for the advice. Really appreciate it."

Nurse Raymond stands too. We're too close together, but I don't back away.

She reaches for my arm, but does not touch me. "Aiden. I was not the only one who called CPS."

"I know!" I spin away and march to the far wall. "Of course I know!"

But the others were when we were younger. When my mother didn't have so much to hide.

Kaylee pops up again. "You almost *killed* him! And if you had, you almost killed *me!*"

"I wasn't dead—"

"Oh, Kaylee, I never wanted—"

"Thank you!" Oona shrieks. "Thank you thank you THANK! YOU!"

I know she's thinking about the fairy tale curse, and it almost makes me smile.

Oona grabs Nurse Raymond's hand and hauls her towards the door. "Thank you! We will obey your every word! Won't we Aiden! Thank you so much! I'm the princess, and I say no fighting now! Thank you! Goodbye!"

She is literally pushing Nurse Raymond out the door, but the woman pauses as though Oona were no bigger than a fly—which she practically isn't.

"Aiden, I am sorry." Nurse meets my eyes from across the whole big room. "You're white. I thought they wouldn't hurt you."

And she's gone.

Oona slams the door. "Right! Now let's be really good!"

"Right," I say. Something inside me turns off. I stop feeling and keep going. "I'll be good."

***

And I am.

At 11:55, I hit the pole.

Then the Green Knight makes a big fuss with his men, and I go and cut a piece of sod yay long.

Then we fight, and it's really scary and it's really hard. He's not made of tin, he's bigger than I am, with a real sword. Every time I swing, I'm sure that my dinky hurley stick is just going to break against his armor. Every time I block, I'm sure that he's going to cut right through me. But the hurley pulls my hand as it swings through the moves, and maybe I pee myself a little, but I just keep going.

My sisters take their cheering seriously. Kaylee found a supply of sliotars, and whenever the Green Knight backs me to the edge of the meadow she throws one at him. Meanwhile, Oona cheers at the top of her lungs and waves that little red mitten like there's no tomorrow.

We keep going and going, but all the fairy tale battles do that. Our feet churn the grass into mud. He knocks me into the mud, but Kaylee hits him with a sliotar and I jump back up. I knock him into the mud, but I can't keep him down.

It goes on and on.

The rage burns deep inside me, like magma. It's not even about the stupid Green Knight, but he's in front of me, and he's trapped Oona, so I whack at him some more.

And then one of my swings just flies through the air, overbalancing me because there is nothing to hit. I blink, looking for him, realizing it is dusk.

"The perch! The sod! The dirt! Get him, get him!" my sisters scream, and I remember.

I scrabble for the hillock, my fingers find the muddy length.

The fog comes down.

I swing the sod.

And a green stone drops at my feet. It's about as big as a football, but lumpy.

Something sparkles in the mud. I lean over, pressing my left hand against my stomach as though I can hold myself together. I'm wet already, so I just kneel in the dirt and scrabble around until my fingers find something smooth and round.

It's a ring. So that's his heart, and Oona's the princess, and now they go together and this is the end.

Chapter 11

We leave in the morning.

After we cross the first bridge, Kaylee builds a little fire. I toss in the battered leaves, which Kaylee remembered to stick in her coat pocket when we left Nisha's cottage.

"Nisha, Nisha, Nisha," I say, which is the magic part. Then I look down at Oona's cheerful, hopeful, face, and I keep going. "We appreciate everything you did for us. Both in the Terrible Valley and back home. You're...really nice."

We all wait. Fat raindrops sizzle when they hit the fire. My sisters pull up their hoods, but I don't bother. I don't wipe the rain off my cheeks.

"Here she is!" Kaylee calls, and Oona runs down the path to throw her arms around Nisha.

I smile. I'm polite. I thank her at every opportunity.

But my stomach is roiling, hot and burning and sick.

Because I've had a chance to think, and now I know what Nurse Raymond means. I thought I smoothed everything over, but I didn't. I was focused on Kaylee, but I didn't fool anyone.

All the teachers, the other moms, they saw us. They thought Kaylee was less than their daughters. They made fun of my mother over their home-cooked meals. They saw that my haircut wasn't even and there were circles under my eyes. They pitied us.

I didn't do anything right at all. I made us a laughingstock.

I should have told Maura the truth in that carpeted bathroom in Hawaii, but I didn't.

I should have called my dad and explained everything.

I should have told the CPS officers everything. The first time they came, when it was this nice lady, and Kaylee and I were both young and innocent looking. They made my mom take a class and they followed up for six months, and every month I lied to them.

I slog along behind the others. My legs hurt with the little cuts, and I hold my arms close to my chest because when they swing free it feels like they're going to pop out of my shoulder joints. Nisha is telling stories to Oona, who is still bright and giggling. Good, keep her going. I'm glad I could take the blows for her.

The rain gets harder, and it rolls off my wool poncho thingy but dribbles down under my collar. We pause under a tree, and Kaylee hands out snacks and I double check Oona's cloak. She's wiggling too much and the front gapes open, so I take off my clasp and put it on her cloak over her belly, so she has two now. I can just hold mine closed.

Nisha holds out her hand. She has an extra clasp.

Yeah, because nothing I do is ever good enough. Because I should have asked for help. Because everyone else could have do better for my little sister better than I could. I don't want to take her stupid clasp.

"Thanks," I say, and pin it through my cloak like I'm supposed to. My right hand is swollen.

We keep walking. They're singing Girl Scout songs now.

We saw you, we saw you, we saw you. The words play over in my head.

We saw you weren't good enough. That's why Nisha offered to drive us home, because she saw a *little boy* who lied about his mother and couldn't keep his sister out of puddles.

Oh god. The summer lunch in the park ladies saw our shoes and Kaylee's dress, and they gave us lunchboxes anyways. I thought we fooled them, but we never fooled them, did we? I am sick with shame. They knew we had enough money for designer clothes and were just taking tuna fish right out of some other kid's mouth. Some poor kid whose parents loved him and were trying their best. Because my best wasn't good enough. Because I was just a *child* who thought as a child and spoke as a child and understood as a child.

The sole of my left shoe has been getting loose, and with every hill it flops more and more, until half the sole is detached from the shoe. It doesn't matter, I'm wet to the knee and my whole shin hurts so much I'm limping anyways. My tennis shoes might be expensive, but they couldn't stand up to Terrible Valley.

I couldn't stand up to Terrible Valley.

Good thing my brothers aren't here. I would have figured out some way to mess them up too. I would have made my dad disappointed and Maura work harder.

People noticed you. You were special.

I never wanted to be special. I wanted to be ordinary, and give Kaylee an ordinary meal and an ordinary hair-style and ordinary, every-day, totally typical love that ordinary, normal children deserve. I wanted Kaylee to chirp "because I'm the princess" with total confidence in herself, instead of glance at me out of the side of her eyes when something goes a little bit wrong. I tried to show her how to be ordinary, but all I managed was to show her how to be scared.

***

"Here's the basket!" Nisha says. "And now, I must leave. I'm not allowed to stay here."

The girls give her hugs.

I blink and shiver. We're already here. Or maybe we've been walking all day.

Oona has a thousand questions, and Kaylee answers slightly different ones so they both talk at once. I shake my head sharply, trying to think. I can't let them just bumble through being all happy and cheerful, like all the obstacles are gone. We can't get to the surface by ourselves. Dylan and Arthur have to haul up the basket, and they're not figments of my memory.

They're real live boys, and they might be nice or they might not be, but I know better than to trust them. Because here's the thing. Dylan's here because he's desperate to take care of Hannah, and Arthur's here because he's desperate to take care of his mother—and when someone is desperate, they can't always afford to be nice. Oona and the ring on her little finger is the key to all their goals. When push comes to shove, they don't care about Kaylee. They don't care about me. And they sure don't give a crap about "honesty" or "integrity" or "being a good human being."

Neither did I.

So. Oona and her finger.

I shake the gad, which is what the rope thing is called.

"They're back already!" It's Arthur's voice from above.

So time apparently did pass differently, even just outside the valley.

"Did you get Oona?" Dylan calls.

"Did you defeat the Patchwork Man? I mean, the Green Knight?" Arthur calls.

"Yes," I call back. "I've got the princess and his heart."

"Me!" Oona wiggles her fingers in the air. "I'm the princess!"

She's the princess, but I'm not a hero. I failed Kaylee, and now I'm all beat up. In the fairy tales, the guys are never sore and limping in the final scenes. It never mentions a headache or itching scabs.

So, I'm not much of a hero, but I'm going to get my sisters home again. Home to Maura, which Mrs Morrisy said was Kaylee's heart's desire.

I give Oona some cheese while we get ready. She balances on a stone, flapping her cloak with the non-cheese hand and talking to herself. I recognize all the signs of a happy unicorn-pegasus.

I hold the basket for Kaylee, and then I lean close to her.

"You're the big sister now." My voice catches low in my chest. "You stay close to Oona no matter what. You understand?"

"Yes, I—" Kaylee stops, and her face tilts from sunny to anxious. "What do you mean? I'm a good sister, aren't I? I've been playing with Oona for days."

"You're a great sister." I squeeze her arm and make myself smile. "I'm super proud of you. But..."

"But what?"

I glance up the hole, to where the boys' conversation is a distant mumble. "You're my best Kay-bear and always will be. But she's the little one now." I jerk my head towards the unicorn-pegasus. "We've got to go up one at a time."

Understanding dawns. She freezes.

"I don't know what's going to happen next, but you stay with her. No matter what. Don't let them take Oona away from the two of us."

Kaylee's face goes fierce. "I understand. I won't let her be alone."

"Are you ready?" Dylan calls. "I've got the deer in position."

"I'm ready," Kaylee yells back.

I hold the basket steady while it jerks into position, and Kaylee lifts up, up, and away from me. Oona cheers.

By the time I tidy up our bundles, the basket comes back down, and Oona comes hopping back over to investigate.

"Can you climb in?" I ask Oona. "Try it by yourself."

If she can do it, and she thinks it sounds fun, then I'll go up next. It means leaving her in Terrible Valley, but it will be just a few seconds and I'll keep my eye on her the whole time. I'll send the basket right back down, and keep her giggling while I pull it up. Then I'll be with both my sisters, all together.

I make it sound like a game, and Oona tries. But the basket is as high as my thigh, so she can't get over the top. I move a stone for her to climb on, but then the basket tips over when she leans on the edge. We try with the basket laying on its side, but then when they pull the gad Oona falls out.

"Good try"—I swallow hard and review my list of rhymes—"Oona Baboona, Queen of the Moona."

She laughs, and I swoop her up in my arms. I nuzzle my face in her hair, breathing her in, just for a second, and then I swing her in a circle and plop her in the basket. Like it's a game.

"I do it!" she says, and shakes the gad enthusiastically.

"That's a great shake," I tell her.

So my last glimpse is of her smile.

I've given them the princess and the ring. They don't need anything else.

I slump onto the rock I set up for her, my hurley stick balanced across my knees. I don't have to wait long.

Arthur calls out, but he doesn't send down the basket. "The cart is full. Remember how small it is? I'm driving, and the others are wedged in. We'll come back for you."

"Wait!" Oona's thin voice pierces through. "Wait!"

"We'll come ba—ack!" Kaylee's voice is thin, with a jolt when the deer must have started up again. "I pro-mise!"

I pull up my hood and adjust my bum on the hard stone. I'll stay here as long as I can, but I know they're not coming back. I know my fairy tales, and the princess doesn't make the choices. The princess waits.

And besides, Kaylee's not the princess. She has never held the steering wheel in her own life. Our parents pushed her around like a bargaining chip, and I didn't do any better. She didn't even belong in this story—even her clever trick with the mitten? I was supposed to call Nisha. I just messed it up.

Arthur is the one driving, he's got Oona and her ring, and he's not coming back for me.

By the time it starts to get dark, all my joints are stabbing and all my muscles have seized up. I'm wet and cold to the bone. There's a little hut in the trees a little ways away. I can light a fire. If there's food, I'll eat it. If it kills me, I guess I'm dead.

I drag myself to the cottage. My sneaker rips even more, and I pause to yank it off and hurl it in the bushes. My left knee isn't working at all, and the places that the Green Knight's sword caught me really hurt.

Nurse Raymond was right. I thought I was clever but I wasn't. I never was good enough, and Kaylee deserved better.

But Nurse was wrong about one thing.

I'm not a child.

I never was.

Chapter 12

There is soup in the kettle, although the fire is out.

I know how to build the fire, so I do. I fetch water. I pour oil in the lamps. I fetch armloads of wood to get me through the night. I wipe up the rain that dripped through the window and under the door, although the floor makes the rag muddy. Everything is pain, but it's going to hurt even worse if I stop.

This is the smallest cottage yet, but at least that means it warms up more quickly...maybe. The wind sneaks in and the fire smokes.

There's a pallet behind the stove, and I wrap myself in wool and furs and fall straight asleep.

I wake up in the dark, freezing. I'm drenched with sweat and kicked off all the blankets.

Everything hurts, but I manage to stoke the fire and put the blankets back on. I try to do a gentle stretch, but I just can't manage.

I wake up again. Dark. Cold. Shaking.

I vomit, and cry, but there's only one choice. I keep on going. Fire, blankets, back to sleep.

And again.

And again.

In the morning, it's not so bad. I clean up the mess I've made, and discover packets of herbs and Lipton tea. A step down, I guess, but still functional. There's porridge in the pot, and I choke that down and sip the tea without any sweetener. Bitter. Like me.

From the doorway, I can just see to the rock I left by the basket. It's raining hard. I'll hear their voices, I tell myself. I can run back to the basket if they come.

When I turn back to the table, I notice a shelf in the corner. On it are all the textbooks I need to finish my homework.

I take out the pre-calculus book. I'm not sure if it's getting lost in the theorems or my fever is getting worse, but I almost manage to stop worrying. About Kaylee or about this stupid Terrible Valley which produces textbooks and teabags and keeps our phones charged to 100% which makes no sense.

I'm too exhausted to hate myself. Or Arthur, or the Green Knight, or my dad, or anyone. I'm just exhausted.

Dark. Chores. Fire. Soup.

Bed. Wake. Too hot, too cold.

My leg is burning so bad, and I fumble to get a coal out of the fire and light the lamp to check it. I can barely see, but my whole calf is hard and hot. My fingers fumble around for the cut.

There's a few, but they're just scratches. From the knee-high tin men. They were so little, they couldn't do anything that would really harm me, so I don't know how my leg hurts so very much.

There's nothing else to do, so I fall in bed. I sleep, or don't sleep. Stare into the dark or squeeze my eyes against the loneliness. I should stoke the fire, but my limbs won't obey.

Light trickles through the opaque window. It makes my head pound.

Water.

Too tired.

Water.

I can't step on my left leg, so I crawl to the water bucket and drink from the ladle. Need to vomit—no. I can't let myself. Drink slowly.

When I get back to bed, there's mud on my knees. Don't care. So tired. So cold. I tuck under all the blankets. Shivering so hard. Dang but that leg hurts. Just a little owie. Just a little.

When I wake again, I'm too tired to move.

They're never coming back for me.

I'm going to die.

Chapter 13

"Aiden? Aiden, my love. I'm here."

The woman's voice is so soft and gentle. She's touching my hair, my shoulder.

This is not Kaylee, and there is no one else who loves me. Maybe I have died. Or maybe it's a dream.

She helps me turn and have a sip of water. I was so thirsty. She wipes my face with a cool cloth. I was burning.

Now I know where I am. I am a child, a little one. Before Florida. Before everything.

I swallow the pills she gives me. I let her wash my leg and put on some cream. I think I fell down riding my bicycle.

"Daddy took the training wheels off," I mumble.

"You're doing a great job," she says. "You're so brave."

She kisses my forehead.

I fall back asleep.

***

Warm light on my eyelids. It smells of wood smoke, not my dad's house in Seattle. There's a rhythmic squeaking behind me. My joints ache and my limbs are throbbing, but I think I can move. One finger. One ankle. Yup, it works.

I skim my eyelids open, just the tiniest amount. Rough linen pillow, my own hands tucked close. They have long fingers and nubbly knuckles with a sprinkling of hair. Man hands.

If this is not Seattle, and I am not a little kid...then who is beside me?

It's not my mom after all. Mom never came back. She didn't.

Something inside me breaks. I don't make a noise, but I cry, and cry, and cry myself back to sleep.

***

I wake again in the afternoon. I have to pee, and my brain doesn't feel as fuzzy any more, but my leg is hurting really bad again.

Okay, I've just got to do the hard thing, and roll over and see who this is. Probably I'll have to be grateful to Nurse Reynolds, or Nisha, who is young and pretty and this would be really super embarrassing. Or some other woman from my past, who has showed up in the Terrible Memory Valley in order to demonstrate that actually I kept f-ing things up and couldn't have made it without her sticking her oar in and doing something for Kaylee that I forgot about.

I take a deep breath and heave myself over in bed.

"Hi, sweetheart."

It's Maura.

My heart and stomach do this swooping thing that I can't make sense of at all.

"I"—don't know what I think, or want, or that throbbing feeling when I look in her eyes—"have to pee."

"That's good, it shows your body is working. Here, let me help."

I'm taller than Maura, but she knows the way to balance herself to support me. She helps me over to the potty bucket (I'm sure they have a better word for it, but that's what I said with Oona), and then turns to the table and hums while I take care of my business. No privacy here.

She helps me back to sitting on the bed, and I'm totally out of breath. She holds some lukewarm tea so I can drink. It's that green sludge again, but it's nice and sweet, and Nurse Raymond's brews did actually help with the aches.

But Maura opens a little box and gives me pills to take with the green sludge. Ah, no wonder I'm feeling a little better.

"There's another anti-nausea and some ibuprofen," Maura explains, adding some new ones. "The effect will be the strongest in another hour or so. Do you think we can try to get to the basket?"

I look at the window, trying to imagine walking that far. It feels like a million miles.

She brushes the hair off my forehead. "I might have lied to the pharmacist, just a little, and said that you've gotten ear infections your whole life and this is just another one. He gave me a couple doses of antibiotic, but it's probably the wrong type and not nearly enough. We need to get you to the doctor."

"My leg's infected? I am gonna die."

"Aiden." She cups my face, and her hands are pleasantly cool. "I'm not going to let you die. We're going to the doctor."

"What if I can't walk?"

"I'll carry you."

"I'm too big."

She pulls my head in to her shoulder and wraps her arms around me. "Haven't you ever heard of those women who pick up a whole car when their baby is in danger? A mother's love is that strong, and I've got a lot to make up for."

I put my arms around her waist, holding her tight. I'm glad she's here. I'm glad it's Maura. "But I'm not a baby," I mumble against her shoulder.

She kisses my hair, just like I kiss Oona's. "You're *my* baby," she says.

It doesn't make any sense, but I'm too tired to figure it out. I lean on Maura, breathing in her warm smell. She's been there for me for a long time. Never trying to push me into anything, never trying to prove herself. Just ready. Waiting for me.

Waiting to be my mom.

"Okay," I mumble. "I can try."

She kisses my hair again. "It's going to be okay," she says. "I promise."

She moves away, tidying up the room, sending me a reassuring smile.

And you know what? I didn't want my biological mother. In the dark of the night, in the fog of pain, that wasn't who I wanted at all. Suddenly, she is nothing to me. Nothing.

***

Maura smears Neosporin all over me, wraps my feet and calves in soft leather shoes like Kaylee has been wearing—oh, that's how the infection got in, my tennis shoe not doing much good—and bundles up our stuff. She throws some leaves on the fire and calls Nisha (wait, what?) and the two of them stand on either side of me and frog-march me to the basket. Maura goes up first, so Nisha can hold the basket for me to get in and Maura can help haul me out of it.

There's not one but two deer, and Maura chatters about the deer as she tucks me into the back of the cart. Kaylee was right. They were the magical kind of deer, it sounds like, and they're all friends. After the first deer dropped off Kaylee and Oona, she went and got Saba. Now Saba is staying at our house watching the little kids, and these are two more of them.

"How does Saba watch the kids?" I ask. "She hasn't got any hands."

"It's only because Kaylee is there," Maura admits, climbing up into the driver's perch. "Kaylee does the things that need hands, and Oisín can translate when Saba needs to say something. She might be in deer form, but Saba is sensible, and she's an adult. She enforces the rules, and if anything goes wrong, she will decide what to do." Maura shakes out the reins. "North to the stars, south to the sun, and onwards to home again," she says to the deer, and a moment later calls back to me. "I feel okay about leaving Kaylee with the hands-on duties, because I'm coming right back, and she knows she can trust a grown-up to make the decisions. Making decisions is the hard part."

Was it, I wonder? Was that the part that was hard?

I rest my aching head against the folded blanket. I can't tell any more. I don't know where I went wrong.

Chapter 14

I've never been so happy to see the battered stones of our lopsided castle, but Maura rolls me straight from the cart into her little car. She snaps the seat belt and piles blankets around me, so maybe I'm not looking so good.

Then someone big is helping me into a wheelchair. I blink. It's dark, but the lights in the parking lot glare and stab into my eyes. I haven't seen anything this bright in ages.

I shiver and Maura tucks the blanket around my shoulders.

It's February here, I remember. It gets dark early.

They wheel me up to the doctor's office, and I kind of remember him. For my first visit, Maura waited in the hall, since I'm sixteen and I didn't want to bother her anyways. This time, I'm glad she stays. I let her answer most of the questions.

I let her make the decisions. She's right, it feels good.

"I really think he will do better at home," Maura says, calm and firm. "I'll bring him back in the morning if he's not improved."

"Or in the night if he takes a turn for the worse. Straight to the ED."

"Absolutely."

So they give me an IV in the clinic and let Maura wheel me back to the car.

She's right. I really need to go home.

I think I have had a gaping wound my whole life, and that is the only way to close it. I need to go home.

I need my family. "They're my superpower," I mumble to Maura, as the car whips along the country roads.

"I know, baby," she answers.

I think I was missing a few words, but I fall asleep before I find them.

***

I wake in the night, like I have ever since I fought three times three hundred tin soldiers.

But this time there is the low glow of a lamp, and Maura is beside me.

"You don't have to stay," I mumble. "I'm okay."

"Your fever is down." She's checking the thermometer. "Antibiotics really are amazing. Let's get you something to drink."

"I can do it." I reach for the water bottle on my own, just to show her.

She lets me, and that almost hurts. I guess I don't need her now. I can take care of myself.

"You can go back to your bed," I tell her. "I'll be okay for the rest of the night."

***

The third time, I wake without thrashing or retching. My eyes open quietly, my brain is working, and Maura is still there.

She is sleeping beside me. When we bought this castle, it came with all the furniture that was too big to move, and that includes these big honking beds. Mine could probably sleep a whole family comfortably. Maura is lying next to me, on top of the comforter, in her usual fuzzy sweater and baggy skirt.

I touch the blanket covering her. It's soft and several shades of blue, and Maura keeps it upstairs. She puts it on her lap when she's sitting next to Oona when she's scared to fall asleep alone. She uses it on her own big chair when I've found her reading before bed. And she brought it into the little boys' room and slept under it when Oisín had strep throat and then Oliver had the stomach flu.

My eyes flit to her bedside table. That's her special thermos, the ones she fills with chamomile tea when she's up with kids at night.

There's her book, between us, half under the covers, as though she fell asleep reading. Like Kaylee said she did, when Kaylee got strep throat and then also got the stomach flu, because Kaylee always gets everything. I was relieved that someone else was with her, because I never knew when it was time to call the doctor. After I was twelve or so, at least I didn't have to convince Mom to make the call. I'd just cough to rough up my voice, and make the appointment like I was Kaylee's father. I was always afraid the nurse would find me out—either that I was just a kid, or that I was calling for something that didn't deserve an appointment.

Maura was right. Making the decisions is the scary part.

So was walking to the grocery store in a storm.

So was accidentally starting a fire in the oven. Kaylee jumped up and down and cheered, while I held the fire extinguisher and debated whether it was worse to risk possibly burning down the house or for sure ruining our dinner and we didn't have more.

Wait. That's another decision.

I hobble to the bathroom, which is way better than anything in ancient times. The prior owner stuffed these little en-suites in the corner of every bedroom, and the toilet wobbles and the sink slants, but I appreciate the gush of water (okay, trickle) that spills over my hands, and squirt on tangerine soap. It's antibacterial. Mm, modern technology.

I take my own temperature.

When I get back to bed, Maura is propped up on the pillows, reading. "Feeling any better?"

"The IV stuff worked. 98.1, totally normal." I take a deep breath and huddle under the blankets. Nice, normal, poofy blankets. No dead animal skins. "You can go now. You should get some sleep."

Maura just watches me with a little smile. "If I didn't know better, I'd think you're trying to get rid of me."

She's got to be tired, and getting tired of me. "Thanks a million—a billion. You've done so much for me and Kaylee, and I really appreciate it. Really."

"Aiden." She turns and brushes the hair off my forehead. "I'm not doing you and Kaylee a favor. This is being your mom."

I squeeze my eyes closed, feeling tears welling up. My breathing is getting shallow, and I'm worried about Kaylee. I want to check on her. Just to be sure she's okay.

"You don't have to," I tell her.

"Isn't that what we decided? All of us?"

"In the courtroom?"

"And afterwards, yes. That I take care of you now."

I hold my breath until the sob passes, then blow it out through pursed lips. "But you don't have to," I repeat. "I lied to you. I lied to everyone."

"Oh, Aiden."

I hold my breath even tighter, braced for everything. She's going to yell, she's going to leave, she's going to throw me out in the February night—and worse, Kaylee too.

Maura strokes my hair. "I figured that out a long time ago, sweet boy. I'm still here. I'm *always* going to be here."

I can't hold it any more. The sob bursts out, and it's rough and ugly. I'm too big to cry like this. I huddle in tighter, and Maura puts her arms around me.

"You're right, I don't *have* to be your mother," she tells me. "I *choose* to be your mother. I choose you every day, for as long as you need me. Forever."

I cry like I'm a stupid little boy all over again.

"And I'm not leaving you tonight," Maura adds, crisply. "So you might as well stop asking."

***

I wake with pain, and Maura gives me pills.

I wake with retching, but manage not to throw up, because I'm taking pills for that, too. Maura wipes my forehead with a damp cloth and helps me take sips of water.

I wake with spasms in my leg. Maura rubs my knee, and then puts a hot pack on it. I go half-way to sleep holding her hand, then jerk it away.

I hate this big-man body of mine. I want to be little, to fit in the curve of her arms, to snuggle down until I'm helpless. I roll away from Maura, reminding myself of all the years I've lived. The magma rolls in my stomach. I'm so tired of being angry. It never does any good.

The next time I wake, it's because Maura is shaking my shoulder.

I reach out, my hand beating empty pillow. "My hurley!" I cry.

"You were dreaming," she says. "There are no more little tin men. There's no more danger."

But the little tin men weren't the worst thing that have happened in my life, and ever since I saw Nurse Raymond, I can't forget it.

"It's over with." I thump my pillow. "It's gone. We came with Maura, remember? We're in Kilkenny now. We are."

I'm still half in my dream until Maura starts to rub my back.

"You're safe," she murmurs, "but sometimes it helps to tell me about it."

"You'll hate me." I can't bear her disappointment. Not hers.

"I won't," she answers, as though it's that simple.

I push aside the covers and go to the bathroom, mostly to make the rest of the dream go away. I turn on the light and push the button on my electric razor, just to prove to myself that they work. I open the window, rattling in its frame. It smells of rain and cows and February.

It's not the Terrible Valley, and it's not Florida.

I shiver and go back to bed. Maura is reading her book and waiting for me.

I fiddle with the covers, glance at her and away, start a sentence and then stop. I'm tired of holding everything in. It didn't help.

"I'm strong enough to hold what scares you." Maura puts the book down and turns toward me. "I know you got used to making things look okay in order to protect Kaylee, but you don't have to do that right now. I'll protect Kaylee. I'll protect you."

I listen to her breathing. It's a little rough, like this is hard for her, too.

Maura's super gentle, but I think I know something about being strong inside, and that's what she is. My dad turned her whole world upside-down, and instead of raging about how terrible he was, she pulled herself together and built a whole new life. In a leaking Irish castle. And she made room for me and Kaylee, and Saba and Oisín, and she keeps telling stories and knitting mittens and staying up with children when they're lonely or sick in the night.

None of that is easy. I should know, because I couldn't do it.

I haven't slept more than an hour or two at a time in days and days, and I'm pumped full of drugs and everything hurts. I'm too tired to resist, and I start telling her a whole jumble about Mrs Morrisy and the vision in my soup bowl, and then Nisha and how I didn't remember she had used her own money or driven us home. From Maura's little comments, I can tell Kaylee has told her a lot of this.

Then I'm up to Nurse Reynolds.

I take a deep breath. I have to turn away, talk into the darkness.

"When we were little, Mom was just spacey. I guess we both thought she was fooling Nurse Reynolds when she said she had to work, but now I think—I think Nurse knew Mom was upstairs the whole time. Mom had family money, she didn't work. Mom just really didn't like sick kids. They made her anxious."

"Hm." Maura rubs my back.

"It got worse when Mom started dating. She changed with every guy. But by then I could mostly take care of Kaylee, so it wasn't so bad. I stayed home when she was sick. It was okay."

Maura waits. "Until Nurse Reynolds came again...?"

I grit my teeth, but I can't hold it in any longer. "I was in eighth grade and Kaylee was still at Larkin Elementary. I guess Kaylee got sick really fast, and Nurse Reynolds talked to Mom and drove her home and stayed the whole day. I didn't know Kaylee was at home. I stayed for basketball practice. I didn't know."

"Sweetie, it wasn't your job. It's okay."

"It wasn't okay! Because when I got home, Mom still wasn't there. And Nurse Reynolds met me in the front hallway, and she started asking questions, and I said the usual things. But she'd spent the whole day in my house, and she'd had to go in Kaylee's bedroom and bathroom and the kitchen, and she knew things. She'd ask me a question, and I'd try to smooth it over, and she was tall like a whole tree in my entryway and kept saying 'that's a lie. Try again.' And I got more upset and my lies got stupider."

It occurs to me, for the first time, that I could have told her the truth. She saw Kaylee all the time at school, but I'd grown and my voice had changed. It occurs to me that Nurse Reynolds was asking "is it you doing this to Kaylee or your mother" and the more I lied the more I said "it's me" instead of "please help."

"She left," I say. "And my mom got home. Mom was dressed up all pretty and in a good mood. I went up real fast to check on Kaylee, but she was sleeping, while Mom got herself some wine. We sat in the living room watching the X-Files together."

I take a deep breath, but I can't go on.

"So, that was when CPS arrived?" Maura's voice is calm.

I shake my head. "It was late at night. It was the police. I guess Nurse Reynolds convinced them to surprise Mom." I spent years praying someone would surprise her. All the visits before, they'd call and make an appointment. Once Dad came to town overnight as a treat, and he called her from the airport. Oh my god. So close. She swooped around and cleaned everything up, and by the time his taxi arrived we were the perfect family again. Mom loved looking like the perfect family.

"The police," Maura repeats gently.

"I answered the door and brought the officers to the living room. Mom offered them a drink. They said they couldn't, but she was so sweet and charming. Super sweet."

I can't find the next words, because I remember how good that moment felt. Mom's hand on my shoulder, making me feel loved and included.

"They apologized for bothering her, but they had to search the house. Mom showed them around, and she made excuses and fluttered her fingers, but they didn't like finding booze and ketchup but no food in the kitchen. They found a broken lamp that clearly had been left there for a while, and dirty cups all over. They were getting grumpier. Mom said some stuff about being a single mom, and how hard it is, and 'boys these days.' She put her fingers in her eyes, you know, like ladies do when they're trying not to cry. Or trying to look like they're crying. And the police were in their heavy boots and clumped up to the stairs, and I was really scared. I didn't want them in our bedrooms! Kaylee was up there. And so I stood close to Mom to protect her, because she was so pretty and fragile and sad."

I was so stupid. I imagined they would take her away. I imagined her pretty little manicured nails clutching the bars of a jail cell, which was awful. But also, part of me was thinking Kaylee and I would be on the next plane to Seattle to live with Dad and Maura and that made me excited, despite how bad it would be for Mom, and I was so mixed up inside.

"Kaylee heard the commotion and came out of her room. She stood in the hallway in her Hello Kitty bathrobe while the police checked our bedrooms." She was watching me. Scared. But not too scared, because I was there. "I tried to go to her but one of the policemen stood between us."

Maura's arm jerks tight. She holds me close to her, but her crying doesn't make her weak. It means that this time, walking through my memory, she's taking some of the burden. Keeping me safe.

"Two of the guys searched our bedrooms, throwing stuff around. Mom held my shoulder and I was worried about Kaylee. They one of the police asked us what was wrong with Kaylee, like what was she sick with today, but the head guy came out of the bedroom and stopped him, and they put their heads together to talk, but that one guy still stood between us. I tried to go to her. I tried! He wouldn't let me, and Mom started to cry."

They had such big boots. Marching up and down on our rugs, leaving streaks. We never wore shoes upstairs. They seemed to take up twice as much space as a normal person, with their chests full of straps and gear and stuff, and broad shoulders, and those huge boots. Stomp, stomp, stomp. I was eight years old again, just arriving in this house, helpless and overwhelmed but knowing that I had to take care of Kaylee or no one would. Mom cried harder and I didn't care about her anymore, I just wanted Kaylee. That look in her face! She needed me.

"I tried to go to her. I'd go around. I'd push through. She put out her hands. She put out her hands for me!"

Just like Oona does now. A little child who deserves to be held and protected.

"Oh, Aiden. Oh, sweetie." Maura is holding me tight, as though I am a little kid and not a big, tall, dangerous teenage guy.

Because I was. The policeman in the hall grabbed me and told me to stop.

"I didn't stop," I tell Maura. "I didn't obey."

She rests her cheek on my hair, making a little humming sound.

"They were just trying to take us into take us into different rooms." I can't help making excuses for them. "They just wanted to see if either of us knew that Kaylee was sick without giving her a chance to explain it to us. They wanted to see if we had the same explanation for the broken lamp and stuff. They were just trying to talk." I take a deep breath, but it's all shaky.

"But at the time, it felt like they were taking you away from Kaylee," Maura says. "And whatever happens, you always stay with her, don't you?"

"Well, this time I couldn't." I hold my breath and try to blow out through pursed lips, but it doesn't work anymore. "I was—they were—" The sob rips at my chest.

"It's okay. It's okay to cry, sweetie." She strokes my hair.

She waits. I hold in the sobs, but I can't say the words.

"Shall I guess?"

I nod, relieved.

"Your mother and Kaylee are both petite, and your mother was dressed up and playing it up to the hilt. You'd just gotten in from basketball practice. You hit your growth early, so you're not a big guy but you looked older than your age back then. You were probably too panicked to listen to instructions, and as soon as you started pushing it was an excuse to push back. And maybe you got more frantic and they got more rough."

"Yeah." They had me on the floor, on my face. And then there was more. Yelling. Someone snapped handcuffs on me. "But that wasn't the important part."

Maura sighs. "You're important, too. But tell me about Kaylee."

"They finally got me quiet. The head guy crouched down and said they couldn't take me out of the house without clear evidence." And please

Jesus, don't give me reason to arrest your underage ass. And that terrified me, because Kaylee was only in fifth grade and she couldn't even make toast without burning herself. So I got real still, and I did just what they said. "They said we just needed to go over a few questions, and then they'd leave. I just needed to go to the dining room with them. That's was all. So the guy held my cuffs and I started down the stairs. The other guy was complaining they'd already spent too long on a bogus call, and clearly kids with this many fancy clothes and electronics were just fine. But the guy holding me was pissed."

I run out of words again.

"And Kaylee?" Maura asks.

"I was almost at the bottom of the stairs." I can still see the lamplight cutting across the floor, feel the smooth metal pulling my shoulder back. "And Kaylee started to scream. Not words. Just screaming. Screaming and screaming, and she wouldn't stop."

Maura squeezes me tight.

"I guess they didn't have her, because she came down the stairs. Screaming. And she fell, somehow. The guy holding me grabbed her so she wouldn't get hurt worse, and she really lost it." I pull in a breath, just trying to get through this part. "I didn't dare try to touch her or even speak to her, because they'd told me not to." She was trying to take my hand and pull off the cuffs, and I didn't hold her hand back. All the signals we had between us, all the glances and pinky-squeezes and silly names—I didn't give her any of them. No reassurance. I didn't dare. "So they pulled me into the dining room. And they took her into the front office. And they asked some questions, and I had some answers."

I take a deep breath. It's over now. "Then they left." But the next day, Kaylee had bruises from throwing herself at the door they closed between us, flinging herself on the floor, breaking another lamp. Her voice was hoarse from screaming. "They didn't actually do anything. It wasn't...anything."

"It was a lot," Maura says. "They called your dad, you know. There was a report."

"What?" How could he know, and not—no, that old anger isn't doing any good.

"Not everything you've told me. It just sounded like...I don't know, a minor bureaucratic inconvenience. It said there had been a call but everything was fine upon investigation. They said that Kaylee might have anger issues, which was not unusual for girls her age, and suggested counseling. He came down to visit the next week, didn't he?"

"Yeah." And Mom had fixed everything by then. Doctors appointment for us both, cupboards full of organic food, new lamps. "Kaylee had appointments with the school psychologist. No extra trouble for anyone."

"Extra trouble is not the deciding factor in parenting," Maura says firmly.

"It's okay. That's the way my mom always was."

"It's not okay," Maura immediately replies. "None of this is okay! If she didn't want to parent you, she could have told your dad. He asked her. We even talked about it together a few times, when we weren't really sure if you two were doing great. He offered to take custody multiple times, and your mother would cry and rage and argue that she keep you both. That everything was fine and she loved you too much to lose you." She sighs. "And he never insisted."

Wait—Mom could have asked for help? Dad started the conversation, but never insisted?

All these days—ever since this started—I've been thinking I was wrong because I didn't tell someone. I've been thinking of all the opportunities I missed and how that ruined Kaylee's life. But Mom—or Dad—

"I should have argued," Maura says. "I'm sorry. I read articles about blended families, and I was trying to respect their parenting decisions. I apologize so deeply that I ever, for one moment, put their feelings above yours. I am so angry with myself."

"You didn't know. We only saw you a couple times a year. And you had the babies."

She takes a deep breath. "You're right. I didn't know. But I could have asked more questions. I could have pushed Roy harder, so he double-checked your mother more often. I should have."

"You always gave us the best gifts for Christmas. You sent texts on game days and choir concerts. You were good." I don't want to be mad at Maura, I want to snuggle down and believe that she will love me forever.

"I always cared about you." She holds me close. "It was a little hard to get to know you, but I cared."

Yeah, it was a little hard because we didn't talk to her. At all.

Speaking of not talking...

I roll onto my back so I can look at Maura. My heart is pounding. "Can I ask you something?"

"Of course."

It's a stupid question, but I can't help it. "Why didn't I tell the truth? Why did I never trust you even when you were always nice? Why did I keep protecting Mom even when the police were inside my house and had handcuffs on me? Why didn't I tell Nurse Reynolds what was wrong? How come I saw Dad a few times a year and I was so angry and I wanted him so much but I never told him anything? Why was I so stupid?"

I can't bear to look at Maura and wish I hadn't pulled away from her.

But she pulls my face to her shoulder. "Oh, Aiden. You're not stupid, never, ever, ever. You are loyal. You are loving. And I suspect your first thought was always that saying too much could make something worse for Kaylee. But listen..."

She waits for me. I sob, and sniffle, and she wipes my face with the sheet.

Finally, she pulls away to look in my eyes. "Aiden, you were never at fault because you were a child. You still are a child. The adults are at fault, today and last year and every single time. Every single time it was an adult responsibility."

"But I could have said something! I should—"

"No." She is absolutely firm. "It is too much to ask a child to betray their mother. Of course you lied to protect her. Of course you wanted to keep your family together. Of course you love her."

"Why?" I bury my head in her shoulder again. The blue blanket is fuzzy on my cheek.

"It's the sacredness of motherhood." Maura strokes my hair.

It was. It is.

"You were eight years old when you became my child," she says. "That's a long time that I have done wrong by you."

"But you weren't supposed to! You didn't have to!"

"Well"—she laughs abruptly—"I am perfectly willing to assign the bulk of the blame to Amber. But you have been feeling guilty? For not doing enough? For not talking to your dad?"

I nod.

"Every one of those times, I take responsibility. I was always the adult. You were always the child. I am truly sorry, Aiden. I could have done better. I take that on."

It's the third time she's said it, and I let it sink in. Feel what that would be like to not carry that blame.

It wasn't Maura's fault, not really. Not at all. When she married my dad, she was young and already pregnant. I'm basically positive he didn't tell her that he had kids until after they were married. Besides, my dad is a whirlwind and a half, all on his own.

But...if it doesn't make sense to blame Maura for how Kaylee grew up....maybe...possibly...it doesn't make sense to blame me.

"It takes a while to figure out, doesn't it," Maura says into my hair. "We don't have to fix it all this morning. We need to change the custody so Amber doesn't have visitation, and maybe a therapist, and you need to talk with Kaylee, and we need more time together. You and I. We have time, Aiden. We have the whole world together."

"Even if I'm almost grown up?"

"Just exactly the way you are." She squeezes me close. "I never knew how bad it was, I promise, until the girls got back from Terrible Valley. They were both babbling, and Kaylee was so worried about you that I finally got her to talk. That was the first I knew, but I should have asked many years ago. I should have been more suspicious."

"My mom wasn't bad." I'm stuck on that word. "She never hit us or locked us in our rooms. She did lots of nice stuff for us."

"Your mom isn't bad," Maura agrees. "I am sure she is a very mixed-up person inside."

Something inside me loosens. I don't like saying mean things about my biological mother. It makes me feel even worse.

Maura rests her hand on my hair. "However! It is very bad for children's socio-emotional development to get food and attention some weeks, but not others. It is bad for children to have to make adult decisions and bear the consequences. Your mother is not some evil fairy-tale villain, but she was...making some poor choices."

She pulls me close again, and I relax against her. I'm getting sleepy.

"Yeah," I agree. "That was bad for Kaylee."

"And it was bad for Aiden." She holds me close. Calm. "But we're going to start making it better. Okay?"

"Okay." I yawn.

"I love you," she says. "I choose you."

"Mm...love-oo-too."

And I fall asleep in my mother's arms. My real mother.

Chapter 15

Morning light. A noise, a smell. Something woke me, and my muscles seize up and then relax.

I'm home. I'm safe. I'm not alone. I should—

"I'm just checking on him," Kaylee whispers. "Is the fever gone?"

Wait, isn't it me who checks on Kaylee?

"It's been gone for hours now." Maura's voice is low and gentle. "Now his body can start to recover."

"Did he sleep okay?"

Wait, it's me who asks—it's always Kaylee who's sick.

"He didn't get much sleep. We'll take it easy today, but I know he's glad to see you." Maura puts her hand on the blanket over my shoulder.

"It was so awful, watching everything and I couldn't even help."

I'm too embarrassed to open my eyes, but I can feel Kaylee perch on the chair by my bed.

"You helped a great deal," Maura says.

"I knew he was gonna be okay in the end," Kaylee says. "Because of the Sword of Daylight and everything. But the stories—they don't make it clear how yucky all the parts in the middle are. That stuff was really hard! He was hurting."

"I'm sorry." I can't help interrupting. "I didn't want to upset you."

They are both silent for a moment.

"Aiden," Kaylee says ominously, "you are not understanding what I am saying. At. All. Zero. Nuh-uh. No way."

And then Maura starts to laugh, and I can't help but smile, and then Kaylee giggles along. She's just so...thirteen.

"I'm going to go get some tea." Maura pats my shoulder, and she moves away. "I'll be back in a few minutes. Do you want anything from the kitchen, Kaylee?"

"Um...I'll have some tea if you're making it?"

"You got it."

I flutter open my eyes long enough to see Maura give Kaylee a quick one-armed hug and drop a kiss on her head. Good. She's treating her like a normal kid who belongs to her. That was Kaylee's heart's desire.

The door closes, and I close my eyes, too. I reach out my hand and Kaylee locks pinkies. I squeeze twice. She squeezes three times. She giggles.

"Kaylee, I'm sorry," I say. "I should have told Dad. I could have—"

"Would you stop it?" She sighs. "You don't need to say sorry to me. Not unless you take the last brownie or leave the toilet seat up or something."

I don't know what to say.

She's sighs again, even more dramatic. "I've been thinking about what you told me to take care of Oona, no matter what, and how she's the same age that I was when you were taking care of me. But I'm, like, practically a grownup, and you were eight. I don't know how you did it."

My eyes spring open. "Well, I did lots of things wrong. For the first few months, when Mom was too tired to make dinner I just fed you crackers. And then—"

"Aiden, would you stop already?" She takes a deep breath. "You were a kid. That's all."

"I know." Her accusations in the cottage burn into me, the truth of them. "I should have told Dad. I should have gotten help."

Kaylee screws up her face. "Would you just stop?"

I sigh. "Stop what?"

She gives one of her dramatic sighs, but I know she's thinking. "You don't have to be a grown-up. And you really don't have to be a hero, that was scary. Can you just…" She gives me a smile, but it's a little watery. "Can you just be my Aiden?"

"Yeah," I say. I smile on purpose, and then I smile for real. "I can do that, Kay-bear-Baloney, eating macaroni while driving a pony."

Kaylee laughs, and that feels good. She's still laughing when Maura comes back, carrying a tea tray, and just the way she looks at both of us makes me feel all warm inside.

But Kaylee gets the last word. She pulls herself upright, takes the mug that Maura prepared just the way she likes it, and casts me a sidelong glance. Not fearful; she's full of mischief.

"Not true," says Kaylee. "I'll take the pasta, but me? I'm driving a deer."

***

"Is he awake?"

"Can we come in?"

"Mummy, is he okay? Is he?"

"I brought you pancakes, Aidey!"

"I brought you a brontosaurus! Rowr!"

I roll up onto the pillows, late morning light streaming across my bed. My throat is sore and my legs hurt, but I feel lighter than I have in days. Years.

I bet it's because the antibiotics knocked the last of those tin-can-men germs. That's it.

"RAWR!!" I say back, opening my arms for my little brothers.

They jump on me, Oliver like a floppy starfish, Oisín pretending to devour my shoulder, Oona giggling and climbing on top of everyone. Saba prances around, cocking her head, flicking her big deer ears, and then leaps onto the foot of my giant bed. Kaylee is right behind the boys, plate of pancakes in one hand and stuffed dinosaur in the other.

I kind of like these little kids with no personal boundaries. I like Oliver's trusting weight on me, although I move Oona's knee farther from my bladder, and she collapses giggling on top of the boys. Saba lays her chin on my feet, and I wiggle a toe in greeting.

"There's plenty of room," Maura says from under her blue blanket, and Kaylee lays herself down carefully, her smile bright and hopeful. Maura squeezes from her side and I squeeze from mine, and all the kids laugh.

"It's a Kaylee sandwich!" Oona squeals.

"It's an everyone-sandwich!" Oliver laughs.

"Rawr!" Oisín munches Kaylee's shoulder and then flops on top of her.

I reach around Oliver and Oona and find Maura's hand, reaching over Kaylee and Oisín.

She holds on tight, and I know she always will. She's our mom.

I spit some of Oona's hair out of my mouth, and look down and across all of them. Funny, they've gotten blurry all of a sudden, as though Oliver has squeezed some tears right out of my solar plexus.

For years, my family was just Kaylee and I. Everyone commented on how much we looked alike, although now I realize that her blonde hair was always neater than mine.

Now, my family doesn't look at all the same. We've got blond hair and dark hair, fair skin and brown skin, and one of us is a freaking deer for goodness' sake. But we all love pancakes and we all believe in fairy tales.

This, right here? This is my superpower, and I squeeze them tight.

And tickle. Just a little bit.

The Two Rings

I wish Arthur would just shut up.

Actually, there's a lot I wish Arthur would do, but me, Dylan O'Neill—I'm just the sidekick. He's got the energy, makes the decisions, and only wants to hear from me if I've got something helpful to say. Right now, I'm pretty much positive he doesn't want to hear that he needs to stop talking, so I hunch into my seat and don't say anything.

Like usual, Arthur is driving, but it's really seriously not like usual, because he's driving a rickety wooden cart, pulled by a deer, who is jogging along above the tops of the trees. We're going above the farms and barns and houses of County Kilkenny, headed towards the council headquarters to speak with the Cathaoirleach. Arthur is brash and confident as always. As for myself, I'm hungry, I've gone days without putting on deodorant or Neosporin on my scrapes, I'm filled with a dull sort of panic that I did everything wrong, and I've got a five-year-old on my lap.

Oona Robinson is holding up her left hand with her right, and she's staring at them as though that hand is gravely injured. But really, her middle left finger is wearing a heavy ring with a red stone, and everyone—including Arthur's current prattle—has made her scared to death about that ring.

I have a little sister too. And I have a girlfriend, Hannah, and we met when we were five years old and I swear to God we're soulmates, although everyone says that what seventeen-year-olds feel is going to change and nothing we have is real. Arthur just has brothers, but I don't like it when girls feel helpless and scared, I really don't.

I juggle Oona on my lap with a tickle, and her rigid form relaxes against me just a little. I feel guilty for touching her, but there's not space in the cart to sit side by side.

We've come straight from the Terrible Valley, and Kaylee insisted we go straight to the castle where the Robinsons live. There was a confusing minute or two in the car park outside the castle, with Kaylee and their mother shouting back and forth, and there was *another* enchanted deer and she was talking to *our* enchanted deer.

Kaylee wanted Oona out of the cart, and Arthur and me to head back to Terrible Valley to get their brother Aiden, immediately, stat, five minutes ago.

Arthur wanted to go straight to the County Hall to wrap up the business with the ring and the reward, and go back for Aiden afterwards. I would have said that Arthur doesn't get a vote given that Kaylee, Aiden, and Oona aren't his family and family is more important than a ring—but I'm just the sidekick and no one asked what I thought. In the end, Oona sided with Arthur. She stuck out her little lip and refused to get out of the cart. She wants the ring business settled.

Kaylee screeched and stamped, and Mrs Robinson said it might be best to finish our story, and Arthur yelled at Kaylee, and I promised Mrs Robinson that I'll take good care of Oona, and Arthur yelled that I have a sister so I'm good with little girls, and Kaylee demanded that Oona get out of the cart, and Oona braced her feet and pouted, and Arthur yelled.

Then the two deer settled the argument. They were standing in the drive with their heads together, and the other deer flicked her ears and stepped back, and then our deer trotted away. Oona tipped into me and Arthur almost fell off the driver's perch, but we all got ourselves settled right as the cart started to slope upwards. Kaylee ran after us, but we were headed into the air so she could hardly grab Oona—or slap Arthur; whatever she had in mind.

Mrs Robinson cupped her hands and shouted "I trust you, Dylan O'Neill!"

So that's a big responsibility. I know Mrs Robinson a little bit, from school events and hurley games and things. She brings homemade snacks and asks how we're doing, then listens like it really matters. So I need to take care of Oona, and go back for Aiden.

All I want is Hannah. My girl. My heart.

But first I have to help Oona finish off her story and take care of the ring. I jostle her into a more comfortable position, hooking my arm firmly around her, and murmur a prayer over her head. Cover all the bases here.

Arthur's a good guy underneath, but in this mood he's ten kinds of trouble. He doesn't see Oona as a person, just a means to the end. Honestly, I don't know what he's planning with going back for Aiden. I should have offered to stay behind while Aiden went in the cart. I didn't get my words together fast enough, and Arthur had us all ready to take off.

I point off the open back of the cart, mentioning landmarks and making jokes while Arthur drones behind us. I left Aiden behind and made Kaylee mad, but at least I can keep Oona Robinson from falling out of the cart.

We trotted over the hills, crossing above the country highways. They wind around, and we head into the city...well, as the crow flies. Arthur drove along the greenbelt above the River Nore, but now we're above the maze of medieval streets in the city center—seriously, no one even looks up?—then he guides the deer in a broad descending circle towards the lawn in front of the council building. We settle with a jolt, and he hops down from the high driving perch. I catch the edge of a limp and the way he shakes out one arm, but he's loose and grinning by the time he reaches us. We've been stuffed in this cart for hours, but he's got to pretend that he doesn't feel a thing. I'm in way better physical shape than Arthur, so if

I'm hurting, then I know he is too. He offers a hand, which is just as well, because we're wedged into the back.

I take an exaggerated stretch, but Oona trots right over to pet the deer. She pets her nose with her right hand, her left held stiff and spread-fingered to the side.

"Thank you for pulling our cart," she chirps. "We love you sooooo much, Mrs Magical Deer!"

Damn, I should have done that, although maybe without the declaration of undying love. But before I can move, Oona steps back, and the deer nods her head and she's in the air, faster and faster.

"But what about—" How are we going to get Aiden?

"I've got it handled," Arthur interrupts.

Oona waves and blows kisses, hopping from one foot to the other.

"Right, team. Let's review our plan." Arthur pounds one fist into the other hand, flexing his shoulders like a boxer. "Hey!"

Oona is hopping more.

"Inside," I say, putting one hand between her shoulder blades to propel us all forward. "Good girl, you can make it."

But it's a long lawn, and Oona turns to me, frantic. "Carry me," she whispers.

I scoop her up and start trotting.

"Hey," Arthur yells, but I let him follow or not. For once, I'm gonna put someone else first.

I bust through the heavy front doors and run through the corridors. Luckily, I've been to meetings here and I know where the toilets are. I plop Oona down in front of the Ladies' and she darts inside like a fish.

"For chrissakes, can't you stop long enough to listen to instructions?" Arthur jogs up, panting slightly.

"Sometimes you can't," I tell him. There's anger boiling in me, somewhere along with the stink and regret. I have to turn aside and examine the fliers on the wall, as though I'm interested in the Council's latest environmental initiative. Luckily there's not many people on this lower level.

Arthur just has three older brothers, I remind myself. He knows crap about girls.

And he was the baby who got taken care of, the devil on my shoulder reminds me.

Shaddup, devil. No one in their right mind would choose to get taken care of the way Arthur was raised.

With that, I manage to wipe my face neutral and turn back to him. He's talking about what he'll make for dinner and whether his sourdough starter has gone flat, like this meeting is already a done deal.

"What about Aiden?" I ask.

"No prob. Pound cake or chocolate sponge?"

"After we get back, I need to go to Hannah's," I say. "Can you drop me off?"

I hate asking another favor, but I really need to see her. Before I face my parents, before I try to fit myself back into my regular life. I'm so achingly tired, and I need to explain everything to Hannah. Everything. I've done this whole wild adventure for her and my life together, and I'm about to get everything I promised her, but it's all gone wrong in the middle. Hannah listens in a way that helps me see clearly, and I'm all mixed up right now.

Besides, I owe it to her. She's a part of this, and she didn't even know what happened.

Arthur rolls his eyes. "Tell you what." He digs in his jacket pocket and tosses me his keys. "You go to Hannah. It's parked on the corner of Weyland. Take it."

I finger the keys. I'll turn seventeen next month, so I don't have my license yet.

Arthur elbows me. "Sure, just don't let the Gardaí see you, eh?"

"When are we going back for Aiden?"

Arthur pulls something else out of his pocket. It's a tiny riding crop, or I guess driving crop. "This is the charm. I can call that deer back any time."

"We should go then. Before Hannah?"

He shrugs. "You go see your girl. The cart's tiny, right? I'll go myself."

"Today, though? It's getting dark soon."

He scoffs. "You think I'm some kinda coward who hides at home just because it's dark?"

"I'm just worried about Aiden."

"I *promised* the girls, didn't you hear me?" Arthur flexes his shoulders. "I'm not the kind to leave a mate."

Except he already did. The cart really was full, but—

"Now *there's* my little princess!" Arthur turns and holds up a hand for a high-five. He really does have a good heart, and he really has had a lot of people try to screw him over.

Oona is holding her left hand stiffly to one side, and her face and dress are damp, like she tried to wash up but mostly got water all over. She's dead solemn, but a tiny smile flickers when Arthur calls her a princess. She was the princess of Terrible Valley, and she can't help but adore the title. Heck, when my sister was five, she would have signed up to be kidnapped if it meant that she got to be a real life princess, too.

But Oona's a soggy princess, and it's February. I duck into the men's jacks to grab some paper towels, but when I come out Arthur is already down on one knee, saying something that makes Oona even more serious and worried.

Damn. I shouldn't have left them.

"Can't have your princess dress looking sad for your big meeting!" I smile and start squeezing the water out of her sleeves. I get only a sad shadow of a sad smile, but five minutes later when we head upstairs, Oona reaches for my hand.

"Remember"—Arthur turns at the top of the stares to glare at us both—"we're not going to mention Aiden or Kaylee. None of it. Remember the story we've all agreed on."

He's been reminding us about this story for the last hour, but there's something different in the way Oona drops her head and whispers, "I know."

What did he tell her?

***

We follow signs to the Cathaoirleach's office, which is a whole suite. The secretary says it'll be a long wait since we don't have an appointment, but we've scarcely sat down when the Cathaoirleach himself opens an inner door, Arthur's note in his hand. His eyes go straight to Oona, then directly to her ring.

"Come back," he tells us. "Tea," he barks at the secretary.

Oona takes my hand (with her right one, since apparently the other no longer functions as a hand) and we shuffle back into the inner rooms. I feel even more scrubby and my stomach growls.

I hate this feeling, like no matter what I do, I'm just silly and useless and childish. I've been arguing with my parents lately, and I always end up feeling this way. I guess the Cathaoirleach hasn't actually *said* that a bunch of rag-tag children could hardly defeat the worst criminal in Kilkenny history. I'm just hearing it. I pull my shoulders up, and I am a tall lad.

The Cathaoirleach glances over Arthur and I like we are so much flotsam, then crooks his finger at Oona. "Show me your ring." His office looks a lot like our headmaster's.

She holds out her hand, looking smaller and skinnier all the time.

"Take it off." He watches her like a falcon.

"I can't." Oona jerks the ring in demonstration.

Slowly, the Cathaoirleach smiles, although it does not reach his steely eyes. "You truly do have a story about the Good People, don't you. Sit down."

We arrange ourselves on some square orange chairs in front of his desk. A young woman in khakis and a hijab comes in with a tray of tea; she looks familiar but I can't place her before she leaves again. Arthur pops three biscuits in his mouth at once.

We've been eating traditional food for the last three days—tubers we roasted in the fire, barley bread, fish from the stream. We weren't starving, but it was kind of strange. I want the biscuits too, but I see a sparkle in Oona's eyes and gesture to her first.

"I'm the princess," she says, almost in a whisper. "I should serve the tea."

"Thank'ee kindly." I grin at her. "Two sugars and three biscuits, little princess."

"I take plenty of milk but no sugar," the Cathaoirleach says, surprising us all with his grave respect for the little girl.

She spills a little on the tray but we all wait while she pours, including the head of the county council. I like him better for it.

When we all have our tea (and Arthur and I have bolted the biscuits, I have to admit), the Cathaoirleach asks a couple questions and Arthur launches into our story.

It takes a long time, and I sit back and watch them both. I keep my hand in my jacket pocket, the tip of one finger in my own ring, like I'm holding Hannah's hand.

The Cathaoirleach is a big scruffy man. I don't even remember his regular name, because he's been the Head of Council for so long people just call him that, the Cathaoirleach. I've watched him give speeches before, and cut ribbons for a new project and stuff, so I know to expect his bushy salt-and-pepper hair and rumpled suit. But there's something in the way he watches Arthur that is unsettling. He leans onto his desk, drumming the fingers of one hand, but otherwise perfectly still. That's normal, right?

He glances at me, and I realize what it is—his eyes are silver. I guess they must be gray and catching the light funny, but it feels like he can see right through me.

Maybe I'm just dreaming, because Arthur keeps spinning his story, as cool as a cucumber.

Here's the way our real story goes: A year ago, the Cathaoirleach announced a reward for anyone who could catch the Patchwork Man, who's been seen stealing things and trying to make off with young ladies. Up until now, they've escaped—or he's let them go. Now, everyone knows the Patchwork Man is Daoine Sidhe, the ones we call the Good People because they're terribly bad, and everyone knows that the old castle was built on a Fae hill, which is why we don't call it by name just like we don't ca ll *them* by name.

One of the Cathaoirleach's political platforms was cleaning up derelict housing, and he promised that the Council would pay for remodeling a house and give it to whoever could prove he caught the notorious thief. Arthur thought that a house would be the answer to his problems and mine—or more like, he realized that he'd have a better chance if we worked together. So in preparation, Arthur and I collected stories, gathered artifacts, and did physical training. But all of that would have been for naught, except when we were searching the castle Hannah got herself tangled up with a different Daoine Sidhe, and made a wish that the Patchwork Man would next appear when Arthur and I were there and ready to catch him.

And he did, and we followed him through the Veil, and we found the Old Wise Woman who gave us gifts (including the ring I have for Hannah), and the magical transportation to the Terrible Valley (that was the deer I forgot to thank), and the instructions for how to get Below into the Terrible Valley where the Patchwork Man was hiding Oona.

And in the end, we came back with the Patchwork's Man heart in a ring on the finger of his stolen princess, just like all the stories say. So that's the story that Arthur is busy telling.

But what really happened? We went to visit Aiden at that castle where they live, and the Patchwork Man came popping right out, almost certainly because Hannah had arranged that with the leprechaun. But naturally, Aiden and Oona were right there too. So instead of choosing some lovely maiden (who's properly grown), the Patchwork Man snatched our mate's little sister. So Aiden Robinson came with us when we followed the Patchwork Man, and then I guess no matter how much Arthur and I wanted to succeed, Aiden wanted it more—because Oona was his *sister*, obviously. But then his *other* sister Kaylee showed up, and I honestly still don't know where she came from or how she got into our fairy tale. It was a whole mess.

Arthur doesn't mention any of that. He acts like our original plan worked, adding just enough details from what really happened to make it believable.

Even though neither he nor I actually made it into the Terrible Valley. The Wise Woman gave all three of us boys gifts, but only Aiden's could defeat the Patchwork Man. Arthur and I camped in the meadow *above* the valley, while Aiden and his assortment of sisters went *into* it.

That part confuses me too. Arthur went down in the basket first, and he came up whiter than a sheet, and while the Robinson sibs were fiddling with the basket, he warned me to refuse to go down. So when they lowered me, I yelled out that I couldn't do it. I thought we were all going to go back, but lo and behold, Aiden and his sister went down easy peasy, and took off, and apparently Aiden was the hero and killed the Patchwork Man and got his heart on the ring which Oona is wearing.

In three days of camping, Arthur never told me what he saw Below. He never explained why, after all those months of preparation, we stopped before going into the valley. I could tell something scared him, bad, and Arthur doesn't like to talk about bad stuff.

But Aiden is American, and he's rich, and he said he didn't want the reward. He said one of us should get the house, so we could go to the Cathaoirleach without him. He really did say that.

I also don't know why we brought Kaylee and Oona back but left Aiden in the Terrible Valley. I didn't expect Aiden to be hurt, so then I froze and wasn't thinking clearly. Arthur's got a good heart, I know he does, but I have to admit that following along with him has gotten me into trouble before, and I have a feeling this might be the worst trouble yet. I really shouldn't have left Aiden behind. I know better.

Crammed in the back of the cart, Kaylee got more and more hysterical the farther we got from him, the fear and desperation coming out of her in waves. She wanted to go straight home and tell Mrs Robinson that Aiden was hurt, and Arthur did what she asked, but of course that also got her out of the way for this performance of his in the Cathaoirleach's office.

Arthur tells the whole story without including Kaylee and Aiden.

Oona looks into her teacup, her left hand propped on the far side of her chair like it doesn't belong to her.

The Cathaoirleach asks questions.

And I get an odd feeling. He was elected the normal way, and he does the normal things on the council. I've attended public meetings, and he came and talked to our secondary school, so I ought to know what to expect. Something feels wrong, and he doesn't meet my eyes again. I don't know if it's because I'm seeing him up close, or because he's let down his guard with nothing but three kids in the room, or because I've been through the Veil and my eyes are different now.

I think...

Maybe...

He's one of the Daoine Sidhe. Not human at all.

***

Arthur laces his fingers behind his head, leaning back, that familiar cock-sure grin in place.

"So that was it?" the Cathaoirleach asks. "The whole thing?"

"Sure. Pretty amazing, innit?"

I have to admit, Arthur is a good story-teller. He had an answer worked out for every logistical detail, and he told it with every emotion correct. Horror, surprise, righteous anger. Listening to him practically made me feel like I was there...as I was, according to him.

"What do you think, Miss Robinson?" The Cathaoirleach turns to Oona with something like a smile. "Is that what you remember happening?"

"Everything Arthur said is true," Oona pops out immediately. "It was all just like that. Exactly. Everything."

"Enthusiastic, isn't she?" Arthur chuckles, laying a hand on Oona's hair. He is so calm it almost covers up her nervous bluster.

"Do you have anything to add, Dylan?" the Cathaoirleach asks.

"No." I drop my eyes to my lap, then worry what that looks like to the man. I'm doing this for Hannah, so I'm going to do it all the way. I find my own easy grin, the one I use for "sure it's no problem, didn't bother me anyways" when customers are rude, and let my head rise slowly, comfortably. "Like Arthur said, him and I have been planning this for months. I'm just glad we could pull it off and ensure the safety of our community."

The Cathaoirleach raises his bushy eyebrows but doesn't ask any more. He pushes a buzzer, and within a few seconds, the assistant is back again.

"Hafsa, would you be so good as to give this lovely young lady a ride home?" the Cathaoirleach says. "She's a trooper, but she's all worn out."

"Of course! Oona, luv, do you want to come with me?" Hafsa holds out a hand, smiling warmly. "I looked up your address and called your mum while you were in the meeting. And I've got a box of biscuits for the car, if you'd like."

I'm responsible for Oona. I should stick with her—but I glance quickly back and forth. The Cathaoirleach has me pinned like a butterfly on a cork-board, like he's not letting me go any time soon. I have a bad feeling and I want Oona out of it.

"You called her mum?" I ask Hafsa.

"I sure did!" Her eyes are perfectly normal. "And I shop at O'Neill's Grocer because you have the best deli counter. You help me sometimes on Saturdays."

"Oh, I remember now." I'm thinking she's a better option than being stuck in a room with the Cathaoirleach, but I'm still cautious. "Do you have a booster seat?"

"We've got a whole supply here, along with biscuits and juice boxes." She wiggles her eyebrows at Oona. "We get kiddies here pretty regularly, and we take them along to where they need to go next."

She definitely sounds like a better option than being in a room with the Cathaoirleach. I turn to Oona, smile, and tug her pigtail lightly. "How about it? You ready to get home?"

She leans closer. "Is it *safe?*"

Prickles run from my skull all down my back, although she only means driving with someone new. Nothing here is safe, but I know how kids are taught to be scared of strangers, so I use the words we did with my sister. "Since she works here, she's kind of like a teacher. Or police officer. It's that kind of rule."

"Ohhhh." Oona sits back into her chair, satisfied. "Thank you, ma'am. I'm coming." She wiggles her feet towards the ground, propelling herself with only her right hand.

"Eh." The Cathaoirleach shakes his head, like he's waking up. "Your ring. Let me see it."

Oona arranges herself carefully in front of the big desk before extending her left hand, slowly, as though it might explode.

The Cathaoirleach bends close, but instead of asking questions or touching her, he just taps the big red jewel with a pencil. "That oughta do it. It'll come off now, like any other ring. Have your mum put it in the bank to save for your university, hah."

Oona tests it, twisting the ring back and forth and putting it off and on a few times, before she thanks him.

I approve of her skepticism. I have my hand in my own pocket, fingering my own ring. It's probably the only good to come out of this whole disaster, and I've been so worried about losing it that I stitched it to the inside of my pocket a couple days ago. The Wise Woman gave it to me for Hannah, although that was part of the story that Arthur changed. He kept his own masonry tools the same and made kind of a joke about it, but he said that I got the Sword of Light. As for myself, I'm glad I have a good ring from a good—well, actually I don't know if the Wise Woman was a Daoine Sidhe herself, or just operated the way-station for them.

Oona finishes making her slow, polite, goodbyes, and gingerly takes Hafsa's hand. Then suddenly she darts back and throws her arms around me. I hug her back, smiling into her hair. She's a sweet one, Aiden's little sister. I'm real glad we got her back.

Once she is finally on her way, engaged in an earnest discussion about which type of biscuits to bring, the Cathaoirleach folds his hands on the desk and grins at us both. There is something odd about his smile.

"I know we're a bit young," Arthur says, "but by the time you finish the remodel on the house, we'll be ready for it."

"You might be young in years, but both of you have gone through enough trials that you have become men in truth," the Cathaoirleach pronounces.

"'Xactly." Arthur chuckles.

Oh, c'mon, man! Don't you see anything wrong with this? Don't you wonder how he knows this much about us?

"Do you deserve a second chance?" The Cathaoirleach is smiling that strange smile. Now that Oona is gone, he looks less grandfather and more wolf.

"I did just fine on my first one." Arthur refolds his legs, cool and confident.

The Cathaoirleach looks at me.

I don't say anything.

"Then you receive the reward you deserve." The Cathaoirleach stands and shuffles to a door at the back of his office.

Judging from the placement of the door, the corridors we walked through, and the glimpses we've had of the secretary's office, this can only lead to a small closet. That's all there's space for. That's it.

The Cathaoirleach puts his hand on the doorknob and looks back at us. "You want to take a tour?"

Arthur moseys to his feet, stretching his back and then tugging his bomber jacket into place.

I stand with him. I need to say something, but Oona was in the chair between us, and those square chairs are kind of big, so we're awkwardly far apart. I should—

"You coming?" Arthur grins at me and strolls towards the Cathaoirleach.

We didn't do anything good, and our fair reward isn't going to be good either! Doesn't he understand?

"Arthur!" I hiss. "Mate! C'mere!" I step backwards, towards the door. The real door.

"And what about your ring?" the Cathaoirleach says to me. "I could help you with that, too."

I take another step away.

"He hasn't got a ring." Arthur has reached the back of the office, next to the Cathaoirleach. "Now what's in here?"

"Your new home," the Cathaoirleach answers, and throws open the door.

It's black. Not dark like a closet that isn't lit up, but total black like the depths of a cave.

Arthur darts a glance at me, the hint of a question in the way he quirks his mouth. I shake my head but he's already turned away.

"Is that so?" Arthur grins, then quick as a snake, his hand darts out and slaps the wall.

The light switch.

The darkness vanishes, and we're looking outside. Flagstone path, evergreen trees and willows with their branches bowed low, rain dripping slowly off every twig, green spears of onions or daffodils poking up through the brown bracken. It could possibly be behind the Council building—I didn't see that side, but the scenery isn't out of place—or it could be anywhere else in Ireland. Or hell, I don't know, Tennessee or Slovakia or something! The fact is that it can't be the back yard, because this is a big rectangular building and *this door leads to the inside and that's the only place it can lead*.

Panic is making me fuzzy and sluggish. I step backwards, closer to escape, and bump into a filing cabinet. It clanks, and I scramble for purchase, knocking some papers on the floor.

Arthur looks at me, frowning.

Good! Maybe that was good! I'll send him signals!

"Do you want your reward or not?" the Cathaoirleach asks.

I shake my head, willing Arthur to look at me. Say no, you gombeen! *Run!* I bump the other door. Kick it. Look over here! Look at me!

Arthur doesn't look at me. "You bet I want it," he drawls, and saunters right through the closet door.

Instead of staring at my best mate's square shoulders and messy hair, I'm staring at droplets rolling down twigs. Dripping onto the flagstone path. Half-grown daffodil spears.

He's gone.

Completely gone.

The Cathaoirleach swings his bushy head towards me, and I yank the doorknob and practically fall out the door. I stumble through the waiting room, knocking into a bookshelf, startling the receptionist.

"Do you deserve a second chance, Dylan O'Neill?" the Cathaoirleach calls after me.

"Excuse you!" the receptionist snaps! "That will be—"

"Do you?"

I bash through the outer door and my legs take over. Jogging down the long corridor, swerving to avoid people with their arms full of file folders or coffee cups, totally shocked as though they've never seen anyone racing through the county offices trying to avoid a portal to *hell*, so help me God.

I skid, my shoes sliding as I swerve around for the staircase. My ring! Hannah! I grab the bannister with one hand and shove the other in my jacket pocket.

Still there.

"I could help you with that..."

The Cathaoirleach's voice echoes—here? In my head? I spin around the bottom of the stairs at top speed, slamming into a middle-aged woman with a box. Lanyards and buttons go flying all over tarnation.

"Sorry!" I sprint away. The main doors are in sight.

"You come back here!" yells the woman.

"Do you want your reward?" calls the Cathaoirleach's voice. This is not normal.

"Real sorry!" I cry, and bust through the big doors.

Cool air. Rain. The long pavement across the broad front lawn.

I touch my pockets—Hannah's ring and oh. Arthur's keys. He's not going to be needing the Polo now. I take off, feet pounding, my stride long and steady.

"Regret," comes the Cathaoirleach's voice, but it's fainter now.

I run.

And run.

I know these streets. As I lope past, I keep checking the buildings, people's faces. Is this real or is it some kind of fake, alternate Kilkenny? The details are right. The people are normal. I always have to jump over this pothole. Same tourists with their same accents. I could turn down thataway to get home, but I keep going.

Hannah first. I've got to warn her, she might be tangled up in this. My blood pounds and visions race through my head. Me protecting Hannah. Jumping in front of a monster. The Cathaoirleach in her drive, and myself speaking up. Yelling. I whisper the things I would say to him, matching the rhythm of my feet. I should have done it for Arthur, but he made his own choice, right? I'll make choices if it saves Hannah.

Hannah.

I run.

There it is. The Polo. I force my steps to slow so I get in one block of cool-down, although my heart won't stop clattering. It's too old for a button fob, so I've got to get all the way up to it before I can make sure the keys still work. Good. I try turn the key in the ignition—it won't go—try harder—oh right, I've got to put the pedals down. Now the engine engages—

Boom. Arthur left the radio blasting, like usual, and a heavy beat assaults me from all sides. A driving metal pulse and—

"Regret," says the Cathaoirleach. "You could drown in it."

He's on the damn radio. He's speaking to the beat, low and pulsing.

"Do you want a second chance, Dylan O'Neill? Regret. Regret. Regret."

I hit buttons all over the console, trying to get the noise to stop. Finally it cuts to silence, and I manage to lurch the car into gear. I have to get to Hannah. Four-way stop, I leap into the intersection and stall. Damn. Damn. Other cars honk, but I've got to ignore them. Just stay calm. Put it in neutral, restart the engine, put it in first, and we're off. Again. It's better as I get to the wider streets going out of town and I can stay in third.

Boom-ba-da-boom. "Regret, Dylan O'Neill. Regret. You could drown in it. You could drown."

I didn't turn that on! I slam the buttons, but it does no good. This is not a normal radio, not a normal guy. He's caught me somehow, and I've got to warn Hannah. The ring was from a Wise Woman. Fae magic to protect her from a Fae fakery.

But as I drive, the familiar hedgerows creeping past, other doubts seep in. I hope Hannah's not mad at me. She never says it, but I feel the tension in her. Disappointment. All the choices I've been making lately are wrong, and this adventure was for sure the wrong-est. Dad says I'm still a child yet, but the Cathaoirleach says I ought to know enough to be a man. Hannah's been hurting lately, more trouble with her parents, and she hasn't even trusted me enough to tell me about it. I've got to be the one she can depend on. I've got to be a man for her, but instead I was uncertain and let Arthur make the decisions for me. I knew it was wrong. I knew it from the first day when Arthur was rude to Aiden, and I knew it when we let Aiden go Below on his own, and I *really* knew it this morning when we left him there.

Oh damn. Who's going back for him? The charm was in Arthur's pocket. Arthur's gone.

I've got to get Aiden back. And I've got to be a good partner for Hannah. I don't know how to do either, but I've got to. So I will. I'll do everything right, from now on.

"Regret. Regret. You could drown in it."

The Cathaoirleach's taunting pounds from Arthur's speakers, all the way to Hannah's house.

***

I jam on the brakes before Arthur's battered Polo scrapes the Rowlands' Mercedes, and tumble up the wide steps to their house. My hand pauses over the bell. Her dad's a surgeon now, and her mum wanted this fancy new build in the country, and now we're all supposed to act like we've got our heads up our arses. I don't have time for "how's the weather, ma'am" and drinking coffee out of a tiny cup. Instead of alerting Mrs Rowland to my presence, I just go in.

The house has a quiet, dark feeling, smelling like air freshener. Mrs Rowland doesn't come popping out of the woodwork.

"Hannah!" I call. "Hannah!

My back is cold with sweat and my heart is pounding.

"Here! I'm in the parlor!"

So she's been practicing. I rush through the dim house until I'm hit by soft, ordinary lamplight and the sleek curves of the grand piano. I brace my palm on the doorway, catching my breath. Just drinking her in.

Hannah was just putting something away, turning to me with a funny little smile. Her hair swings softly by her pixie-like chin, and she's wearing her favorite jumper with holes in the elbows. I know the velvet of her skin, the magic of her smile, the feel of her lithe body nestled up to mine. I may be a rubbish boyfriend, but I love her so much. I'm going to do things the right way now. I am.

"What on earth happened?" Her eyes rake me up and down, widening slightly at the condition of my jeans. "Come on in and—"

"I'm fine. It's yourself who needs to be careful." I can't let this catch her up, with the—

But she draws herself up, her soft mouth going firm.

Crap. I stuck my foot in it again. "I didn't mean—look, I brought you this, Henny luv."

Hannah's face loosens slightly with the childhood nickname. I'm twisting the ring in my pocket, and give the thread a firm yank. I hold out my hand and her eyes light up. She draws close, which is just where I want her, resting her hand on my arm. Her touch steadies me. Makes the world real again.

I open my hand to show her. It's a little ring, gold and silver knotted together, completely different from Oona's chunky brazen jewel.

"Oh, you didn't have to buy me a ring!" She leans closer, smelling sweet and comfortable. "I've already told you that I'll marry you, and we're trying to save up."

Despite that, I can tell she's not really upset. I close my hand, needing to explain first, just as her fingers brush against mine. I feel the magic then—wrapping around us, together, safe.

"It's not that...I mean, of course we are." I take her hand, caressing her fingers. It's going to fit her fourth finger, and that feels special. She's smiling as I slide the ring on. "There's a whole story, but first I want to—"

I blink.

"Make sure you're safe," I say to the vacant room.

My hands are empty, my arm cold where Hannah was touching me just seconds ago.

She's vanished.

Jaysus, Mary and Joseph—what have I done?

* * *

To read more

What happened to Hannah, and what does Dylan do with his second chance? Order *The Boat on the Lake of Regret* here for all retailers

https://buy.bookfunnel.com/hzxiszq79z

or here for the Kindle version

https://www.amazon.com/dp/B0F9HYQLGB

He has one last chance to be a fairy tale hero.□
But she didn't agree to be the damsel in distress.□

When her longtime boyfriend unexpectedly slides a ring on her finger, Hannah is whisked from her everyday bedroom to a medieval ball. Hannah knew that Dylan would do anything to prove to her parents that he's husband material, including going into the Fae world—but she never agreed to go through the Veil herself.

Now one of three princess sisters, Hannah is paired with now-Prince Dylan. But, homesick and blindsided, she pretends the Veil has wiped him from her memory.

As her prince scrambles in vain to be the right kind of hero, Hannah ignores her instincts and follows her new sisters onto a mysterious boat—which promptly sails them into a land of giants, magical traps, and enchanted pianos...and away from Dylan.

Read now to journey back to medieval Ireland, complete with the Fae and mythological monsters, in this fairy tale adventure and sweet "it was always you" romance.

Author's Note

I set Aiden's historical reference point in the same world as Saba's, so in Heroic Ireland. Admittedly, many of the details (such as how the houses were set up or what people wore) were written down in the 8th-12th century, and Aiden's story mostly takes place in the Below world, so it's a rather vague time period.

Hurley

Hurley was first mentioned in the mythological cycles set BCE, and still is overwhelmingly popular in southern Ireland. Although I knew it could be confusing for my American readers, it is impossible to write about a teen boy living in Kilkenny where hurley does not play a significant role in the story.

A hurley stick looks similar to a hockey stick, but somewhat shorter, with a small leather ball. It is played on a field similar to soccer, and players hit the ball between teammates or dribble on the top of the stick as they run. It is fast-paced, complicated, and rather violent.

The Knight of Terrible Valley and Lawn Dyarrig

I have kept all the logistics of this fairy tale while changing the emotional details to fit Aiden and his family. For instance, the hero and two others (brothers/friends) leave their normal house to find the Knight of Terrible Valley, stay overnight with a helpful old woman (in the original, it is her daughter who is kidnapped), then she gives them a sword and a magical horse, who takes them to a special meadow.

The description of going "Below" is quite interesting, and similar scenes are found frequently in Irish folklore, complete with cutting the turf and needing to build a basket and pulley system. Although I invented the description of the tin can men and the houses, the heart of the original story is also the hero's journey through the Terrible Valley. When he arrives, the Green Knight is away and the kidnapped woman tells him exactly how to defeat her captor. The battle barely merits a few sentences; if the hero follows instructions, then he wins. The climactic drama is when his companions leave the hero in the Terrible Valley and how the hero returns home. Since I had changed the family situation, these logistics are different in my version, but the plot energy is the same.

Obviously, I added a lot more characters, but the structure of the plot is close to the original.

ABOUT the AUTHOR

Characters you connect with. Adventure. Love. Family. And endings that are more than a sugar rush. □

When Christy Matheson is not throwing ordinary characters into fairy tales, she is busy raising five children. (Very busy.) She writes character-driven historical fiction with and without fantasy elements, and her "fresh, smart, and totally charming" stories have won multiple awards.

Christy is also an embroidery artist, classically trained pianist, and sews all of her own clothes. She lives in Oregon, on a country property that fondly reminds her of a Regency estate (except with a swing set instead of faux Greek ruins), with her husband, five children, three Shelties, one bunny, and an improbable quantity of art supplies.

Please join Christy in conversation about books and determined women throughout history.

Join her newsletter to get free stories, art giveaways, & puppy pictures. https://sendfox.com/ChristyMatheson

And you can always find her at: christymatheson.com

www.ingramcontent.com/pod-product-compliance
Lightning Source LLC
Chambersburg PA
CBHW030643260626
47157CB00007B/2466